Everyday Spirits

by Chris Gregory

This is a work of fiction. All the characters in this book are fictitious, and any resemblance to actual persons is purely coincidental.

Cover Art by Lizzie Knott – https://www.lizzieknott.com[1]

---

1. https://www.lizzieknott.com/

This is a work of fiction. Similarities to real people, places, or events are entirely coincidental.

EVERYDAY SPIRITS

First edition. May 21, 2022.

Copyright © 2022 Chris Gregory.

ISBN: 979-8223994213

Written by Chris Gregory.

Other books by Chris Gregory

Science Fiction by **Chris D Gregory**
Seconders
Second Generation
Distant Son

Rescue

Urban Fantasy by **Chris Gregory**
Everyday Ghosts
Everyday Spirits
Everyday Legends

Historical Fiction by **CD Gregory**
Crystal
Resister

Pendragons
Uthyr Pendragon

Dedication

For people with spirit and for those in need of it.

Prologue

University Hospital Lewisham, Larch Ward, May 2018

There she is again, my Anna. I'd recognise her anywhere and anytime: that tumble of fair brown hair and those shrewd green eyes peering at me from underneath. She looks a little older, though not quite as tired as she looked ten minutes ago. Worried too. I understand, it's the first time she's come to see me since I died. Before I die.

Anna hesitates at the end of my bed and pulls her dreadful baggy coat around her. Not quite as many patches as the last time I saw it, but just as scruffy. She wears it like armour. With an effort I raise my hands to her and smile. She smiles back with a beam that makes me feel like the world is a good place. She comes to me and hugs me tight, burying her head in my chest. When she lifts her face to me it's streaked with tears, so I go to brush them away.

"Hello, sweetie," I say. "You know what happens next," I gesture to the drip full of pain killers attached to my wrist. "But you know you'll make it. You'll get to find heroes of the past... and become one."

"You do know then!" she exclaims. She seems vindicated because she guessed I knew and a little outraged because I didn't say.

"Yes," I nod. I've shielded you so long my dear, but you're an adult now. You're no longer my baby and I can't shield you forever. I'm sorry I didn't say anything when you were younger."

"Why? Why didn't you listen when I told you about the ghosts of the other family, still there in our home in Blackheath? Why didn't you admit I'd seen a young woman sitting on the steps outside our house talking to herself? Why did you let me think I was the only one who knew I could do this?"

I let her questions tumble out like a wave crashing on the shore and wait for the ebb. "Times change and some things become harder to accept. The world is a different place to when my mum was growing up."

"Your mum?"

"Your Grandma, Élise. She could do what you do."

Anna sits up, holding my hands and looks at me in wonder. "She could walk between times, like me?"

"Yes. It seems she taught you. When you were small."

"I..."

"...don't remember," I take a deep breath. I feel drained, but she deserves to know now. "You would have been four and I doubt you remember much. But I remember taking you to see Élise in her little mobile home by the sea in Pagham. She liked you. There weren't many people your grandma would tolerate, but you were one of them."

"She died when I was barely five."

"Yes, she passed away peacefully in her sleep. What a lovely way to go." I close my eyes for a moment and consider how delightful it would be to die that way. I shouldn't be envious, but I am. "A few months before she died, I took you to see her. I came back from a walk along the seashore and found you, sat on her lap, eyes shut, a frown of concentration creasing your little forehead. 'Shh' she put her finger to her lips, 'she's seeing', and I knew exactly what it was she had been teaching you to do."

"What did I see?"

"After a few minutes you opened your eyes, and they were wide with wonder. 'Sailors,' you said. 'Wind. Big waves.' The next day I took you with me for a walk along the shore because I wasn't keen to let Mum teach you more. When we reached the old Mulberry Harbour wreck on the beach at Aldwick you started jumping up and down and pointing at it. 'Big wind!' you said. It was a beautiful sunny day, barely a breeze. 'Sailors in big waves', you insisted. When I got back to Mum's place, she told me all about the harbour sections that broke loose in the storm just before D-Day, back in 1944. They ended up on the beach at Aldwick where the seamen tried to rescue them, but this one stuck fast and stayed there ever since."

"I saw the storm before D-Day?"

"That's what we worked out."

"Did your mum teach you how to see?"

I'm running out of energy. I rest my eyes a while then open them again, to see how concerned Anna looks. She squeezes my hands so I must be strong. "No. She could already see how things were changing. How the modern world would reject such a gift and treat it like a mental illness or worse. Perhaps she had second thoughts when she saw you that day. Perhaps she wanted you to have the gift, so it didn't die with her."

"But I still don't understand why you didn't talk to me about it."

"It wasn't safe," I admit. I can see she suspects there's more to tell. Of course she does, she's smart, like her grandma. But there are some things I cannot just tell her. Some things she must find out for herself. "Go talk to your grandmother," I say gently instead. "She grew up in a small Normandy town called Vire. Her maiden name was Couteau."

"Élise Couteau. Vire," Anna repeats to herself.

I can see from the set of her jaw that she intends to go there. She intends to find out everything, she's stubborn and determined like that. I can't help being worried for her so, despite my misgivings, I add, "If you find yourself in trouble, pray to Saint Michael."

She frowns. "You're kidding me," she says in a flat tone.

With an effort I shrug. I'm utterly exhausted now and tell Anna that I need rest. She cries a little more, then hugs me and stands up to leave me sleep. My eyes are shut but I know she's still looking at me, so I murmur, "And always remember I love you."

The Man in the Jacket

Brightmoor Street, Nottingham, May 2022

"This is where you're going to sit?" asked Doctor Briars. She peered down at Anna through her spectacles and brushed a loose curl of black hair back across her dark skin.

"Yes, against this wall," said Anna. "It's out of sight from the street so hopefully no one should see us."

The evening sun had sunk behind the offices above them, and the hum of traffic was muted. Anna settled into a corner of the under-croft, at the edge of the empty car park. It was a little warm to be wearing her black oversized overcoat, but she knew it would be cold where and when she was going. The same place but in October 2019.

"What exactly am I looking for again?" asked Doctor Briars. Anna could tell that her employer, and ever more her friend, was still sceptical. Who wouldn't be? But she had already revealed so much to Angela Briars, she seemed like the logical person to ask to watch over her. The only person.

"Not sure. That's why I need you to watch."

"And you want me to record you on your phone," Angela waved Anna's new Samsung in her left hand, raising one eyebrow.

"Please. Thank you, Doctor Briars."

"Angela. You must get used to calling me Angela. For heavens sake, I'm squatting in a backyard filming you on a journey to the past, we can't get more informal than that. Can we?"

Anna made a crooked smile from the corner of her mouth. "Thanks, you're a star."

Angela shook her head with amused exasperation. "Look, I'm filming you. Perform!"

Anna closed her eyes, self-conscious. Even though it wasn't the first time she had searched for this particular moment in the past (she had made a trial journey last week), it was the first time she had been watched and recorded. It felt weird. And a lot harder.

Anna peeked through one eye.

"I'm still here. Get on with it!" tutted Angela.

Anna closed it again and focussed. First, she tried to clear her mind, make it as blank as she could in the circumstances. Then her mind's eye looked down... The shadows across the yard rolled backwards. The moon rose in the west and set in the east, all in reverse time. The cycle of shadows and stars ran faster, like a video rewinding. Now she was aware of the shadows lengthening, heading back into winter, now they were getting shorter as she emerged into autumn, then summer. The year looped backwards again and, as the shadows lengthened for a third time, she slowed them looking, searching. She could feel a cold breeze on her cheek, see the moon climbing down, back behind a cloud, hear voices at the end of the street. One of them was hers... screaming.

Brightmoor Street, Nottingham, October 2019

Anna leapt to her feet and ran towards her scream. She could picture the struggle in the doorway on the corner of Cranbrook Street beyond. In October 2019 she had been attacked. A man had tried to rape her. Her whole body trembled at the thought of it. How many times had she dreamed of footsteps following her down a street in the sodium-lit gloom, her shadow moving around her as she passed each lamp? How many times had her heart raced as she saw a second shadow moving behind hers? How many more times would she have to lurch forward in bed, gasping for air after a hand clasped her mouth shut and pushed her into a doorway? Anna knew she couldn't stop the nightmares, but she could do something to box them into a corner of her mind.

Up ahead was a familiar little girl in a light grey slip standing near the corner and waving. It was Beatrice, who had pulled her out of a pit and showed her Victorian Nottingham. She saw a woman running towards the girl. It was Anna. It felt appallingly weird. She could see herself running towards herself: oversized overcoat flapping madly. Behind her was the man in the jacket, staggering, yelling. Anna felt a sliver of ice slide across her spine. She ducked into a doorway and flattened herself into it.

First the little girl ran past her, waving for the other Anna to follow. Then the other Anna ran past, eyes wild, hair streaming across her face. Anna lunged forwards and curled herself into a ball on the hard tarmac road and instantly had the wind kicked out of her as the man in the jacket tripped over her and fell, swearing. Before he could recover Anna pulled a cannister of pepper spray from her pocket and squirted it at his eyes.

"AARGH!"

"Stay down," ordered Anna. She heard other Anna yelp and knew that she had fallen into the pit where little Beatrice would revive her in another time. So strange. She wondered how authoritative her voice sounded while her heart was in her mouth and her hands were shaking. But the man was helpless before her, rubbing his eyes and making them sting even more.

"Whattheheckareyou..."

"Shut up! Listen."

"Areyoucrazyyou... AAARGH-STOP-NO-F..."

Anna shot another squirt of pepper in his face "I said shut up. I know who you are."

"Wha?"

"I followed you back to your home. I know where you live, I know where you work. I found out what your name is, Adrian Alexander Price, and I'm going to make damned sure the police know it too. Unless you do as I say."

"..."

"Good. You're listening. I'm going to be watching you. Everyday. Like a ghost from the shadows. And you're never ever going to do anything like this again. Are you?"

The man stopped writhing momentarily to shake his head.

"ARE YOU?"

"No."

"No, what?"

"No... Miss?"

"I'm going to assume that's the first time you've shown any respect to a woman which is why it didn't sound convincing. No, what?"

"No, Miss!"

"That's better."

"Who the f..."

"None of your business. Give me your jacket."

"What the f..."

"Take your bloody jacket off and give it to me."

"But it's cold."

"Yes, and I'm freezing. Give me your jacket."

Adrian Alexander Price stopped rubbing his streaming eyes for a moment to pull his jacket off and hold it out in the direction of her voice. Anna took it.

"Now your tie."

"Wha..."

"The tie. You're not behaving well enough to deserve a posh jacket, let alone a swanky tie, so take it off."

Adrian Alexander Price unknotted the tie and held it out for her.

"Now get up and go home to The Park. You don't deserve to live there either."

Adrian Alexander Price hesitated, cowering, shaking from the cold now as much as the shock.

"GO!"

He struggled to his feet and staggered against the wall of the house beside them, wiping furiously at his eyes. Before he could see anything from them, she was gone. He had no idea who she was.

Brightmoor Street, Nottingham, May 2022

Having looked up within the field of vision of her mind's eye and tracked the sun and moon as they chased each other forwards across the sky, Anna found herself huddled against the wall of the under-croft and opened her eyes.

Angela had fallen backwards and sat on her bottom at the edge of the car park with one hand over her mouth and the other holding Anna's phone out towards her, as if it were a crucifix, she was using to ward off evil.

"Hey, Angela, are you okay?" Anna rushed over beside her and put her arm around her shoulders. Angela craned her neck to keep Anna in sight every step and kept staring at her. "What happened?" asked Anna.

"I was hoping you'd tell me," Angela muttered and handed Anna her phone. It was still recording so she stopped and re-played.

Anna never felt comfortable watching herself, but at least it wasn't as hellish as seeing herself run towards herself screaming. For the first few seconds she was just sitting there, in her oversized overcoat on a warm May evening, with her eyes shut. Opening one eye to peek at Angela then shutting it again after being told to get on with it. Then she saw her eyelids fluttering, her eyeballs moving rapidly from side to side under her lids. It was unsettling, as if she were watching herself have a fit. Then her body started to fade out like a ghost and there was a shriek which must have come from Angela. Anna could understand why she might be a wee bit upset. Anna's body kept fading until it disappeared altogether, like some particularly fancy piece of CGI. The camera angle jerked away. That must have been when Angela fell over backwards. After a few seconds, her body started to fade into view again, gaining substance rapidly until she was fully there. Holding a jacket and a tie.

'Hey, Angela, are you okay?' she heard the recording of herself say, so she hit the pause button. "Wow! I guess you're a bit freaked out?" Even Anna was.

"Just a bit. It's the first time you called me Angela."

For a moment the two just looked blankly at each other, then Anna burst out laughing. After a few moments Angela joined in. They laughed so hard they shook, and as the shaking subsided, they looked at each other again. New respect for each.

"Where the hell did those come from?" Angela pointed at the jacket and tie beside Anna.

"From a man who didn't deserve them," said Anna, sourly. Angela stared at Anna until she explained. Fully.

"You could have been killed!" chided Angela. "You knew he was dangerous. If I had any idea what you were doing, I'd never have..."

"No, you wouldn't," agreed Anna. "Which is why I didn't say. But I got him. I scared him, like he scared me and maybe, just maybe, he might never try to rape anyone again."

"That was the most reckless, stupid, brave and downright weird thing I've ever known anyone do. Don't ever do it again!"

Anna didn't answer that. She knew that fewer than one in thirty women who report a rape see their attacker charged and fewer still would be prosecuted. What chance would she, homeless at the time of the attack, have of getting justice? Anna had her own unique solution.

"God bless you Anna Partington, there aren't many women who'd go back and confront their attacker like that or live to tell the tale."

"S'pose so. S'pose there aren't many who can go back."

"Of that I'm sure. I'm really sorry, Anna."

"For what?"

"For ever doubting you could time travel."

"I'd have doubted it if I were you."

"You were like... like a ghost. You just faded out and came back again. Holding that jacket and tie, out of nowhere." Angela paused, a shrewd and calculating look on her face, then shook her head.

"What?"

"No, that was really wrong of me to even think of it."

"Go on, what were you thinking? Really, I don't mind."

"It was a terrible thought. I was thinking how much we could all discover if you were to go back to important moments in time to investigate the past. Real facts about the past, no educated guesses from fragments of pots and belt buckles. But that'd be exploitation."

"It's what I've spent my life doing, in case you don't remember. Go on, name a time and place. I'll go take a peek for you. You deserve it after helping me."

"No, Anna. Every time you do it, you put yourself at risk. I won't have you doing that on my account."

"How 'bout I tell you all about it when I come back from a journey of my choosing?"

Angela adjusted her spectacles and considered. "Deal. But no more stunts like that." She paused again, understanding dawning across her face like a shaft of sunshine. "That's what you've been up to! Researching that family tree of yours, and the questions you were asking me. You're going on a search for your family, aren't you?"

Anna nodded.

"Oh…" Angela put her hand to her mouth. "You're going to see your mum again, before she died of cancer."

"Yes," Anna's voice sounded small.

"You haven't tried to do that yet?"

"No."

"Come here," Angela hugged her tight.

Family

There she is again, thought Anna, Eleanor. Mum. She looked thin. So pale. She'd forgotten this or perhaps pushed it to the back of her mind. Anna felt nervous. What if Mum worked out that Anna had returned from the future and freaked out? In her condition! What did Anna think she was doing? She was more scared of facing her mum than the creep of Brightmoor Street. Thank God, she thought, she's smiling, putting her hands out in welcome. Her mum's arms were so scrawny and festooned with tubes and hospital tags! Oh Mum, look at what that disease has been doing to you.

"Hi Mum," croaked Anna, and pulled her oversized overcoat around her.

"Hello, sweetie," Eleanor said quietly. "You know what happens next," and gestured to the drip full of pain killers attached to her wrist. "But you know you'll make it. You get to find heroes of the past... and become one."

"You do know then!" exclaimed Anna, relief flowing through her rigid limbs.

She looked so tired, so drained, but Anna was desperate to understand. She waited, holding her mum's hands, and encouraged her while she talked about her grandma Élise and how she taught Anna to see when she was only four. Anna had the vaguest of memories of a storm by the sea, of sailors struggling with a huge floating platform and waves as high as a house. But it was as if it were someone else's memory. In a way, her four-year-old self was someone else. Eleanor encouraged Anna to talk to her grandma in the past, telling her maiden name and where she grew up.

"Élise Couteau. Vire," Anna repeated, committing the names to memory. She'd always known her as Grandma and she'd never thought to ask where she'd grown up, though she couldn't miss her French accent, even after so many decades living in West Sussex.

And then her mum said something that took Anna completely by surprise. "If you find yourself in trouble, pray to Saint Michael."

"You're kidding me," frowned Anna, searching her mum's face for signs of mischief and finding none. She felt uncomfortable. Anna didn't think her mum was religious, any more than she was. Perhaps the drugs were taking their toll, but she seemed lucid if utterly exhausted. Perhaps she was afraid of her imminent death. Who wouldn't be?

Her mum shrugged. It reminded Anna of the Gallic shrug her grandma would give sometimes, which could mean anything and nothing. "I need to rest," she said simply.

Anna wondered if she would ever see her mum again and the thought overwhelmed her. She tried to cuff away tears as she leaned forward and wrapped her arms around her. Slowly, after a long embrace, Anna stood. She felt unsteady, her vision blurred. Her mum's eyes were closed, and she looked peaceful.

"And always remember I love you," Eleanor said, her eyes still closed.

"Love you too," whispered Anna.

Blackheath, London, May 2022
Anna couldn't ignore their old home, so near the hospital. She took the 108 bus across the northern edge of Hither Green and got off near the quaint old Victorian station building at Blackheath. She walked up Tranquil Vale, feeling as calm as the name of the street, and stopped to peer at the clothes in the Shelter charity shop. She

was finally admitting to herself that she needed a summer top, rather than cycle through her tatty T-shirts forever, and that she could afford to buy one at last.

She had spent three years descending the spiral into poverty and homelessness. And three years climbing out. It seemed so long ago she found it hard to remember going shopping with her mum. When Eleanor was diagnosed with cancer, Anna's life sprung a slow puncture. First, she willingly gave up her limited social life to shop and cook and take her to chemo sessions. Then her mum was too ill to work, and they couldn't afford the nice house in Blackheath. Then they moved to the council flat in Catford. Then her school studies suffered. Then her mum died. Then she was taken into care, which she hated and ran away. Then she found that squalid B&B. Then she begged a friend to let her sleep on the sofa because she couldn't stand the drunks who crashed around the place in the middle of the night, nor the used needles dropped across the floor of the shared kitchenette. Then she outstayed her welcome and lost a friend. And another. Then she got on a coach to Nottingham to find her aunt, Jane. And in a very strange way she found her. And Robin Hood, whom she fell in love with.

But that is another story, thought Anna and turned her attention back to the second-hand top, dark green with a light green leaf pattern, in the window. It was only a fiver, and the cash would go to a good cause. One of several that had seen her through the tunnel and out the other side. Anna had her friend Angela to thank for that. Doctor Briars had listened patiently to Anna as she told her improbable story, while both were patients in Nottingham's hospital. Angela had been waiting for a mastectomy. Anna didn't know that at the time, she only found out later, but somehow it made her feel closer to Angela. Both scarred by cancer: one of them inside and one inside-out. Angela gave Anna her first job: tour guide at Nottingham

Castle. She loved it, and at last it meant she could afford to buy a few things new. But Angela understood that Anna was on a mission now and had given her blessing to take some extended leave.

Anna touched her bank card to the reader by the till. It felt odd to have a bank card again, almost as if she had been re-admitted to a private club. Not far from the truth. She found a small cubicle at the back of the shop to change into the top then stuffed her old T-shirt into the pocket of her oversized overcoat. She wasn't wearing the coat, just carrying it. Too warm to wear a coat in May, but old habits died slow. It always paid to have a warm coat to hand, just in case.

Further up the street she turned left, skirting the benches around The Crown, into her old street, Southvale Road. Familiar Victorian terraces embraced her, leading her downhill and around the corner to the right. Close to the far end, near the primary school she'd gone to, was their old home. A smart black door in a white, flat arched surround with a matching set of flat arched openings for the sash windows above and beside. She had no idea who lived there now. In a way she didn't care. It was quiet so she sat down on the steps, next to the black iron railings to gather her thoughts and memories.

Her father was an absentee for most of Anna's life. Life with her mum had not been idyllic. They loved each other, but they would argue too, more often as Anna grew into her teens. It made her wince now. She'd been a stroppy madam sometimes and occasionally her mum had made a surgical strike with an acid observation or sarcastic quip. In hindsight it seemed pretty normal, but at the time it stung, and Anna would fly off in a rage then use her ability to go searching the past for the ghost family who lived in the house a generation before. That wasn't normal. It was also one of the many reasons Anna became so isolated from her few friends and ended up on the streets when all the threads came loose. If only she could go back and tell herself that...

Anna closed her eyes and watched the sun roll back to the far eastern end of the street. Then night, then day, then a blur as the seasons rolled back. She counted each summer going backwards until she would have been five years old, then slowed and stopped and looked around herself. Anna was getting good at this now. Recent history she could navigate with some accuracy, it was the more distant past that she still blundered around.

For a few moments she just sat there, basking in the summer sunshine on her old doorstep, imagining she was five again and the world was still exciting and fun. It warmed her. She began to hum to herself, a tune she remembered singing at the primary school just over to her left. The school was quiet, so it must be a weekend or a holiday. She chanced a peek over her shoulder. A little girl with tangled light-brown hair stood against the sash window, nose pressed to the glass. Anna smiled and stuck her tongue out. The little girl stuck her tongue out too, then giggled. She reached up on tiptoes to pull the top sash down. Anna's heart lurched with fright in case she fell, but the girl grasped the frame and pulled it steadily down then waved a hand over the open top.

"Hello," said the girl.

"Hello, Anna," said Anna. Somehow meeting your five-year-old self was not nearly as off-putting as meeting your twenty-year old self. It was just as she had thought, you're a different person when you're that young.

"Do you know the tall pretty girl who lives here?" five-year old Anna asked.

Twenty-year old Anna knew her younger self was talking about the ghosts of the family who had lived there a few decades ago. "Yes, I do. She sings songs and she's soft-spoken and kind."

"Yeah."

"But don't forget you have good friends to play with in the school over there. Alice, Parminder, Gemma."

"They can't see the other boys and girls in the playground."

Anna could remember watching the children from the past in old fashioned long shorts and pleated skirts. "I know. It's our secret. But Parminder and the others can throw balls to you and chase you and play hide-and-seek."

"Yeah."

"Make sure they know you like them, especially Parminder and Alice." It was their sofas in Hither Green and Catford that Anna had crashed on when the B&B became too depressing. "They're stars."

"'kay."

"Shall I sing you a song?"

"Yeah."

"What shall I sing?"

"Umm. You choose."

She was tempted to suggest Pat-a-cake. It was the first thing that came into her head, and it reminded her of rescuing the bakers' girls from the fire in medieval Nottingham. Her heart lurched as she remembered who else was with her then. Her Rob. Frightened of fire, but courageous in the face of corruption. Scared of the future but safe in the past. Would she ever see him again?

"Go on," urged her young self.

Her audience was waiting and a little too mature for nursery rhymes. She stood up and put her hands against the windowpane. The girl placed her hands by Anna's, on the other side. Then she started to sing a song that her mum had taught her. One that her mum had been taught by her own mum. Élise.

"Je serai bientôt de retour
    Prenons patience...
    Attends-moi, mon amour,
    Dans ce beau coin de France,

Qui fut témoin de tant de jours
Pleins d'insouciance..."

Anna didn't understand all the words she sang in French, but she knew that she was calling on her love to wait for her. She sang softly to young Anna who smiled and listened, little hands against the glass, against hers. She also sang to Rob and wondered if he really had died or if he might still be alive somewhere in medieval Nottingham.

Eventually she heard her mum calling time for lunch. Anna nearly ran after her five-year-old self, then stopped and sat down with a bump. Her mum's voice. She realised that although she had said goodbye to her that morning, she would carry on meeting her every time she travelled back to see their shared past. Time to go.

Bognor Regis, May 2022

The train was late leaving Victoria. Anna didn't care, she didn't need to be anywhere on time. She was able to think about who to see, where, when and in which order. She was going to Pagham to find her grandma, dead for over fifteen years, to ask her some leading questions.

Anna had many questions about her strange time travelling ability and it was a revelation that she had a family member she could go back in time to ask. The question that burned fiercest was what had happened to her dear Rob. Rob Ahmed had been another homeless wanderer on the streets of Nottingham, just like Anna. He hadn't been the easiest person to get to know. Anna would admit that she wasn't either. But if it hadn't been for Rob then she seriously wondered whether she would have made it this far. He was an accidental time traveller, just like Anna, and together they discovered her ancestors in medieval Nottingham, fought injustice and helped the poor. The awkward orphan, Rob Ahmed, had become the legendary Robin Hood, and she loved him. And missed him.

She had returned from medieval Nottingham back to 2019 because she had so many questions to ask, and she wanted to see her mother again before she died. Anna had returned alive, holding Rob's body. It tore her heart in two. She hoped with all that was left of her heart that he was still alive, enjoying the medieval Greenwood with their friends, Tuck, Ruth, and Little John. She hoped that seeing him dead in 2019 didn't extinguish his life in 1215. The discovery that her body journeyed with her when she time travelled suggested that Rob had died. But she clung to a hope that he might have that other existence in the past. The obvious thing to do was travel back to the point in medieval time, just after she left, to see if he were still alive. But Anna couldn't face that. What if he was dead? It would be like losing him all over again. Worse still, what if she couldn't find any evidence of him having been there at all? No. She had to find out another way, ask someone who understood time travel better than she did. Not only did she want Rob to be alive, but she also wanted to return to him in the medieval forest village. She loved him. She had promised him.

After being held at rural Barnham for a while, the train pulled into the gently crumbling station at Bognor Regis. Not the most auspicious start to a time travelling odyssey, but we all start somewhere, thought Anna. She wandered down Station Road, into the pedestrianised high street lined with a motley mix of takeaways, tanning parlours, and bargain shops. She was sad and unsurprised to see a young guy sitting against the white-washed glass wall of an empty shopfront with a begging cup held despondently over his knees. She was only surprised she hadn't seen others. She dug inside her pockets and found a few coins. She made a point of looking him in the eye and smiling as she gave. She knew from bitter experience that was worth more than the coins.

Ahead of her was a glass roofed arcade. Apart from a cluster of people sitting down to a fish and chips lunch at the near end, most of the units had posters promising retail delights to come. It was all but empty. Just like so many high streets she had seen away from London, Bognor's was suffering. Perhaps more so because it was an unfashionable seaside resort. She emerged onto a service road and a barren wasteland of tarmac beyond. It was only the hint of sea and the cry of seagulls that enticed her to negotiate them. After fighting her way across another road and enough railings to hold back a seaborne invasion, she made it to the beach. 'Beach' was a generous word for a bank of pebbles stretching further than she could see to left and right, but there was seawater only yards away and she always got excited at that. Anna half ran, half slid down the stony bank, threw off her shoes and waded into the water up to her knees, giggling.

It was a long time since she had been to the seaside. She used to love it as a kid, and she felt like a kid again now. No need to be anywhere soon, no work to be done and no one telling her what to do. To the west was the old seaside pier and arcade. It reminded her of the arcade at Goose Fair in Nottingham where she had such a wonderful evening with Rob.

Rob.

If only he could be here to share this with her. She waded back to the pebbles, found a clear patch without sweet wrappers and tar, then lay back to let the sunshine dry her.

The sun was low in the sky when she woke. Must be early evening, she thought. She was hungry, so she walked to the pier and bought a bag of chips to eat while she wandered on westward, in the direction of Pagham and the setting sun. About half a mile along she passed a line of little beach huts all painted different shades and colours. A few were still open, their proud owners sitting in the doorways with a thermos flask or a can of beer and a newspaper. It made her smile. The obvious question was why sit in a hut at the beach on a sunny evening? But she knew the answer was that they wanted to be able to sit and watch the sea when it wasn't sunny. The fact that it was sunny now, didn't alter their habit of sitting in a hut. A peculiarly English answer to a peculiarly English question.

Further on she saw a rusted metal hulk emerging from the retreating waters. Anna veered off the pebbles to take a closer look. It was covered in tiny barnacles and lodged deep in the rapidly draining sand. She wondered if it was a shipwreck, but it didn't look the right shape. Something about it felt familiar but she wasn't sure why. A cross brace had all but crumbled away and there were three clusters of barnacled bolts sticking up in the air, which looked like it had been attached to something. Then it came to her. This was the section of Mulberry Harbour that she had seen break free in the storm before D-Day, her first memory of looking into the past as a four-year-old.

It was always a strange mix of wonder and reassurance to find physical evidence of her ability. She gave it a gentle pat and turned back to her path along the beach. Another couple of miles further on she found a familiar lane leading north, off the beach towards the harbour. Past the bungalows and the café was the enticingly named Lagoon Road, a narrow potholed track lined with scruffy shrubs and more bungalows. At the far end the bungalows petered out into a large open bank of shingle and scrub, sandwiched between the harbour and the sea. A forest of dinghy sails bobbed and drifted across the harbour. There were a couple of shabby old cabins with draughty windows, bitumen roofs and peeling weather boards. Paradise on the south coast, thought Anna with a wry smile. The one on the right was where her grandma had lived.

Anna found a quiet spot on the lane beside the cabin where she could slip back in time unnoticed. She counted the summers going backwards till she judged she had the right year, though she wasn't sure what day it was. It was a sunny afternoon, the air smelled salty and fresh, and there was a thin elegant elderly woman with a neat white bob, a smart skirt and cardigan, holding a watering can over a bed of dahlias. Her Grandma. Anna wasn't sure how Élise would react to a visit from her granddaughter, all grown up when she had only been four last time Élise looked, but of all the people she knew, at least Élise would have some frame of reference to put it in. Just as she hovered by the hedge, her grandma looked up and saw her.

"Ah, Anna, you have come at last. Sit here on the garden bench, I shall bring you coffee."

Not Quite Everything You Ever Wanted to Know…

Pagham Harbour, Sussex, 2006

So many questions. The first one was: "How do you know who I am?"

"I would have thought that was obvious, my dear," said Élise over her shoulder as she walked to her kitchen. "Because I have met you in your twenties before."

She left Anna to mull that one over while enjoying the beauty of a lovingly tended English garden. Lovingly tended by a French woman, in memory of her departed husband. Her grandad Jim had died when she was only one, so she had no memory of him other than the photos that Élise and Eleanor had kept around their homes. Anna wondered what Jim had been like. Every photo portrayed him with an easy smile, as if he'd just shared a joke with the person taking the shot. She imagined she would have liked him and wondered why she hadn't asked more questions about him before.

Élise returned with an elegant coffee pot and two small cups on a tray. Coffee served French style. No lactations to change the flavour or dilute the caffeine kick. Just a bowl so full of sugar it made her teeth jangle. Anna smiled and took a cup, she found she needed it to revive her from the journey.

"You have many questions," stated Élise, looking at Anna over the top of her black-rimmed glasses.

"Mm. Yes, I do." Anna took a long sip of strong black coffee to jump-start her thoughts. "Why did you teach me to see the past when I was four? And did you teach Mum?"

Élise shrugged. "I just felt I should. And no, I did not teach Eleanor."

Anna wasn't sure if her grandma was being completely open. "Why not?"

"Because it is a danger as well as a blessing. The twentieth century saw so many changes. People have changed. Before that some treated time travel as witchcraft and the worst that was likely to happen to the witch was being burned at the stake."

"Shi..." Anna put her hand to her mouth, "Sorry Grandma, but what could be worse than that?"

"Don't be such a prude, Anna, just learn to swear in French, it is far more elegant and satisfying. There are many things worse than one person being burned as a witch. Thousands of people could be burned or tortured or incarcerated indefinitely while being treated as if they are sick in the mind. Persecutions are not new, but the twentieth century has perfected them, raised them to a great art form with ordinary people as their unwilling canvas."

Anna could hear the anger in her grandma's voice and had her first hint that she could be a formidable woman. "What we do is that dangerous?"

"Of course! You think our travels go unnoticed?"

Anna remembered how her ancestors in medieval Nottingham had put it all together and how she had to admit her origin in the twenty-first century. She realised she had been lucky. They were good kind people. She could have been unlucky... "I guess not. But why is it not talked about?"

"Because it frightens those who cannot do it."

"We frighten them?"

"Absolutely! Imagine what you could do with such a talent. Nudge a few thoughts here, remove a few obstinate people there, blow the embers of a revolution that had never been recorded in any of the history books. Until you return and re-read them, et voila! Vivre la revolution!"

"Oh my God." It wasn't that the thought hadn't occurred to Anna before, it was just that she hadn't followed it. She remembered her dear friend Ruth discouraging such thoughts in the medieval Greenwood. "They fear us. Rich and powerful people fear us."

"Absolutely. We are…" Élise searched for the right word, "…incendiary. And there are many more rich and powerful people around now than there were a hundred, two hundred, three hundred years ago. Unfortunately, the poor have remained poor, and we, the time travellers, have become even fewer."

"But there are more than you and me?"

"Oh yes. We come from a family of time travellers. And there are others."

Anna wondered if Rob had come from such a family. "Is it hereditary? Something genetic? Or does it have to be learned?"

Élise shrugged again, that Gallic shrug. "A little of both, I think. I am told that someone can be taught without any history of travellers in their family, but I believe it helps if you do."

"So why me? Why protect Mum and then teach me?"

Élise looked away, as if she didn't want to answer. "I saw you looking."

"What do you mean? I was only four, what did you see me do?"

"You had that look that told me your body was here, but your mind was elsewhere. I never saw Eleanor do it, but I recognised it in you, so I taught you a little focus. Just a little, so you could better control it."

Anna still wasn't sure how much Élise was letting on, but she thought over this information. So long as she could remember, she had been able to see into the past if the circumstances felt right, but they had always seemed random events. As if they were the most colourful pictures in a picture book that she flicked through at a whim. Her life changed when she was attacked by the man in the jacket. She fell down a hole in the ground and little Beatrice had helped her out into Victorian Nottingham. Not a vision, not an observation or a dream, she had been there. Walked the gas-lit streets, supped the parsnip soup, felt the heat off the burning castle and the whack on the back of her head from the flat of a cavalry sabre. "So, how did I go from seeing to travelling?"

"Because you are a natural." It was said with some contempt for the stupidity of the question, but Anna detected a hint of pride. "You are descended from the family Couteau. You understand how the word translates to English?"

Anna's French was rudimentary. She was no linguist, but she rummaged her school French and guessed: "Knife?"

"Exactly. You are a knife. You cut through time; you cannot help it. And now you are here because you have many questions, and you know to come here because your mother said she saw me teaching you. I knew she saw me teaching you, so this meeting was inevitable."

Anna studied Élise's face, stern yet compassionate. Old, yet still sharp. As sharp as a knife. "Will you teach me more?"

"I am too old," she waved away the request with her hand.

"You seem pretty perky to me."

"I do not have time. Hah! Such irony!" Élise looked away, across the harbour towards the bobbing sails. "I have enjoyed all the time in the world, but now I have so little."

Anna remembered. Élise had died early the next year, peacefully in her sleep as her mum had said. "You know."

"Yes of course I know. I have travelled forward and seen my end. I do not wish to go there again."

"You said you had met my current self. Before now."

"The nineteen-forties, in my hometown. That is another reason why I taught you a little focus. What more harm could I do?"

"Did you teach me there? Then, in Vire?"

Élise shrugged.

"Did you?" she persisted.

"I did not like you then. I was... how you say, prickly."
"But you did, didn't you?" said Anna, her eyes narrowing.
"Perhaps."

Anna tried to draw more from her grandma that afternoon, but Élise became more evasive and frustratingly vague. Any questions about what happened to time travellers' dead bodies seemed taboo in the light of her own imminent demise, as gentle as it might be. She felt frustrated. Her grandma had said so much and yet she had left so much more unsaid that it made Anna's new knowledge almost useless. Not quite everything she ever wanted to know about time travelling and now she was afraid to ask.

Anna yawned and realised that late afternoon in 2006 was middle of the night when she left 2022. Élise showed her to a tiny spare bedroom, barely able to fit the neatly made single bed, and Anna collapsed into a world of strange dreams. Stormy waves, brightly painted beach huts floating out to sea, chip shops full of people muttering secrets, a woman in a long dark coat revealing the glint of a knife beneath its folds, and something mournful that lurked at the very edge of her thoughts. Or rather a cold and pitiless absence...

She woke once with a start, clutching her chest. It was pitch black. No streetlights, but she could hear the waves breaking on the shore outside. She listened to the waves for a while and lay back. They calmed her. Eventually she drifted away again, a deep and dreamless sleep this time.

Her grandma greeted her in the little sunlit kitchen with coffee, toast, and homemade rhubarb jam. Simple but delicious.

Élise was wearing a different blouse with a lower neckline. As she was buttering the toast, Anna caught a glimpse of a scar running up the back of her neck. It looked old yet deep. She wanted to ask how Élise got it, but somehow it felt too private.

"You are going to Vire now," Élise stated. Anna noticed how she pronounced it: Veer.

"Yes," said Anna.

"I will be difficult to talk to but persist. I sense that you are sufficiently stubborn Anna Partington."

"I am," she admitted, then realised that Élise had used her chosen surname, her mum's maiden name and her grandfather Jim's surname. The name on her birth certificate was Fitzwalter. Presumably, she had told Élise that in the past. "You don't think it odd that I avoid my father's name."

"In the circumstances, I think it wise."

"What do you mean?"

"Like many other questions I have left annoyingly unanswered," Élise said with uncanny self-awareness, "this one is best answered by my younger self. Better you go and see and understand more fully than an old woman can tell. But I will tell you one thing before you go, for all the good it will do. Take great care what you do in the past. Remember that every act has consequences. Every act of everyday. Some may be good. Some will be bad. You may think you are acting with good intention, but you can never ever know exactly what your actions may lead to."

"So, like, don't kill anyone," said Anna, remembering how she shot Sir Gisborne with an arrow to stop him from killing Rob. She still had mixed emotions about that. She had been forced to. Rob had frozen with fear when he saw Gisborne's flaming sword and if she hadn't acted Rob would have died. But instead, Gisborne died. Anna felt numb at the time, a shock at the taking of a life, no matter how evil or deserved. But she had also felt a strange and shameful strength: standing up to an abusive bully. Until now she had only dwelled on these emotions. Now Élise had added further guilt for the consequences of her actions.

"Especially that," said Élise, fiercely. Anna looked Élise in the eyes, trying to determine the thoughts behind them. Anger? Fear? Regret? She wanted to ask if Élise had ever killed anyone but that was not an easy question to ask anyone, particularly your grandmother. "Remember," continued Élise, "all acts have consequences."

Anna just nodded. "Thank you, Grandma. I look forward to meeting you for the first time in Vire."

Élise's face softened. "Take care, my dear." And she took Anna's hands in hers then kissed her softly once on both cheeks. "Bon voyage."

The Little Cats

Caen, Normandy, May 2022

Seagulls circled. The sea-breeze blew hair across her face. Anna held the deck rail and leaned out to watch the shore crew conjuring order from the chaos below. It had been a smooth crossing from Portsmouth, for which she was greatly relieved. She was slightly ashamed to admit that anything more than a stiff breeze on a ship made her seasick. Ironic for a time traveller.

She queued with the other foot passengers for the shuttle to take her to the official border. That was another thing that felt strange: having a passport again. Her old one had expired while she was sleeping rough, and it had taken ages for her to organise a new one. She may be able to cut through time but there was no circumventing the wait for Her Majesty's Passport Office, if you had previously been of 'no fixed abode'. The officer in the booth examined her photo then stared at her until she felt uncomfortable.

"Bonjour," she offered.

He gave a curt nod and waved her on. Anna had developed a deep suspicion of people in authority. She had seen how easy it was for them to abuse it, especially when dealing with the vulnerable and homeless. She tried to understand that it was a boring job, and it must be difficult to respond to the hundreds of people he saw each day. She put it out of her mind and went in search of the bus for Caen and looked up the times for the next one that would take her on to Vire.

What little she saw of Caen did not differ from any modern city. High rise apartments, shiny office blocks, retail parks and traffic. Lots of traffic, all through the centre and out to the ring roads. She caught a fleeting glimpse of gothic church arches and old stone walls, but they seemed swamped by the twenty-first century.

Vire, Normandy, May 2022

The road out of Caen towards Vire was a refreshing contrast. Rolling hills, hedge-lined fields, herds of cows and the occasional stand of tall white wind turbines turning gracefully in the breeze. It seemed a shame to forsake all that for another retail park on the edge of Vire, but once they were climbing the hill to the town centre, it felt more like her notion of a French market town. Two long lines of neatly planted poplar trees gave way to a cluster of houses, a couple of small hotels, a little café on the corner of the junction and an open space with more trees. Far less traffic than Caen, and many of the parked cars were discreetly tucked away behind flower troughs and neatly trimmed hedges. She thanked the coach driver and hopped off, finding herself opposite a small round tourist office with a conical roof. Someone had put a little thought into that, and not just its location. Anna noticed a line of flags on tall white poles in front of it. German, Spanish, British, French and a red and yellow one she took a moment to recognise. She had seen it before, in medieval Nottingham. Worn on the tunics and shields of Sir Gisborne and his men.

Anna's knees almost went from under her, and she staggered to a wooden bench, clutching her modest rucksack and her oversized overcoat. An elderly man come over and said something to her in French which she guessed meant 'Are you okay, love?' She nodded and smiled and mimed being out of breath. The man smiled too and wished her 'bon vacances'.

Looking more closely, she noticed there were only two yellow lions on the red flag, not three, but the similarity was uncanny, and she wondered if there were any historical connections. She got up and crossed the road to the tourist office where the friendly lady on the counter assessed her with an expert eye and addressed Anna in embarrassingly perfect English.

"Welcome to Vire, how may I help you?"

Anna took a moment to organise her thoughts. "Hello. Er, I'd be very grateful for a list of places to stay. Economy, please."

"No problem," she said and produced a list, conscientiously going through it to point out prices and where to find them using the map on the back. "May I help you with anything else?" she concluded.

"Yes, where's the nearest library?"

"Ah! A scholar! Take this road to the roundabout and turn right into the main square, Place du Six Juin Dix-neuf Cent Quarante-quatre. There you will see a large gateway and clock tower, our Porte-Horloge. Take the road to the right of the Porte-Horloge, Rue de Chênedollé. The Médiathèque is just around the curve, next to the music school on the right-hand side."

Anna thanked her and set off up the road. It was lined with cosy bistros, chic clothes shops, a florist and a boulangerie. The comparison with poor run-down Bognor was stark. Was Vire immune to the ravages of internet shopping, economic depressions and pandemics, or did the French place more importance on shopping in person? She looked in the window of the boulangerie. An Artisan Boulanger, no less! Anna's mouth watered at the wonderful aromas and display of confections. She dug in her pockets for some of the euros she had bought on the ferry and used a mix of schoolgirl French and pointing to buy an early lunch. She couldn't help nibbling a corner of the baguette on the way to the public square. It was delicious. And the éclair melted in her mouth. What must French people make of Greggs, she wondered? Best not ask.

The square was a sunlit space with little flags that danced on overhead lines radiating from a pole over the flower festooned roundabout. The buildings around it had stone walls and regular windows, neither old nor new, just oddly timeless. One end was dominated by an impressive medieval gatehouse with a tall clock tower standing over it. The Porte-Horloge the visitor centre woman had spoken of. Anna crossed the road and walked right up to it, running her hand across the stonework. It had corbelling and crenelations on the tops of the turrets and ivy grew up the side of the nearest tower. It was easily the oldest thing she had seen since she arrived, which struck Anna as a little odd. Surely the French had as many historic buildings as the British? She touched the edge of an arrow slit near the base and sensed something cold and deeply sad. She pulled back her hand and stepped away. The sensation took a while to fade. It felt familiar yet she had no idea why.

There were handy seats in front of the Porte-Horloge, so Anna sat down and finished her lunch while studying the gatehouse. It was charming, obviously medieval, and somehow completely out of time and place. Why did it seem so isolated there? And what had she sensed when touching it? She wiped the crumbs from her lips and set off up Rue de Chênedollé in search of answers.

Médiathèque, Vire, Normandy, May 2022

The road began so narrow Anna wondered if she had the right one, but it widened at the top and she caught a glimpse of the countryside beyond. She realised Vire was high up on a hill as she could see sunlit fields for many miles.

The Médiathèque was a fascinating mix of old and new. A modern glass entrance lobby took her under a low canopy, along the side of an imposing traditional brick structure with stone dressings and plinth. To her left the old building unfolded like a dolls house into a generous atrium where she saw several levels of bookshelves scattered with coffee tables, magazine racks, and a media centre. A middle-aged man and a young woman sat at the desk smiling.

"Bonjour Mademoiselle," said the man in the red shirt and glasses. The young woman asked her something she guessed meant 'How can we help?'

Anna did her best to reply in her limited French, cursing herself for not paying more attention in school, then handed them the letter she had carried all the way from Nottingham in the pocket of her oversized overcoat. Thankfully, Doctor Angela Briars had far better French than Anna. She also had a basic understanding of various old French dialects so that she could conduct her research, when not running the visitor centre at Nottingham castle. When Angela understood that some of Anna's family came from France, she had insisted Anna take the letter with her and explained that it was a simple introduction, 'to whom it may concern', explaining that Anna was assisting her with scholarly research.

Whatever Angela had written, the letter opened the already welcoming doors to the Vire library wide to her. The man in the smart red shirt took Anna up the stairs and found her a comfy chair with a computer, next to a glass wall with a view over a small garden. After putting her oversized overcoat on the chair and offering to look after her rucksack at the desk, he took her on a grand tour of the Médiathèque, politely ignoring the state of her oversized overcoat on their return and how it made the place look untidy.

"My name is Auguste, please do not hesitate to ask if you need anything, Mademoiselle."

Anna almost blushed. She couldn't remember any time she had been treated with such genuine respect and courtesy. She found it a little overwhelming and just kept saying thank you. Just as she was settling in, the young woman returned and re-introduced herself as Jeanne Rajaonarison. She was small, dark skinned with a frizz of black hair and a stylish summer jacket.

"Here is your card, it allows you access to all the local history files and many of the national online archives," she said. "Would you like me to help you navigate the system?"

Anna was aware of her mouth opening and closing like a turbot. She'd always felt at home in libraries, but she'd never been made such a fuss of in Nottingham Central Library. She was usually grateful that no one had noticed her or thrown her out for looking scruffy. She gathered her thoughts. "Yes... please, I'd be really grateful."

Jeanne made sure Anna understood it all and asked if there was anything else she might need.

"Well, outside the tourist information office I noticed a red flag with a pair of yellow lions. I know I can look it up now, thanks to your help, but do you happen to know whose flag it is?"

"Oh yes, it is the flag for our region. They are two leopards. We call them the little cats."

"I saw a similar one with three cats."

"Les treis cats, it is used by Upper Normandy. We are in Calvados district, Lower Normandy."

"Okay," she paused, trying not to give too much away, "I've also seen les treis cats in a medieval context. In England."

"It was the flag for William the Bastard." Anna's eyebrows shot up, surprised at Jeanne's choice of honorific. Jeanne laughed, "You call him William the Conqueror. We know him by his dubious birth!"

"Ah, okay. But did anyone use it in England after him?"

"The House of Anjou: Henry the second, Richard the First and John."

It was on the tip of Anna's tongue to say she had met King John and he didn't seem half as bad as people made out, but remembered herself and said, "Oh! So, they all had connections to Normandy?"

"Indeed, England and France were at war for over a hundred years because of their claims to Normandy."

"Oh dear, I am sorry."

Jeanne laughed again. She laughed easily and often, and Anna warmed to her. "It was William's fault, not yours!"

Anna knew that Jeanne must be over-simplifying, yet it was a compelling thought. "I can see why you call him the Bastard!"

Jeanne found that hilarious and led Anna over to a little break out space for coffee. The more they chatted, the more they found they had in common. Jeanne had come to France from Madagascar and spent a few years hand-to-mouth before Auguste took a risk and offered her a job at the Médiathèque. He said he was happy to ignore the lack of permanent address as he recognised someone who had a love of books and learning when he saw them. Just like Anna, Jeanne loved books and had been given an unexpected and all-important hand up. Now Jeanne had a small flat on the edge of Vire and had been granted French citizenship.

Anna shared a little of her experiences on the streets of Nottingham and told her how Doctor Briars had offered her the tour guide job she enjoyed so much.

"Have you a place to stay yet?" asked Jeanne.

"That's my next task. The lady in the tourist information place was really helpful."

"You would be most welcome to stay with me for a few days, just until you find somewhere suitable."

"But... that's too generous. And you barely know me."

"I have read your introduction from a doctor of archaeology at the University of Nottingham, and I know that it is good to have a little help in a new place."

"I... well... thank you, so much. I'd really appreciate that." Anna was a capable young woman. She had survived many experiences she should not have had to endure so she was prepared to make her own way. However, she was quietly thankful and relieved to have found a new friend so quickly on her first day in Vire, especially one who understood Anna in more ways than her own language.

Later that afternoon, comfortably settled in her spot by the garden view, Anna found a medieval map of the town that showed the Porte-Horloge had been one of many gates in the town walls, surrounding an inner castle keep, or donjon. That explained to her why it had seemed so isolated, standing away from the other buildings from another time. She followed a link to the local archive records which went back to William the Conqueror's day. Anna just thought of him as The Bastard now. Harsh but fair. By chance, a familiar name caught her eye among the nobles of twelfth century Vire. Gisborne.

Anna nearly had her own litter of little cats.

1944

Vire, Normandy, May 2022

Anna had fallen on her feet. She wanted to keep Jeanne as a friend and not outstay her welcome, unlike her stay with Parminder in Hither Green. The very next day she set off from Jeanne's flat on the northern edge of Vire to explore and find a guest house. Jeanne had suggested Anna try the small family hotel opposite the train station, near the bottom of the hill. There was a bar at the front and the barman called his wife over to help. Madame Guérin showed Anna to a single bedroom tucked away at the back, overlooking their sunny garden. It was clean and bright as it faced south and Madame Guérin seemed friendly, so Anna took it. She had more important things to do.

Climbing back up Rue du Calvados to the town centre, she passed an elegant house set back from the street with ornate white railings and a tall gable with a round window that looked as if it had been lifted from a grand chateau. It seemed much older than most of the buildings in Vire, though not nearly as old as the castle gate. She wondered who it would have been built for and who might live there now.

Further up were a scattering of little shops and restaurants with glimpsed courtyards beyond. The road broadened beside the tourist office and the bus station where she had arrived the previous day, so Anna knew where she was and started to build on her mental map.

This time she crossed straight over at the floral roundabout and sauntered down the hill, past the glassy Hotel de Ville towards a mix of bars and Norman Creperies. Near the bottom she saw another medieval tower peeking from behind some apartments and a little greenery beyond it, so she took a right to investigate. She could see the Porte-Horloge back up the hill and guessed that the tower must be another remnant of the old medieval town walls. She didn't dare touch it in case she felt that unsettling melancholy again.

At the edge of the tree lined pavement, she saw two boys feeding ducks next to an open body of water. There was an elegant footbridge and what looked like a weir at the far end of the pool. Above her to the right was a steep wooded hill with a footpath winding up it. There must be a decent view from it she reasoned, and Anna was rewarded with an excellent panorama of the pool and the southern edge of Vire, cradled within a valley. At the top was a rocky outcrop with stark stone ruins. A sign explained that these were the remains of the donjon, or keep, of the medieval castle started by the Norman and English King Henri (Henry) the First. Ivy climbed one side and an open fireplace was visible halfway up the wall on the other. Anna wondered if the floor of the room it served had gradually crumbled or whether some catastrophic attack had brought half the keep down and exposed its inhabitants, clinging farcically to the edge of the fireplace. Anna remembered the brutal bombardment of Nottingham Castle while she was trapped in an oubliette within, then swiftly put it out of her mind.

She could see a bandstand on the open space beyond and the centre of Vire behind. Two elegant stone pavilions framed the route like gate guardians. A local history map told her the entrance to the medieval keep had been there before. The square on the other side was full of market stalls and shoppers, busy buying their groceries for the weekend under the shadow of an elegant gothic church. Anna wandered the stalls, eyeing the rich variety of vegetables, breads, and cheeses. A wonderful smell wafted across and she noticed a line of people chatting in front of an open-sided van where a blonde-haired woman was busy cooking. Someone walked away nibbling the end of a steaming crêpe and discreetly wiping chocolate sauce from the corner of their mouth. Anna had to wipe away a little dribble as she joined the queue. When her turn came Anna did her best to ask for a crêpe in halting French.

"Caramel or chocolate sauce, love?" the blonde woman said in a south London accent.

"You... you're not French?"

"Dartford, dear. I reckon you're from south London too."

"Blackheath."

"Ooh, well posh," she laughed. "You here on holiday?"

"Yes. Not that posh though. Well, I suppose Blackheath is but I'm not. And it's kind of a working holiday."

"I was just pulling your leg. Vire's a good place, take a little time to look around the countryside too. I'd better serve my regulars, so caramel or chocolate?"

"Oh! Sorry, chocolate please."

"I'll add a spoonful of Chantilly. Three euros please."

Anna thanked her and took her crêpe before remembering to ask her name: Tricia. It struck her that Tricia was a brave woman, cooking crêpes for the French! It was delicious.

After licking the last of the sauce off her fingers she wiped them on the edge of her oversized overcoat, always carried with her, and peered inside the large church. Notre Dame de Vire. It was dark compared to the square and it took a few moments for her eyes to adjust. Light crept through clerestory windows and bounced off the walls onto the nave below. Behind her was a large ornate rose window. She took a moment to sit in a pew at the rear and absorb the peace. As she did so Anna sensed a strange absence. Anna would have put it down to the sombre nature of churches had it not been for her experience the previous day. It felt a little like the melancholy of the Porte-Horloge yet dispersed, less... personal.

Anna left and followed the market stalls back into the centre then found the street to the Médiathèque. She thanked Jeanne for recommending the hotel and remarked on the English woman selling crêpes.

"There are many English who settle in Normandy," Jeanne said. "I suppose it is the shared history and being so close to Britain. Did you enjoy your walk around the town?"

"Very much. Amazing view from the donjon on the hill."

"Vire is surrounded by valleys, cut by the river Vire. I think that is why King Henri built his donjon here."

Anna would have wanted to ask more about the medieval castle, especially after having seen the name Gisborne among the list of local nobles, but her real quest was finding the young Élise. Her grandma had mentioned that she worked in a bookshop during the war.

"Do you know where I might find out about the shops in Vire in the forties?" asked Anna. "Particularly the bookshops?"

"I think there are some street photos from the thirties, but I doubt you will find much after 1940. There won't be records of shops from 1944 until the fifties at least."

"Oh, why's that?" asked Anna in all innocence, then closed her eyes as she realised the stupidity of her question. "The war!"

Jeanne nodded. "There wasn't much left after liberation. The whole town had to be rebuilt." She took Anna over to a book on the local history shelves and pointed to the photo on the cover. The battered shell of the Porte-Horloge stood in an empty wasteland. Behind was a ruined tower and the carcass of the church she had just visited, Notre Dame. No shops. No houses. No people.

Anna sank into a chair and leafed through the book in silence. Photos of a thriving market town with crowded streets contrasted starkly with harrowing scenes of destruction. A lone figure stood on a mound of debris which may have been their home. The gable wall of the church without any roof surrounded by a sea of rubble where she'd bought her crêpe from Tricia. Jeanne left Anna for a while and returned with coffees.

"I never realised," whispered Anna.

"It took me a while to work it out," said Jeanne. "The locals do not say much about it. Most of them were born after the war anyway, but even those who were there say little. Though they always put the flags across Place du Six Juin Dix-neuf Cent Quarante-Quatre each year to celebrate liberation."

"Sixth June 1944. D-Day. The bunting in the main square." Anna remembered the radial lines fluttering in the breeze over the floral roundabout.

"Yes. They are proud of their independence. And happy to see British and American tourists here."

It all made sense now. The neutral timeless architecture of the main square. The isolated feel of the Porte-Horloge. The rarity of historic buildings. Vire had been devastated in 1944. "I never realised the Nazis destroyed so much."

"It was not the Nazis who did this." Anna looked at Jeanne blankly. "It was the Allied bombers."

Anna shook her head as if denying the records of history. "But... why?"

"Vire is a crossroads, just like most towns. It was held by the Wehrmacht, the German army, and the Allies wanted to destroy the roads to slow and trap them."

"But the French people..."

Jeanne shrugged. It reminded her of Élise when something defied explanation. "Many died. Most became refugees. Eventually they rebuilt."

"Surely the Allies tried to warn them?"

Jeanne leaned across and leafed through the history book until she found a page with a reproduction of a leaflet printed in French. "They dropped copies of that," she said, "but they all missed Vire. They fell on the fields and a few nearby villages. It might have helped if they had printed 'Vire' on the leaflets but all it said was 'this town', which was not particularly useful. A few locals brought copies to a meeting of the local Council that afternoon, but they decided to ignore it."

Anna hung her head, feeling shame at the actions of her ancestors. "And they welcome British and American tourists?"

"Oh yes. The Americans liberated Vire, and the British liberated many other towns in Normandy. There is a plaque that honours the American soldiers on the hill opposite the donjon."

Anna was dumbfounded. She didn't know which was more difficult to understand: the resilience of the French citizens of Vire who rebuilt their homes from the rubble or their forgiveness for those who bombed their homes into oblivion.

At the end of the afternoon, as the sun caressed the tree-tops, she crossed the valley and climbed the hill to find a memorial dedicated to the fallen soldiers who brought freedom to the people of Vire. She sat cross-legged on the patch of grass beside it, looking at the donjon among the trees and the pool below. She wondered what the view would have been like in June 1944. She wondered what Élise had been doing then. And she realised she would have to travel back to 1944 to find Élise. There would be nothing left of Vire after that date for many years to come. Much earlier than 1944 and Élise would have been a young girl, not a young woman, with fewer answers for Anna. The only viable window in time to find her grandma would be during the occupation.

"...and he was very handsome," finished Jeanne and wiggled her eyebrows, making them all laugh. Jeanne was giving her verdict on the star in the latest Hollywood remake of Robin Hood to her friends, Yvette and Renée. She had invited Anna to join them at the cinema, just up the road from the Médiathèque, and relax afterwards with a glass of wine in the brasserie opposite. Anna appreciated Jeanne talking in English, it was a thoughtful gesture and there was no way she could keep up with them otherwise. They didn't seem to mind as the film had been in English with subtitles and they were still in the zone, poking fun at the American take on Olde England. Anna refrained from saying what she remembered of real life in medieval Nottingham, and she was distinctly unimpressed with the choice of male lead. She had fallen in love with the real Robin Hood and there was no one to hold a candle to him in her eyes. Braver, more self-effacing, and a sense of social justice that burned so bright that any film character seemed insincere.

"... Anna? Hello, Anna!"

"Oh! Sorry, I was miles away." About three-hundred miles and eight-hundred years.

"We were asking what you thought of him. The hunky Robin!"

"He was nice, I guess."

"Nice! Is this an English understatement?" asked Yvette, laughing.

"Not really my type," smiled Anna.

"And who is your type, Anna Partington?" asked Yvette salaciously. Jeanne giggled and Renée rolled his eyes.

"Dark, brown eyes, unassuming and cantankerous."

"What is this 'cantankerous'?"

"Bloody difficult but charming with it," explained Anna.

"Aha! Like my Renée," nodded Yvette sagely.

Jeanne thought this was hilarious. Renée was bewildered. Anna smiled and looked wistfully into her wineglass.

Afterwards Jeanne walked Anna back to the hotel. "See you tomorrow in the Médiathèque?"

"I'll be away for a few days in Rouen," lied Anna, "to meet a friend," she added, which was slightly nearer the truth. "I really enjoyed this evening, thanks for asking me along." And that was the truth.

"It was good to have you with us. Thank you for teaching us a new word, Anna Cantankerous Partington," she laughed. "Bon voyage!"

Anna found her room and prepared for the voyage. Before dawn she would go to the garden behind the hotel and look for a discreet corner to hide in and search for the past.

Vire, Normandy, June 1944

Counting summers had been a challenge. Anna wasn't sure if she had counted seventy-eight or seventy-nine, but she could tell it was a summer's evening, close to sunset. She dreaded the thought of trying to keep her focus while counting off eight-hundred-and-seven if she were ever to search for Rob. Anna wondered how she had navigated back to 1215 in the first place. Had it been luck, or had she been guided by her ancestors?

She stood up out of a thriving vegetable patch and took her bearings. It had been a laurel bush in 2022. She found a narrow alleyway between the houses that led out to the street in front of the station. The single-storey glass station pavilion was gone, replaced by a two-storey period façade with shutters. A plume of steam rose from the tracks behind it. A steam engine. It was tempting to look, but she wanted to get to the town centre before the shops closed. Her grandma might be leaving.

EVERYDAY SPIRITS

The Rue du Calvados felt narrower, crowded with little stone houses. An elderly man in a flat cap passed her on the other side of the street, head down, no eye contact. Further up the hill on the left she saw the white railings of the elegant house she had noticed after finding her hotel room. It was only when she drew level that she saw the flag hanging from the first-floor windows. For the second time in Vire the sight of a flag chilled her spine. There was no mistaking this one: a black swastika on a white circle in a blood red field.

Welcome to occupied Vire. Anna had stumbled on the local headquarters of the Wehrmacht. A German soldier stood sentry outside the door, so she decided not to linger, putting her head down like the old man and walking on up towards the town centre.

The road was cobbled. A handful of vintage cars and an old farm truck were parked against the kerb. A few cyclists whizzed past her on their way down the hill out of town. Shopkeepers pushed brightly coloured canopies back into their housings with poles and pulled the wooden shutters back against the shop windows. The pharmacist was about the only one still open, everyone else was going home. Was Anna too late to find Élise that day? She hurried to the junction expecting to see the flowers on the roundabout and the main public square, but instead she found herself at cross-roads, with an equally narrow street leading off either side. The buildings felt much older, some of them looked as if they had been gently crumbling there for hundreds of years. At last, she saw a familiar sight to her right: the Porte-Horloge with its ancient clock tower and gateway. It was jammed in between the shops either side, not standing alone anymore. She knew there had been a couple of bookshops on Rue Saulnerie, near the church, so she headed on with purpose.

At the medieval gateway she was stopped by a tall German soldier. He wore long black boots, a dark grey-green uniform, a cap, and slung over his shoulder was a business looking rifle.

"Papers please." His accent was Germanic, it sounded a little like the Saxon accents she had heard in medieval Nottingham. He seemed tired. Testy.

Anna froze. It hadn't occurred to her that she would need a form of identity in occupied France. It did occur to her that he was either speaking French or German, yet she was understanding him as if he spoke English. She wondered again what happened in her mind that allowed her to understand and be understood.

"Er, I forgot them," she tried.

His demeanour changed from tired to irritated. "Come with," he said in a curt voice, and gestured back the way she had come.

"I can go get them."

"No. You come with me," and he gripped her firmly by the elbow marching her back along the street to the cross-roads. He seemed agitated now.

Anna didn't like being manhandled. She didn't like people abusing their authority. She snatched her arm away from him and was about to run when she was struck by the butt of his rifle from behind. She fell to the ground, her head bouncing off the cobbles with a smack. Anna struggled to fill her lungs with air then let out a groan of pain and anger.

The soldier hauled Anna to her feet again and pointed the barrel at her. There was no arguing with that.

Within a couple of minutes, she found herself back at the swastika-bedecked chateau, sitting on a hard wooden chair in front of a German officer who regarded her with a mix of suspicion and fascination. He was quite young, probably early-twenties, had dark hair and wire rimmed spectacles. He looked more like a librarian or bank clerk than a soldier. She reminded herself that was what many of them had been until 1939, when they were called up to serve the Fatherland. He looked more like an administrator than a fierce invading warrior. Again, that was likely what he spent most of his time doing. That and dealing with tiresome locals who forgot their papers.

"What is your name, Fraulein?"

Anna was under pressure. "Marie Ann Couteau." It was a half-truth, borrowing her grandma's maiden name and replacing her christened first with a French sounding version of Mary.

"Couteau?" The officer seemed genuinely surprised and interested. "You do not sound French."

"I was brought up in England." True enough.

"You are related to Élise?"

Good god, he knew her. "Yes. She's my gr... cousin." Oops, nearly messed that up.

"So, I shall call her here. She will vouch for you."

Oh no. What if she said, 'I've never seen this woman in my life', which in 1944 would be perfectly true. "Mm," nodded Anna and wondered if it would be a good time to start praying to some random saint.

There's a Storm Coming

Vire, Normandy, June 1944

An elegant young woman stepped through the office door, accompanied by the sentry, flicking back her dark hair. She pursed her lipstick lips to smile at the officer who stood and went to kiss the white gloved hand she offered. She wore a matching light grey jacket and skirt that looked as if they might have been tailored from a man's suit with reasonable skill, and she carried it off with more. Her heels were poised in polished high heels, with stockings which must have been expensive for that time, unless they were borrowed like the material for her suit. Her hair flowed to her shoulders in Lauren Bacall curls that seemed to Anna as if it may have been carefully arranged to look natural. Anna's hair just flowed. All over the place. The young woman was gorgeous, and she knew it. Neither man could take their eyes off her. Nor Anna for that matter, but for a different reason. Despite carrying herself as if she were in her early thirties, Anna had worked out the woman had to be only seventeen or eighteen.

"Thank you so much for attending Mademoiselle Couteau," said the officer.

"My pleasure, Lieutenant Lehman." The woman's pleasure faded as she turned to look at their detainee. Anna was being assessed, rapidly and astutely, by this self-assured young woman. Younger than her. "Ah, so good to see you," she declared and leaned forward to kiss Anna slowly and deliberately on each cheek. "Who the hell are you?" she murmured in Anna's left ear, so quietly she barely heard, and the men would have had no chance.

"Cousin Marie Ann Couteau," Anna whispered as the young woman screened her lips from the soldiers with her head at Anna's other cheek.

"What brings you here from Saint-Sever, Cousin Marie?" she asked bright and clear.

"I was hoping to talk to you about our local history, Élise. I thought you might have something in your bookshop. I'm so sorry I forgot my papers and caused all this trouble."

"No trouble," said Élise, waving away Anna's apology. Her eyes said otherwise. They were skewering Anna to the wall of the office. "Let me take you back to our apartment. We can bring your papers to the Lieutenant's office tomorrow, can't we?"

"No hurry, Mademoiselle. It is a long walk so any day this week would be fine," Lieutenant Lehman smiled and bowed to Élise.

"Thank you," said Anna. The officer nodded affably but the sentry carried on eyeing her with suspicion. Anna returned his gaze with a rebellious frown and felt a dig in her ribs from Élise beside her.

Up the hill, out of sight and sound of the Wehrmacht headquarters, Élise stopped and turned to Anna. "Do not ever do anything as reckless as that again! I do not care if they put you on a train to the east or stand you up against a wall with a blindfold but understand this. For every idiot like you, there will be at least five innocents who will lose their freedom or their life. The Allies plan to invade in a matter of days, and the Wehrmacht know it. They are looking for any sign of trouble, no matter how small," Élise put her white gloved forefinger and thumb together so close that a swatted gnat wouldn't have passed through. "I do not know who you are, but I can take a good guess at how you got here and from when." Her eyes narrowed, daring Anna to contradict her. She obviously recognised a twenty-first century time traveller when she saw one.

Anna took a step back. She felt as if she had been physically assaulted and, she now realised, with good reason. "I'm your granddaughter," she said eventually. "And I really am sorry. I didn't think."

Élise's beautiful dark eyebrows rose momentarily then returned to a menacing glower. "I do not suppose that Marie Ann Couteau is your real name."

"Mary Ann Partington. But I prefer Anna."

"If you wish to live then you are Marie Ann Couteau now. You had better remember it. One slip and there will be blood on your hands. Not just yours."

Anna nodded. She didn't do contrite, but she was making a passable attempt at it.

Élise turned on her elegant heel and stalked on up the hill. After a few yards she stopped and looked back at Anna. "Well? Are you coming to our apartment or not?"

Chez Couteau, Vire, Normandy, May 1944

The apartment was above her bookstore on Rue Saulnerie, a few hundred yards past the Porte-Horloge. The door from the landing opened onto a kitchen-diner-living space with a dim silhouette of Notre Dame against the skyline opposite. Candles threw a flickering half-light across the walls and ceiling. A small wooden table was set for two. A fair-haired young man about the same age as Anna stood and offered his hand.

"Good evening, Mademoiselle. My name is Henri."

"My brother," explained Élise. "She calls herself Marie Ann Couteau. My cousin from Saint-Sever."

Henri nodded to show that he understood her cover story.

"Pleased to meet you, Henri," said Anna shaking his hand. "I'm actually..."

"... very hungry," cut in Élise with an icy glare, "but she should know that we have little to share." Anna was starting to understand the severity of occupation, and if Henri only knew her cover then he couldn't give her away.

"On the contrary," smiled Henri, "we had a gift this afternoon. A rabbit freshly caught. I was about to prepare our supper and I am sure it will serve three."

Élise put her hands on her hips and looked at the ceiling. "It seems you are staying. But only for tonight. Tomorrow I find your papers and you take them straight to Château Jeannin." Seeing Anna's puzzled face, she added, "The Kreiskommandantur. The German headquarters, where I went to retrieve you."

Anna resented being referred to as if she were a click-and-collect package. She turned to Henri and said, "Thank you, I appreciate it."

"And after you must return home," said Élise, firmly.

"But I've come specially to find you. I have so many questions to ask."

"They can wait. I am busy."

"Running a bookshop?"

"Surviving." Élise turned to her brother and gestured to a door with her eyes. He nodded and took the rabbit carcass and a meagre handful of vegetables into the back room with a knife and a chopping board. When he closed the door, Élise turned back to Anna. "Sit."

Anna objected even more to being talked to like a beagle. She stood firm. Élise rolled her eyes.

"Do you have any idea what happens in occupied Normandy now?" she asked, folding her arms like a stern headteacher.

"The Allies win. The Nazis are driven out of France."

"There is a storm coming. I know. I have travelled forward in time to see it and I have returned with whatever information I could find to do whatever I can. There are British, American, Canadian,

French, Polish and heaven knows how many other nationalities, hundreds of thousands of soldiers all preparing to board ships and sail the channel, as we speak. Many of them will sail to their death. For every allied soldier that dies on the beaches of Normandy a German soldier will die too, and more French civilians will die than all of them put together. We are trapped between two armies who are intent on annihilating each other. After four years of occupation, suspicion, brutality, and semi-starvation, we will be bombed by Allied aircraft. We will be shelled by Allied artillery. Our homes will be destroyed, and we will be left with nothing but what we stand in. And you want to ask me some questions?"

Anna stood holding her grandmother's hostile stare. "Why don't you leave? If you can time-travel like me, why don't you get out of this time?"

"You think I should leave my brother?"

"He can't..."

"No! He is not a time traveller like us. And our mother is dead. The German troops entered Vire four years ago. She stood in the road to shake her fist and curse at them, and she was shot dead on the spot. The SS were making an example. Her name was Estelle. Our father was taken for forced labour at the Siemens munition's factory in Essen the same year. Yes, the same Siemens that you will all blithely buy refrigerators from in the future. We have not seen or heard from him since, nor will we. I have searched the future. It is likely he died in one of the Allied fire-bomb attacks on Essen. His name was Étienne. So, who is going to look after Henri? Who is going to look after our home, our town, our people?"

Anna saw the rage in Élise's beautiful face. She also saw her fear and vulnerability. She looked like a frightened teenager acting bravely, hurling defiance at the world. Anna stepped forward and took her hand. "I didn't understand, but I do now. I am so sorry. For my great grandparents and for everything that you and Henri endure now. I shall go after I have shown the papers tomorrow. I shall find you some other time and perhaps we can make a new start."

Élise looked down at her hand in Anna's. She seemed surprised. Some of the rage faded from her eyes, her face began to relax. "Please. Take a chair. I shall call Henri."

Henri chatted amiably about how lucky they were to have been given the rabbit, the length of the queue at the boulangerie, the price of swedes at the market stalls and the weather. Beautiful today, but rain due that night. Anna suspected he overheard a little of their discussion and certainly sensed the tension when he returned. He seemed like a natural-born peacemaker. The world could do with a few more of them, she thought.

That night she slept on a nest of coats on the floor, including her oversized overcoat. It had rarely left her side for the last five years and had all the stains, rips, and loose threads to prove it. About midnight she heard a distant grumble. She got up and stood at the window, peeking out behind the black-out curtains. There was a flicker on the horizon, and she counted the seconds until she heard the thunder. Was it thunder, or the sound of distant guns? Had the invasion started already? No. They had to wait until the storm subsided, she remembered.

Anna realised with a jolt that this was the very same storm that she had seen as a four-year-old child from the other side of the channel, on her first journey into the past. She was literally in two places at the same time. How could that be? And yet she had seen herself twice now. It defied any laws of physics that she understood. But hey, so did travelling backwards and forwards in time. Another question unanswered.

There was a ghostly white flicker of light on the horizon followed by a rumble, closer than the first. A few drops of rain rolled down the panes of glass. Here came the storm.

Élise had been out to 'find' Anna's papers before she was even awake the next morning. After a cup of ersatz coffee, one part coffee beans, five parts unidentified granules, Anna put the papers in her pocket and left to report at Château Jeannin. The rain was still falling, ponding on the cobbles, and running down the gutters. She pulled her oversized overcoat over her head and ran down the road to the Château.

A column of military lorries laboured up the hill. As they passed, she saw rows of soldiers sitting in the back, peering out through the canvas covers at the rain. Anna remembered watching a column of British army trucks, headlamps on, driving up the motorway on a wet Sunday afternoon in modern day England. They had the same sense of grim clandestine purpose about them. Perhaps those trucks had been part of Rob's regiment? Perhaps it had been him in the back of one of them, on his way to Afghanistan?

After finding a military clerk to present her undoubtedly forged papers, she stood outside the white railings looking left and right. Right was downhill, towards the vegetable patch she had emerged from. Left was uphill and the centre of occupied Vire. It was a straightforward decision. She had already promised Élise that she would go, but Anna's stubbornness made her hesitate. Just long enough to hear a child sobbing.

Anna followed the sobs to find a small boy, about five or six years old, sitting on a doorstep and huddled into the doorway out of the rain. "Hey, what's the matter?"

"I can't find my mamma and pappa."

"What's your name?"

"David."

"Where did you last see them?"

"At the station."

"Did they get on a train?"

"I don't know. The soldiers sent me away."

Anna put her hand out, "Shall we go look for them together, David?"

He took her hand and nodded, wiping his runny nose with the other hand. They descended the hill while Anna held her coat over both their heads. She could hear the chuffing of a steam train pulling away and saw a small group of people being dispersed by German soldiers holding guns. She stopped an elderly couple walking towards her.

"Excuse me. This little boy has lost his parents. Do you know if they might have been on that train?"

They looked at Anna as if she were mad and dangerous, then at the boy, clinging to her arm. "The boy has no parents," said the man in a hoarse voice.

The woman gave him a sharp glare then looked down at the boy with pity. "Can you tell me your surname?" she asked.

"Barron."

"God bless you, child," she seemed to steal herself, closing her eyes then opening them to look squarely at the boy. "Your parents have had to go away. Perhaps this nice young woman will look after you until they return?" she asked looking back at Anna.

Anna didn't know what to say. The woman was giving her a meaningful look. David. Barron. David Barron sounded... "Oh God!" Anna's free hand flew to her mouth, the other hugged little David tight. Tears started rolling freely down her cheeks. "Oh God, oh God, no!"

The woman reached her hand out and cupped Anna's wet face. "God sent you." She turned back to her man and they walked slowly back up the hill.

Anna had read about the holocaust. She had watched the documentaries and the heart-rending films. But she had never held a five-year-old whose mother and father had just been chained to a cattle wagon and taken on a gruelling journey across central Europe to the gas chambers of Dachau, Mauthausen and Auschwitz. Perhaps, if they were lucky, they would die of dehydration or disease before they arrived. She wanted to scream. She felt like collapsing on the street and beating the cobbles with her fists. With a punishing effort of will she wiped her face and knelt beside David.

"Your mum and dad left a message with that nice woman." A lie. "They had to go away for a while." They were forced and will likely never return. "I'm going to find somewhere safe for you to stay." Perhaps this at least would be true.

David nodded and trustingly put his hand into hers.

Concealment

Vire, Normandy, June 1944

Anna suggested David take her to his home. Perhaps there would be neighbours who could look after him. As they walked David told her about the game that his parents had played with him that morning. Hide and seek. He had been hiding in the loft when he heard banging at the door. He heard an argument that he didn't understand, and then he heard heavy boots coming up the stairs. After some shuffling on the landing the loft hatch lifted. He had hidden well, right into the eaves, with sacking over him. After a while, the loft hatch closed, and the boots stomped down the stairs again. Then the house went quiet.

He climbed down and searched all over for his mamma and pappa, but they were gone. He remembered them talking about a train journey the previous evening and something else about the people at the mill in the valley. He had run to the station, in the rain, to search for them but a soldier caught him in his arms. The soldier had told him very quietly and sternly to run far away. He wasn't sure if the soldier was angry with him or with someone else, but the soldier wouldn't let him anywhere near the platform, so he had to go. He had walked up the hill then found a step to sit on because he didn't know what to do next. That was when Anna found him.

Anna wondered if the soldier at the station had been the same one who searched the loft and if he had 'overlooked' the lump under the sacking in the eaves.

David led Anna along Rue des Cordeliers, to the far end which dropped steeply into a wooded valley. For a moment she felt the same sensation of mournful emptiness that she experienced at the Porte-Horloge, yet more indistinct and impersonal like at the church. She looked around her at a large building with a chapel and impressive grounds, then at the trees that lined the road. There was no obvious source of such a feeling, and she put it down to the sick worry she felt in the pit of her stomach for poor David. At the end of the road David stopped and pointed to a small cottage. There were only a couple of other houses nearby and no reply when Anna knocked at either of them.

"Can you remember what your parents said about the people in the valley, David?"

He shook his head.

"Do you know their name?"

"Monsieur and Madame Hamel, I think."

"Do you know where their house is?"

David nodded and led Anna by the hand down a narrow, vertiginous lane. At the bottom was a rough track with a muddier one leading off into the woods at the bottom of the valley. Rainwater ran off the leaves and splashed on their faces. Anna slipped in the mud a few times and was glad of David to steady her. In a small clearing she saw an old mill and mill house by a fast-running river and a scattering of rough stone outbuildings. David pointed to the door of the mill house.

Anna knocked and waited. She could hear a voice from inside, "Who is there?"

"My name is Marie. I have David with me. Please may we come in?"

The door cracked open and a nervous looking man in his fifties peered out. He looked at Anna then David, hand in hand under the soaking oversized overcoat and beckoned them in. "Please, sit down here. I shall fetch towels and blankets."

The room was low with open beams and sacks of flour standing against the stone walls. There seemed to be another floor above, like a mezzanine. There were chairs at the far end and they each sat, shivering despite it being summer.

The man returned with a woman, perhaps late forties. Her hair was not quite as grey as the man's. Her face was a picture of anxiety as she knelt beside David.

"Have your mamma and pappa gone away, David?"

He nodded.

"They're on a train to the east," said Anna tonelessly.

The woman stared at Anna and nodded slowly. She took a handkerchief from her pocket and dabbed at the corner of her eye. Then she applied a broad smile and turned back to the boy. "Well, David. Would you like to stay with us for a while? Until your parents return?"

The boy nodded.

"Good. Have you had anything to eat today? No? I shall fetch some soup and bread. How about you…"

"Marie. Don't worry about me, I understand food is scarce. You have another to feed now."

"We can manage. It is a perk of our job," she gestured at the bags of flour.

"Thank you, Madame… Hamel?"

"Yes. Please take some lunch with us."

The soup was thin but tasty. Not as thin as the watery concoction her friends in medieval Nottingham had endured while being taxed into starvation, but not enough to live on. She was glad of the freshly baked bread, still warm. The Hamel's suspicion thawed and gave way to curiosity. 'Marie' volunteered the bare minimum and made up the rest to avoid connecting her to Élise and Henri.

"You have a long walk back to Saint-Sever, Marie," observed Céleste. "Why don't you stay here until the storm passes?" The wind still lashed the windows, so it didn't take much persuasion. The Hamels were tucked away from the centre of Vire. No one ventured down the muddy track to the mill unless they had business there. She felt hidden and safe.

Anna slept alongside David in the loft over the mill. Sections of mill machinery ran right through the middle of the room. She was woken by the sound of voices talking urgently below and pulled on her clothes to investigate. David was up already, looking out of a tiny window at the loft gable. At first Anna thought it was still raining but she realised it was the rush of water from the river beside the mill.

The Hamel's looked up when Anna descended the loft ladder, as if unsure whether to share what they had been saying.

"Good morning," said Anna. "It seems a little brighter today."

Madame Hamel nodded. Anna could tell the cogs were turning. "There will be much happening today. I think it best you stay here with us and David. Keep off the roads."

"Is it dangerous?" asked Anna.

"Perhaps."

Anna could tell they knew something. She remembered the column of army trucks full of soldiers she had seen the day before. The weather had cleared, but she suspected the storm was just starting.

"Please forgive me, I'm a little confused. Would you remind me what day it is today?"

"It is a Tuesday. Sixth of June."

D-Day. The thunder had arrived. "Thank you. I believe you're right; it may be a good idea not to travel. I'd be grateful to stay a short while."

The Hamels gave Anna a strange look. Had she said too much? Did they think she was a spy and party to knowledge she shouldn't have? Or did they just find it odd to be asked what day it was? But then how did they know what was happening? There was no social media or instant rolling news in 1944. How could they have found out about the invasion? Did they have a radio stashed away somewhere?

Anna and David went for a short walk beside the river, taking care not to stray too far. It was cool, shady and the grass squelched underfoot by the riverbank. She heard a steady drone reverberating around the valley and David pointed up through a gap in the tree canopy.

"Aeroplanes!"

There were dozens in a tight formation, wingtip to wingtip. Anna had no idea whose they were, or where they were going, but she was sure they must be war machines. They walked on along the riverbanks until they came to a tall stone viaduct that crossed the river valley. Anna didn't want to wander too far and was about to return when she caught a glimpse of movement at the parapet above. A sweep of flowing black hair. A graceful poise. Was that Élise?

"Go back to the Hamels, David. I shall see you back there."

He didn't object, he seemed more interested in following the swirls and eddies in the water, throwing stones in which made a satisfying splosh. When he was out of sight Anna climbed the steep slope, through the trees to the edge of the viaduct. Railway lines stretched in either direction. A few hundred yards to the west she saw a young woman walking beside the tracks. Anna hung back beside a pine tree and watched. There was something very odd about her behaviour, especially given what was happening at the coast. She could tell it must be Élise and she was crouching down beside another pine tree, waiting.

About ten minutes later a pair of men arrived. Flat caps, open shirts, and a box carried between them. They laid the box beside the tracks and started lifting sticks out, laying them carefully alongside the rails and binding them with rope. They unwound a wire from a spool then ran it back into the trees where they hid. All the while Élise was watching from the pine, and Anna was watching them all.

Anna had a foreboding. There was a distant whistle, a plume of white steam rose above the trees, the sound of an engine grew louder as it trundled towards Vire station. A moment later the front of the steam engine appeared from around a curve in the track, between the trees. Anna braced herself, clinging to the pine. There was flash followed a fraction later by a resounding boom. The engine emerged from a ball of flame and sloughed off the rails, sweeping saplings away from the edge of the wood. Tonnes of screaming steel scythed past Anna, down the side of the valley. The engine slew into a stand of tall pines which bowed but held it halfway down the slope and the wagons behind it snagged on more trees and ploughed into the wet soil. Steam erupted from the stricken locomotive enveloping the side of the valley in cloud.

Anna saw Élise slip away into the woods beyond. The two men had vanished. She realised with horror that if she stayed where she was, she could be found and held responsible. She ran.

Halfway back she saw David running towards her.

"What made the big bang? Are there soldiers?"

"There will be," she said and swept him up into her arms, hauling him, kicking, back to the mill.

She found the Hamels standing beside the mill, looking for their return, and fretting.

"Quick! Both of you inside now and hide!" called Monsieur Hamel.

"Hide David," said Anna, "I have to find someone else."

Before they could argue she was running hard up the muddy track which was now drying in the morning sunshine. Her mind was in turmoil. Who was driving the train and what was it carrying? Who were the men who laid the explosives and why did they blow up the track? Were they Allied troops or resistance fighters? What part had Élise played? Had she been there to keep watch for the men, or had she been spying on them? The only way Anna would find out was to find Élise, whether her grandma wanted Anna's involvement or not.

She guessed that Élise would be heading back to her bookshop to act as if she had been there all along. Anna climbed the steep lane and hurried along the Rue des Cordeliers towards the town centre. She could see the clock tower on the Porte-Horloge and the gothic arched tower of Notre Dame above the rooftops, so she could see where to go. At the Place de Castel she slowed and turned into Rue Notre Dame, realising that she was back in the occupied part of Vire, and she should not be drawing attention to herself. She also realised that she was passing the spot where the future cinema and brasserie would be built and she had been there only a couple of days ago with Jeanne and her friends, laughing and drinking wine.

The market square was empty apart from two soldiers on patrol. A sinister quiet had descended on Vire which made Anna feel conspicuous. She dug in her pockets and pulled out the papers she had been given only the day before. The nearest soldier nodded at them and gestured for her to get gone.

The shutters on the Couteau bookshop were closed. Anna was about to turn back when she caught sight of a woman and a soldier under the archway of the Porte-Horloge. The woman held a bicycle and she seemed familiar, so Anna walked closer then slid into an archway by a charcuterie. The shop was open but there was no one inside and there were no joints or cuts hanging up in the window display, just a handful of the local tripe sausages. Anna was beginning to wonder what was happening.

The long sweep of black hair on the young woman under the arch seemed a little less carefully placed, perhaps even windswept from a run through the woods, thought Anna. The soldier she talked to appeared to be the same lieutenant who had interviewed Anna. Lehman? Élise seemed animated. She was pointing over her shoulder, perhaps in the direction of the railway. Lehman was nodding, making notes in a small black book. He put the book away then looked around as if checking to see if they were being watched. Anna was an expert at invisibility, she had spent several years as a ghost on the streets of Nottingham, so he did not spot her behind the stone column. Lehman lifted Élise's hand and kissed it. Then Élise leaned forward and kissed Lieutenant Lehman on both cheeks, paused to hold his gaze then walked away towards her bookshop.

Anna had even more questions now. Was that a typical French gesture or was Élise in love with Lehman? The way she looked at him said more than 'Salut'. Why had she been pointing north, towards the railway, where Anna knew she had just been, and why had Lehman been taking notes? Was her grandma a collaborator? Was she betraying her own people?

The Airman

Occupied Normandy, June 1944

Élise mounted her bicycle and rode away while Anna pulled back, out of her sight. Anna noticed an untended bicycle leaning against the other side of the archway. She checked the charcuterie again and saw no one. Nobody in the square apart from the soldiers. Sod it. Anna begged the absent owner's forgiveness and took the bike, swung her leg across and pushed off, wobbling on the cobbles before she hit a rhythm and found her balance.

She took care to follow Élise from a distance, watching to see which turning she took before approaching that junction herself. Having wound through the centre, Élise cycled the road that ran northwest, down the hill. Anna hoped the brakes worked when she saw how steep it was. She winced when they screeched, and she pulled in behind a tree. Élise showed no sign of noticing Anna. The sound of a bicycle braking was commonplace in nineteen-forties Normandy, but the streets were uncanny. Deserted apart from a few people scurrying away from a Wehrmacht truck. It laboured up the hill past Anna and the soldiers stared at her from the cabin, making her skin prickle.

There was a tunnel under the railway and Élise followed the road through, corkscrewing down to a bridge over the river, into a small hamlet named Martilly. Above and to the left, Anna could see the railway viaduct among the trees. It was swarming with troops. A plume of steam spiralled lazily into the sky and she could hear the harsh bark of orders. She put her head down and followed Élise through the hamlet and up a gentler incline beyond.

The road ducked under the railway again then ran almost straight for several miles. Now they were in open countryside and Anna hung well back so she couldn't easily be spotted or recognised. Hedgerows and fields rolled past. The bucolic scene should have been enjoyable, yet she was unsettled by a sound like distant thunder. There were few clouds and no sign of another stormfront, so there could only be one explanation. It was the Allied bombardment of the beaches, over thirty miles north.

Ahead Anna could see the spire of another town and to the left was a forest that swept up over a hill. Élise turned off the main road onto a track that led to the forest, so Anna followed, beginning to puff as the gradient made itself felt. No gears on this forties bike. She reached a crossroads just inside the forest and stopped. She had lost sight of Élise so she peered down the three exits, wondering which way her grandma could have gone. The road ahead was straight and there was no sign of anyone. The road to the right disappeared over a hill so she couldn't see if Élise had gone that way, but it seemed unlikely as it was pointing back towards the main road they had just departed. Anna turned left. Around a bend the track opened up with a clearing to one side. She caught a glimpse of movement at the far end of the road and, hoping it was Élise, pushed harder on the pedals to catch up. The trees closed in on her and the banks rose higher on either side. After a short descent she could see another clearing and the hint of water. And a tank.

Anna clenched the brakes tight and slid into bushes that raked her skin. She dragged the bike upright and pulled it further off the road into the forest. She was shaking. No doubt some guys would have been wondering which make of German tank it was and what the camouflage and markings signified. She'd met a few like that. All Anna could say was she'd seen a bloody big metal tank with a bloody big gun, and she needed to get as far away from it as possible. The ground rose steeply as she pushed her way through the shrubs.

It opened out a little so she could see a lake and around the edge were at least twenty tanks with their crews busy loading ammo and equipment into them. Was this a supplies camp? And where was Élise?

Anna ducked behind more bushes and pressed on up the hill. As she neared the top her feet went from under her, and she slid into a steep-sided gulley filled with scrub and leaves. The bike landed heavily across her and she fell back biting her lip, to stop cursing out loud. She sat up and pushed the bike off her then became aware of the same cold mournful sensation she had experienced at the Porte-Horloge. What was going on? Was it a panic attack of some kind or was she picking up strange sensations from her surroundings?

A figure stood over her and she turned sharply, ready to run. Then she recognised Élise. Her grandma put her finger to her lips. "Stop crashing around the forest like a wild boar," she whispered, "you will give us both away."

There were many questions Anna wanted to ask her but the first one in the queue was, "What are you doing here?"

Élise put her fists on her hips. "Why are you following me? I've seen you for the last four miles. I thought you agreed to go back to whenever you come from."

Anna explained briefly about David but said nothing of the derailment or watching Élise with the lieutenant. Instead, she said she wanted to ask her help with David, which had been true up until she started suspecting her grandma of collaboration.

"That doesn't explain why you followed me here," said Élise, angrily. "My God, I have enough to do today!"

There was a shout. Élise glanced over her shoulder then ran. Anna climbed out of the gulley and saw soldiers about a hundred yards away, pushing their way through the shrubs and undergrowth. She abandoned the bike and scrambled off, in between the trees and along a broad ridge. Despite her panic she noticed the ridge seemed oddly straight and even, as if it were manmade. The sorrowful sensation she had sensed in the gulley was still there, perhaps getting stronger. She tripped and tumbled off the side. Shaking her head, she saw a regular four-sided enclosure, like the walls of a building that had been overgrown and forgotten. Where was she? Where had Élise gone? Anna scrabbled to her feet and ran on, but the shouts were getting louder, nearer. As she clambered up the far ridge a man yelled 'Halt!' and fired a shot at the ground beside her.

Anna stood and faced them, hands in the air. Half a dozen soldiers ran towards her as the one with the gun kept her in his sights.

"Where are the others?"

"What others?" answered Anna.

"There are always others. Which way did they go?"

"I don't know what you're talking about, I was just…"

Anna was stunned by a vicious swipe from a rifle butt and blacked out. When she came to, she was in the back of a lorry with bad suspension, lurching along the forest tracks. She found her hands tied behind her back and a pair of soldiers sitting on the bench opposite, clinging to it to avoid being bounced out of the cabin. Her head throbbed and she could feel a trickle of blood running down the side of her face.

An engine roared overhead. The soldiers craned their necks to look up. The engine coughed, stopped, restarted then there was a mighty crash of falling timber and whipping branches. The lorry screeched to a halt and there was arguing and shouting with the soldiers in the front. One came round and ordered the two in the back out, then stood over Anna with a pistol pointed at her head.

The soldier looked like he might be more senior, a sergeant or something, and he seemed like the kind of person who had no tolerance for difficult prisoners. Anna just pressed herself against the back of the bench and stayed quiet. It was an effort for someone as lippy as her, but the fear concentrated her mind.

Outside she saw a few sheets of paper floating out of the sky. Weird, she thought. A few moments later the two soldiers returned, dragging a man who looked as if he might be dead. He was bleeding heavily, and one arm hung in a way that turned her stomach. They hauled him onto the floor of the lorry and climbed in after him. The sergeant looked down at the man as if he were something a dog had done then took a piece of paper from the nearest soldier, one of the sheets that had been floating from the sky. He read it, threw it on the floor beside the bleeding body, then returned to the driver cabin. The lorry lurched forward again. Anna peered at the body, wearing a short fur lined leather jacket, khaki trousers, and boots. A pilot? Was it his plane she heard crash through the forest? She thought she could see a slow rise and fall of his chest. He was still alive.

Anna looked at the sheet of paper on the floor beside him. Her French was letting her down again. It was frustrating that whatever happened in her head when people spoke didn't work when she read. But it looked oddly familiar. By the time the lorry trundled to a halt, she had worked it out. It was the warning that Vire would be bombed.

Saint-Sever, Normandy, June 1944

A low moan came from the cell next to Anna's. She guessed the airman was regaining consciousness. There were airbricks at the top of the wall between their cells that allowed a little of what passed for ventilation in the summer. She imagined that just made the cells even more drafty in the winter.

"Hello!" called Anna.

"Huh?"

"Who are you?"

"... Pilot Officer Partington," said a groggy and slightly spiffing forties Home-Counties voice. "Who are you?"

Your granddaughter was what she nearly said, after recovering from the shock. Luckily, she avoided that blunder and answered, "Marie Couteau. Have they done anything to stop your bleeding?"

There was a pause before he replied. "I have a bandage on my head and my arm's in a sling. They both hurt like hell, but I think I shall live."

Yes, you will. "Good. Can you stand?"

There was a shuffling sound. "Yes, I'm on my feet. How did you know I was hurt? Did you see me come down?"

"I heard you. Only saw you when the soldiers dragged you over to the lorry and threw you in with me."

"I was out cold. Why are you in here?"

"Being in the wrong place at the wrong time." That happened a lot to Anna. It was almost a calling.

"What rotten luck! Seems I'm here for being on the wrong side. Or the right side, I hope." Anna hoped so too. "Too bad I got jumped by a Messerschmidt. I must have missed the blighter coming up behind me."

"Too bad you missed Vire as well."

"What?"

"Your warning leaflets. They all missed."

"Damn!"

"Is that it? Hundreds of innocent French civilians are going to be bombed to hell and all you can say is 'Damn'?" Anna put lashings of sarcasm into the word.

"Well, I dare say a few may be caught up in it now."

There was a dangerous silence before Anna let rip. "A few? What the hell do you think is going to happen when they drop several hundred tonnes of high explosives on a densely populated town? Do you think each bomb will pop out of the plane, look left, look right, flap its little wings, and find a Nazi shaped helmet to fall on? NO! They'll go all Newtonian physics and fall straight down on the nearest people that happen to be cowering miserably underneath and rip them to shreds, regardless of what nationality they are, what age, what gender and what kind of hat they're wearing. There is no side when you bomb a town there are ONLY DEAD PEOPLE!"

There was a bang on her cell door and a warning from the guard to keep her voice down.

"AND YOU CAN PISS OFF BACK HOME!"

Another bang and a yell to shut up.

"...I say... you sound a trifle upset, Marie," observed Pilot Officer Partington.

"AAAAGH!" she screamed. The guard opened the door and pointed his rifle at her until she stopped. She scowled murderously at him until he left.

"I wonder if you may have had some unfortunate first-hand exp..."

"Shut up!" Anna slumped down onto the floor, head in her hands.

"I'm sorry... I failed," the airman said miserably. "I only had the one job to do, and I muffed it. I expect you have friends or family in Vire?"

If only you knew...

"I'm so terribly sorry," he added. It sounded like he meant it.

Anna wept silently. She was thinking of the black and white photos in the history book. The wrecked church, the heap of rubble that used to be someone's home, the wasteland that had been a busy shopping street. Then she thought of the Hamels and little

David. Then she thought of easy-going Henri and haughty, scathing Élise. Regardless of what side Élise was on, she didn't deserve to die. Nobody deserved to die. Anna felt so helpless. She knew the bombers were coming but there was nothing she could do to warn them. Was there?

She stood up and started banging on the cell door. "HEY! HEY YOU OUT THERE! I HAVE INFORMATION."

"What are you doing, Marie?" asked the airman.

"I'm trying to do what you were supposed to do. What time is the air raid coming?"

"I can't tell you that!"

"Then why were you dropping leaflets all over northern France and not on the very town they were about to bomb?"

"They're going to be bombing lots of... blast."

"WHAT? You mean they're going to be bombing lots of towns tonight? You mean that Allied bombers will not be murdering hundreds of civilians, they'll be murdering thousands?" Anna carried on banging on the door until the guard opened it and pointed his rifle at her again.

"'Piss off back home' is offensive," he reproached. "I heard what you said."

"Pointing a gun at an unarmed woman and locking her up for no good reason is offensive. I've got vital information about an attack on Vire. Take me to your senior officer. Immediately!"

The soldier scratched his chin. He seemed to be considering Anna's demands. "Stay there," he said and left, locking the door again.

"Where do you think I might be going?" she asked the door.

"I'm having no part in this," said Pilot Officer Partington.

"Shut up," said Anna.

A moment later the soldier returned and opened the door again. He had an officer with him who had the air of certain people she had met who wielded authority without care. In medieval Nottingham they invariably wore shiny breastplates. In nineteen-forties France, they seemed to come wearing long shiny boots.

"You have information," the officer said.

"Yes," said Anna. She didn't know all the towns the Allies were going to flatten but she knew one with utter certainty. "Vire will be bombed tonight. You have to warn everyone, get all the civilians to safety."

The officer raised an eyebrow. "How do you claim to know this?"

Because I saw the photos. "Because the airman in the next cell was dropping warning leaflets meant for Vire."

"The leaflets stated 'this town'. They could mean any town. They could be propaganda to make us all run around like chickens without heads."

"It's your head," Anna looked him in the eye. She was fed up being intimidated by men with a little authority and swagger.

The officer returned her gaze, judging, calculating. "Bring the airman to my office. I wish to talk to him."

Oh hell, thought Anna. What have I done? My grandad is Biggles and I've just sent him to be interrogated.

Prayer

Saint-Sever, Normandy, June 1944

Anna prayed. She didn't think she believed in God. She certainly didn't think of herself as religious and yet she was desperate and could think of nothing else to do. It was embarrassing, like she had spent all her life denying God and now the chips were down, she was sneaking in a special request just in case he really was there after all.

"Dear God," she started in a whisper. She'd heard a vicar start like that so it must be the right form of address. A bit like starting a letter or an email. More formal than SnapChat but not a 'Dear Sir/ Madam' situation. Though of course He could be a She, she thought reasonably. Or a 'They'? Keep your mind open. "I know I'm not a believer," she continued. "I'd understand if you thought 'who the hell is Anna Partington to be asking favours off me?' Sorry, ignore the 'hell' bit. Not your department. Look, it's not for me, it's for them. For David, the Hamels, Henri. Yes alright, for my arrogant young grandma, Élise as well, whatever side she might be on. And for all the people who live in Vire. Even for the German soldiers because, dammit, they may be on the side that started this evil war but they're still human beings and they'd probably rather be back home than here. So, I'm begging you. Look, I'm on my knees and I'm begging you, if you're real and if you're even half listening then please... save them."

After a moment's thought she added, "And try not to let my grandad get beaten up, it's probably not his fault he missed Vire, but it's my fault he's getting interrogated now. I'm sorry. Oh! And if St Michael's real and listening then I'm begging you for help too. I just need some kind of miracle to happen and I'm desperate... Amen."

As Anna hung her head, feeling stupid and fraudulent, she started to have a feeling as if someone were watching her. She looked up and behind and maybe it was her imagination or maybe it was just stress, but she thought she caught a glimpse of something white which faded rapidly and vanished. She decided she was conjuring things from her overactive imagination and rocked back on her heels, hanging her head again. Then she heard the lock in the door click. It swung slightly ajar.

"You're kidding me..."

"That is what you said to your mother," came a whisper from the other side of the door.

Anna stifled a yelp and stood up, then slowly approached the door, pushing it further open with one finger. She looked down the corridor, behind the door, over at the other cells. Not a soul.

She shook her head. She had imagined that she had been watched. The soldier hadn't locked the door properly and it clicked open. The whisper she heard was in her head. But... she had just been praying. No, it was a coincidence, it was too absurd to be anything else. Besides, she had been praying for the people of Vire to be saved, not for her to be released. But if God didn't exist then who else would save them?

Anna crept down the corridor towards the door they had come in. Halfway down she heard voices from behind a closed door. She recognised them: the officer and her grandad. Oh hell! I can't leave him here, thought Anna. But how could she get him out? She couldn't knock and say thanks for having them both, but it was way past time they should be going. Okay, she decided, a diversion.

She crept up to the exit door and peered through the window beside it. No one outside, but there was a pile of firewood logs on the doorstep. She crept back to the officer's door, banged loudly on it and yelled, "HEY! LOSERS! COME GET ME" then ran for her life, slammed the door after her and heaved the largest log over to jam it against the door, wedging it firmly between doorstep and door. There were shouts from inside and boots running up the corridor. She picked up a smaller log and ran around the side of the building where she could see a light shining from a window. A peek revealed her grandad sitting on a chair by a desk and a soldier at the door, observing his comrades who were still cursing at the blocked exit. Anna banged the window then ducked to one side. Inevitably the soldier opened the window and leaned out. Inevitably Anna swung the log and knocked him unconscious. Inevitably he lay slumped across the cill so she couldn't get in.

"Sorry," she muttered to the soldier. "HEY!" she called to her grandad. "Are you coming or what?"

Pilot Officer Partington ran to the window, dragged the soldier aside with his good left arm and clambered out. She could see livid purple bruises across one side of his face, and she winced. "Look!" he said. "A bike," he pointed to a motorbike and side car parked in the street beside the building. There was a menacing machine gun mounted on the side car and a black and white cross on the panel. "Jump in."

"In that?" Anna was no fan of motorbikes, one of her friends had had a bad accident on one. And riding around occupied France in an over-armed Wehrmacht motorbike seemed downright provocative.

"Come on," he said, jumped on the bike seat and kicked at the starter pedal.

"How come you get to drive?"

"Can you?"

"No, but I have more arms than you."

"We'll muddle through. I'll do clutch, you do brakes and throttle. Get in!"

Anna could hear the log being hacked loose from the door, so she leapt into the seat and leaned forward to grab the right handlebar as her grandad kicked the beast to a roar. She revved the engine and they lurched forward, just as an irate officer and two soldiers rounded the corner and started shooting.

Like the movies, the first shot hit the edge of the side car and went pang. Unlike the movies the second shot hit her grandad in the shoulder that had already been broken and he yelled with pain. But he kept riding. Trying to keep a grip of the throttle, Anna swung the machine gun around and pointed it at the soldiers who scattered like chaff. Which was satisfying because she had no idea how to fire the thing and didn't think she wanted to, anyway. A moment later they swung behind a building and on towards the main road.

Anna clasped the brake to read a signpost with 'Villedieu-les-Poêles' to the right and 'Vire' to the left. "LEFT!" she yelled, then revved up again.

Her grandad veered left, almost tipping the bike, and clutched his arm swearing. It was bleeding freely again.

"You ride. I'll bind it," called Anna above the roar of the engine. Good job it was the arm nearest her. She unwound part of his sling with her free hand and pulled the sleeve back, telling him to stop flinching while she tried to wipe the worst of it and wrapped it back around the wound. It would have to do for the moment.

"Thanks," he said. "For getting me out. Probably didn't deserve it."

The sun was getting low. The bombers could be arriving over Vire within a few hours. "With any luck you can make amends," she gripped the rim of the side car. "What time is the attack on Vire coming? You're going to have to tell me now."

"I wasn't given details. Deliberately."

"But it's happening tonight?"

"There's no need for stealth, we're all over the coast of Normandy now. It may happen before it gets dark."

"What? You mean it could be happening now?"

He nodded miserably.

There was a deep dull boom from the forest up to their right. A moment later Anna saw thick black smoke billowing up above the treetops.

"What the hell was that? Has it started already?"

"Not us," he said.

"What do you mean?"

"Can't see any planes, so it can't be the bombers."

"Then who?"

"Could be the Resistance."

Anna remembered seeing the tanks arming and refuelling by the lake in the forest. A fuel and ammo dump made a perfect target. Was that what Élise had been doing? Or was she spying on them too, passing information back to her lover lieutenant?

"Better open that throttle up," he said.

Anna obliged and regretted it. While he crouched into the handlebars, she was thrown back into the side car seat. They parted with the road at the top of the next hill and came down with a crunch that nearly knocked Anna senseless against the machine gun. She sunk lower into the seat and gripped the lip of the side car with her free hand, gritting her teeth. It was making her sick with the fear and lurching around, but she refused to complain. A couple of stray chickens ran for their lives leaving half their tail feathers under the front wheel.

"Jim," he said out of nowhere.

I know, she thought. "Hi Jim." She wanted to add 'I'm Anna', but decided it wasn't the time.

They returned through the hamlet of Martilly, and she could see the soldiers up on the viaduct still trying to haul wrecked wagons off the line to repair the track. As they climbed the hill towards the tunnel, she saw half a dozen trucks coming towards them, no doubt going to Saint-Sever to scout for the Resistance after their latest strike.

She spotted a dirt track off to their side, "Turn right!"

Jim veered off the main road and bumped and bounced along the track, jarring Anna's teeth with every impact. It climbed the hill and passed under one of the viaduct arches, right under where the soldiers were working to recover the steam engine. She held her breath. There was a half-hearted 'hey' from above and behind them, but they were into the woods that lined the valley before anyone else called out.

Anna recognised the dirt track to the mill. "Down that track to the right," she called.

Jim fought for control as they slid and slipped sideways down the muddy track. He lost the fight about thirty yards from the river and rammed into a pair of tree trunks, throwing him onto the ground. He lay there howling with agony, his arm bent at a strange angle again.

Anna clambered out of the battered side car and went to cradle his head. Monsieur Hamel had heard the racket and ran to them.

He didn't need to be asked, he motioned for Anna to lift Jim's shoulders while he put his arms under Jim's thighs and back, standing slowly. Together they carried him into the Mill where Madame Hamel cleared a bench and searched for fresh towels and water.

"Bombers are coming," warned Anna. "You all have to find somewhere to hide."

"Luftwaffe?" he asked, confused.

"No, Allied bombers."

"But they are on our side..."

"... and are going to bomb this town flat!"

The Hamels stood looking at Anna, faces blank.

"It's true..." Jim stammered, eyes watering, "er, c'est vrais." He struggled as much with his French as his pain.

Madame Hamel raised a hand to her mouth, "Why?"

Jim and Anna searched each other's face for an answer.

Monsieur Hamel shrugged, "Where can we go?"

Through clenched teeth Jim said "They'll hit the centre. We should be alright here."

"Is their aim as good as yours?" asked Anna pointedly.

Jim rolled his head painfully to look at her. "Pretty much," he tried to smile and winced.

"We're all going to die," she murmured to herself.

"There will be a pathfinder. They drop flares on the target, the centre of town. The bombers following will aim for the flares. Much less chance of being hit here than in the centre."

In the centre. Henri. "I'm going to find one of my family and warn them," she said.

Jim shook his head and winced again. "Don't," he managed.

"I have to," she turned around and saw David looking wide-eyed at the wounded airman stretched out on the bench with blood seeping across it onto the floor.

Madame Hamel put her arm around him and took him to his bed. Monsieur Hamel nodded at Anna as if to say that they had things under control.

Anna squeezed his hand, "Thank you, Monsieur Hamel."

"Pierre," he said. "And Céleste," with a nod in the direction of his wife. "Good luck Marie."

The bike was wrecked. She grabbed some branches that had fallen off the tree it had crashed into and threw them across it to make it harder to see, then half-ran, half-staggered up the hill towards the 'target'.

She felt as wrecked as the bike by the time she reached the top of the hill. It was punishingly steep. She stood holding her sides, gasping for breath for a few moments under an old chestnut tree and looked back across the fields to the north. Sunlight slanted across them throwing long shadows that revealed the rolls of the hills and the hedges that lined them. Dark smoke rose above the horizon like thunder clouds and the rumble sounded less distant than before. It was hard to see against the smoke, but she thought she could see a score or more of little black dots in the sky, above the horizon. They flew close together like a swarm of mosquitoes or a flock of birds. They reminded her of the planes that had flown over her and David that morning... warplanes. Bombers.

Anna ran. Ignoring the stitch in her side and the rasp of her breath and the pain in her shins from struggling up the hill, she ran and ran along Rue des Cordeliers.

Turning the corner into Rue Saulnerie she saw the clock tower caught by the sun on the Porte-Horloge. Almost eight o'clock in the evening. Surely the bombers couldn't be coming so soon. She banged at the door of the bookshop and hammered on the windows. Henri peered from the back of the shop, recognised Anna and came to open up.

"Marie! What is the matter?" he asked.

Anna barely had breath. "Bombers. Coming now. Got to warn everyone. Help!"

"Bombers? Whose bombers, and why would they..."

"Please, Henri, NOW!"

Henri hesitated, trying to comprehend, but seemed to understand the urgency in Anna's eyes. "Hôtel de Ville," he said and pulled the door after him. They ran through the gateway beneath the clock tower.

A soldier approached them. "Papers."

Henri waved his at the soldier, "Bombers! Tell everyone to look for cover."

The soldier paused, confused, and looked up. Henri and Anna ran on. The streets were in shadow, but the rooftops glowed with the evening sun. On the steps of the Hôtel de Ville they were challenged by two more guards. Henri tried explaining the imminent attack, but they obviously thought it was some diversion or trick. Anna plunged past them before they could stop her.

She flung open each door along the corridor but there was no one in. It was evening, why should they be? Finally, she found one middle aged clerk still toiling at his desk.

"Please, Monsieur, there are bombers coming now to attack Vire. You must raise the alarm."

He looked shocked, as if some random young woman had run in off the street and yelled something obscene at him. She had.

"Please, Monsieur, we have no time."

He scratched his head. "Why would we have a siren?" he asked reasonably, "we are already occupied, so who would want to bomb us?"

Anna didn't know whether to scream or cry. She had no reasonable answer to give the baffled clerk and no way of warning the people of Vire. "Run!" was all she could say. "RUN!" she screamed at him.

The clerk hovered at his desk, sorting through papers to put into his leather briefcase. Anna grabbed him roughly by his wrist and dragged him out of the office, papers scattering along the corridor behind them.

Outside the soldiers were still arguing with Henri and Anna almost collided with them. "BOMBERS! RUN FOR YOUR LIVES," she yelled.

One soldier pointed his gun at her and the other searched the sky in confusion. Several window shutters were thrown open and heads peered out from behind. The soldier pointing his gun was about to say something when a low flying plane roared over their heads and a sickly green glow lit the forecourt, shadows wobbling at weird angles. The pathfinder. Flares.

Anna started yelling again and Henri joined in. Several more windows around the square were thrown open as more people looked out at the mad shouty people and the flares. The soldiers stood frozen in the garish light, watching the receding pathfinder.

A gun shot. Anna crouched involuntarily, then peeked through her fingers. The soldier with the gun had fired a shot into the air and was firing again. "GO! OUT OF VIRE! GO NOW!" he bellowed at the heads in the windows, then started to run down the hill to the south.

The other soldier faltered, like a child whose older brother has just run off and left him, then he started to run too. The clerk clutched his briefcase to his chest and followed. A few moments later some doors around the little square were pushed open and half a dozen locals jogged down the hill, in the same direction as the soldiers and the clerk.

Anna could just see the clock on the Porte-Horloge. Three minutes past eight. A moment later she heard a deep throbbing drone as if dozens of engines were all vibrating and running in and out of synch with each other. Each throb grew louder. Anna prayed.

A Memory

Vire, Normandy, 6th June 1944

A whistling whining sound overlaid the throbbing of the approaching engines. Anna, Henri, and a few remaining watchers at the windows froze, listening, judging... how soon and where would the bombs arrive? She felt it a moment before she heard it. The ground shuddered as if rejecting the foreign objects dropped from the sky. A thud vibrated the air against her chest and a deep grumble built towards an ear-splitting crescendo. Gouts of smoke and debris were hurled into the air above the rooftops, caught by the sun, glowing bright orange as if set alight by its rays. The eruptions advanced on them like a monstrous tidal wave hurling storey-high chunks of wall and showers of roof tiles like confetti.

Anna felt a grip on her hand and a lurch as she was dragged away. Henri was yelling at her, but she could only see his lips moving. Anna was barely aware of him dragging her across the small square in front of the Hôtel de Ville, she was mesmerised by the advancing wall of shrieking raging destruction, like prey hypnotised by the sheer irresistible power of the predator.

Into a narrow side street, sun blotted, thunder echoing off walls. Henri pulled her right, up another street, ground shuddering, darkness enveloping. Bursting into daylight, engines thrumming straight above, bombs whining, straight down. Pulled left. Porte-Horloge behind, crammed with people, huddled, scared. Eruption of flame and debris, whole building crumbled, sliding into the street across the Porte, engulfing it in smoke. Ran on, deafened, terrified. Ground shaking like earthquake. Second building crumpled inwards, third cascaded into street. Fourth one right behind them. Blinding white. Punch of hot air; hurled upwards, weightless for moments then dashed like thrown clay.

Pitch black.

High pitched whine. Ears singing.

Someone crawling, all grey and covered in dust, shedding stones and bricks. Talking at her. Can't hear. Shook her head. Pain. Pulling her arm, speaking, pleading, something urgent. Why? What more can happen?

Pulled to her feet, swaying. Lurching forward. Line of red flowed down over right eye. Blood? Warm and wet in hand. Staggering, tripping over chunks of something. Someone? Grey and red and torn and soft. Someone. Was someone. At doorway. Door came away in man's hand. Henri's hand. Ears still ringing, whining. Sound like hang-up tone, no answer, no one there. Books. Shattered glass. Bookshop? Door with staircase behind, black down there. Stumbling. Hands grabbed her, steadied her, guided her down. Dark.

Safe?

Anna collapsed on the stone floor. There was a stutter of dim light, and a candle lit the inside of a narrow tunnel with stone arches. Henri pulled his jacket off, flicking the dirt out with a cloud of dust, then wrapped it around her shoulders.

She was shaking. Henri put his arms around her and held her tight. The whine in her ears was easing. She was still bleeding freely from her forehead, and it was beginning to hurt. More blood dripped from her ears. The floor of the cellar was trembling. She could just hear droning above the ringing in her ears, coming from above. Then a series of dull impacts that shook dust from the tunnel walls and ceiling. Getting louder. Getting nearer.

Anna quaked violently. Henri hugged her tighter. Each impact made her jolt and Henri jumped with her. There was a savage boom and one end of the tunnel imploded in a ball of dust and crushed stone. The cloud rolled towards and over them, coating them in another cloying layer that gummed Anna's blood against her face. She spat it out of her mouth, coughing, choking. Then she leaned forward and retched. Her body shook like a beaten dog. She whimpered.

Again, she felt Henri put his arm around her and ease her back against the curved wall of what remained of the tunnel. He took his jacket off her shoulders, shook the dirt out and wrapped it around her again. Then he took his sleeve and started wiping the dirt out of her eyes, off her cheeks. And then he brushed the chunks of plaster out of her wild hair before tearing off a strip of his shirt, binding it around her head until the blood stopped oozing.

Just as she was starting to gather her wits the droning thrumming engines returned followed by more whistling. Anna clenched herself into a foetal curl and moaned. The impacts felt different, less deep. The explosions were lighter but followed by a terrifying whoosh, like a huge flame igniting after gas left hissing. She heard screaming.

Anna curled tighter, trying to shut it away. But she could only think of Rob. His father and brother burning to death in the firebomb attack on their home. The sound he remembered was the screaming. High pitched, agonised, tortured screams.

"No! No, no, no, nooo!" Anna sobbed.

This was not war. This was not a battle, not a raid, not an engagement. This was pitiless evisceration. Somewhere at the back of Anna's mind was a phrase that she had heard her mother, the historical researcher quote. Total War. Mindless reckless hate unleashed upon every home, every field, every creature whether sentient or not.

Anna didn't know when the screaming subsided and her shaking calmed to a trembling, then stilled. Her head lay in a small muddy puddle of dirt mixed with tears, sweat and vomit. Henri was curled against her back. The drone of engines had gone.

How long had they lain there, covered in dirt in the dark? Anna had no sense of time, a recurring paradox for her. The air stank of smoke and something like roasted meat, but nowhere near as pleasant. The candle had burned out long ago and the chaotic detonations and screaming from the bombardment had been replaced with an eerie silence. No, not quite silence. If she listened hard, she could hear the crackling of flames and distant calls as if a few were searching for their family.

Anna pushed herself up into a sitting position and leaned back against the tunnel wall. Everything hurt. She felt her head and found the bleeding had dried up with raw scabs forming on her forehead. She picked clots of dried blood out of her ears which still sang.

"Henri?"

"Here," came a weak reply.

Anna shuffled towards his voice on her bottom, afraid even to stand in case she tripped over rubble and fell. She felt for his hand and held it. It was cold. Her heart skipped. "Henri? Henri are you hurt?"

"Lost a lot of blood. But I will be fine. Just need to rest a little longer."

Anna felt his forehead which was cooler than hers. "Where are you bleeding?"

"My side."

Anna put her hands either side of his chest. Her left hand came away drenched. "Oh my God, Henri, you're bleeding out! I had no idea."

"Neither did I." Anna imagined his good-humoured smile and shrug in the darkness.

"I'm going to fetch help," she said and felt around for the stairway they had descended.

After blundering around for a few minutes, she discovered steps beneath jagged chunks of rubble and stones. She clambered upwards on all fours, not trusting herself to stand. About ten steps up she found the way blocked by broken timbers and masonry. She tried levering the shattered joists, but they were wedged between stones and bricks. They were trapped.

Returning to the bottom of the steps she called to Henri, "Is there another way out?"

"The tunnel runs beneath Rue Saulnerie," he croaked. "It has several entrances from the shops with basements. One end was blocked by the bombs, but the other might be free."

Anna couldn't remember which end caved in during the bombing, so she turned right from the stairs. After crawling a few yards, she found a mound of debris which went all the way up to the soffit of the tunnel. She turned around and half crawled, half crouched in the other direction, feeling for obstructions. She found another mound of rubble and was starting to think that both ends were blocked when she discovered a gap around the side. Perhaps the stones had come down the stair of another shop but had not filled the tunnel. She squeezed past and made her way on again.

Anna found half a dozen such mounds of rubble and a couple of open stairways, but both were blocked about halfway up. The stink of smoke and cooked meat was starting to make her feel nauseous. She thought she could hear someone moaning and wailing somewhere up at street level, above. It was then that she worked out what the cooked meat smell was. Burnt human flesh. She tried to throw up, but it was a dry retch with a dribble of bile.

Gathering what little strength she had, Anna crawled on in search of a way out. It felt as if she had been blundering around in the darkness for hours and she had no sense of where she was. She was on the verge of giving up when she felt the edge of a stone step and caught a hint of light coming from above. Hand over hand she climbed the steps, trembling, panting, wiping sweat from her face. She realised it was getting hotter as she climbed, as if she were ascending into an oven. There was an old wooden door at the top with slivers of flickering red light slipping in around the rough edges. Anna felt for a handle. The door was warm. She found a hot lever, turned it, and pushed. The door opened a crack but no more. It was jammed against something hard. She could smell smoke and feel the warmth of flames nearby. Anna banged on the door and yelled for help.

No one could hear her. She slumped down beside the door, drained, thirsty, and frightened. She also felt a familiar sense of despair and loss. The same feeling that she experienced beside the Porte-Horloge. Up to her right she could just make out the shape of a vertical slit in the wall with a wider hole halfway up it. An arrow slit. She was in the Porte-Horloge, trying to get out.

A disturbing thought struck Anna. Was the reason she sensed such despair and absence from the gateway on her arrival in Vire because she had died here, in 1944? Had she experienced a memory of her own death? She shivered as the walker crossed her grave. No. She refused to believe it. She was going to live. Henri would live, if only she could attract attention and get the door open. She filled her lungs and started screaming.

There was a call from nearby. A man's voice, somehow familiar.

"Pierre?" returned Anna, now hoarse from screaming.

"Marie?"

"HERE! IN THE PORTE HORLOGE!"

"Marie, I thought you dead!" A few moments later and she saw half a face and an eye peering in past the edge of the door. "Hold tight, I shall fetch help to clear the stones away."

"Thank God, Pierre! Thank you. Please hurry, there is another down here. He's bleeding heavily."

"Back as soon as I can," he called and was gone.

Anna lost track of time again. Her mind passed in and out of conscious thought. At times she was aware of voices and the scraping of heavy stones outside, at others she dreamed strange and disturbing scenes of raging fires and screaming parents and lost children wandering around a barren smoking wilderness. Some dreams slid sideways into galloping horses with nightmarish riders clad in metal holding lances that they wielded to skewer hapless people as they ran. Some lances pierced two, three or even four people through their ruined bellies as if they formed some horrifying human kebab. The smell of roasted flesh filled her nostrils and made her gag. Then the dreams slid again, and she saw limp bodies tumbling into a deep pit where limbs flayed uselessly across blank eyes and slack open jaws. Dreams or memories?

Anna was woken by the sensation of being carried. She half opened her eyes and waved a hand saying, "Man in the tunnel. Bleeding. Please..."

"There are others searching for him. Quiet now, you are safe."

She was being carried by Pierre and another man she didn't recognise. They were staggering up and over huge mounds of stones and twisted timbers which smouldered. As they carried her away, she saw fires burning, an old couple wandering aimlessly, hand in hand, a child staring vacantly from the top of a heap of rubble, clutching a teddy bear, and a singed dog beside him barking. Not one house stood. Not one shop. Vire was only an idea held by those who remembered it.

Bridges

Vire, Normandy, June 1944

Jim stood at the top of the dirt track cradling his sling and staring at the smoking hill on which Vire used to stand. Anna was fading by the time Pierre and his friend had carried her down the hill, but she would remember the look in Jim's eyes forever. His bottom lip trembled like a small child betrayed by his parents. His eyes were red rimmed, raw, and glistening with rage. It took some moments for him to refocus on Anna, lying on a stretcher cobbled together from coats and broom handles. He grasped her hand with his good right.

"Thank Christ! It's been two days. We all thought you dead," he said.

"Not yet," she managed. Two days. She could have been there for two weeks for all she knew.

He walked alongside the stretcher party, still holding her hand. "The murderers used phosphor bombs," he managed through gritted teeth. "They dropped enough high explosives on Vire to level it, then came back and dropped incendiaries."

Anna nodded. She had heard, and then she had seen...

"How will they ever forgive us?" he asked and looked at Pierre with abject remorse.

Pierre just motioned for Jim to keep walking with them back to the Mill. There they laid Anna on the bench she had left Jim on. Céleste set about cleaning her up and covering her wounds. Pierre invited Jim to sit with his friend, Thaddée, and asked David to help make some coffee for them all.

"I'm so sorry," whispered Jim nursing a mug in his lap.

Pierre shook his head and put his hand gently on Jim's good shoulder. "It is war."

Anna wondered at the Frenchman's pragmatism. He had seen his hometown brutally crushed. Searched the ashes for friends and carried her past their charred remains. Her vision narrowed like the walls of the dark tunnel she had crawled, then blinked out.

When Anna woke, she learned they had found Henri. He had been breathing when they fought their way through to him in the tunnel, so Pierre and Thaddée had carried him back to the mill. But his breaths came slower and shallower, and he had slipped away by the morning.

She pulled herself up from the makeshift bed, against Céleste's warnings, and went to sit beside Henri's body. Anna held his hand and spoke softly to his memory. "Thank you, Henri. You saved my life. You held me. Thank you." She became aware of a presence at her shoulder and looked around. Élise.

Anna drew back. The expression on her grandma's face was unreadable. Pierre stood behind Élise and made a gesture to Anna that they should leave, so she followed him up into the mill room above, where the huge mill stones stood silent, disengaged from the wheel. They sat on the edge of one.

"She is alone now," said Pierre. "No family."

"You know her?"

"We know Élise and Henri well. We knew their parents."

"I'm so sorry."

He shrugged.

Anna wondered how to ask her next question. "Élise seems... close to one of the officers. At the Château Jeannin."

Pierre looked at Anna as if assessing her meaning. "Élise is a young woman. The lieutenant is a young man."

"But... he's part of the occupation."

"We have had three Commandants. Commandant Scharf was sent to placate us with his excellent French. Commandant Hubner turned a blind eye to the little things while we supplied him with fine bottles of Calvados. Commandant Noeding must now do as he is told by the SS. Some of the lieutenants have been harsh, but Lieutenant Lehman has not."

Anna studied Pierre's face, trying to comprehend his life during four years of occupation. Day to day survival which depended on diplomacy, bribery, and the mercy of those in power. "You do not mind that they are close?"

"Lehman is a Jewish name. He is not Jewish, but I understand that his great grandfather on his father's side was. That makes him only one eighth Jewish blood, therefore he has passed their test." Pierre emphasised the last word. "Each time the Commandant receives another letter ordering him to fulfil the quota for Vire and its commune, he passes the order on to his lieutenants. Lieutenant Lehman tells Élise. Élise tells the families to hide."

A wave of relief flooded through Anna. "I see," she nodded.

"But they must obey orders, so always people are found. Perhaps not as many, but the orders are obeyed."

Anna hung her head. "David's parents," she said quietly.

"They knew they would be discovered eventually. They begged us to look after David. We told them they did not have to beg." Pierre stood up. "I shall make coffee."

She could hear voices talking softly below. A few minutes later Élise climbed up the steps carrying two cups and handed one to Anna. "You suspected me," she said, her tone flat.

"I didn't know what to think," Anna answered honestly.

"It is right to be suspicious, that is how you survive here. But I am no collaborator. And Werner is not a traitor to his country, nor is he a monster."

"Unlike the people who ordered the bombing of Vire," said Anna, looking at the floor.

"Vire is not the first, and it will certainly not be the last. This is a war, Marie."

"But they were Allies. How can they do such a thing?"

"Those planes were American. The planes that annihilated Caen and Le Havre were British. They are here to drive out the occupiers, to liberate us."

"How can you liberate the dead?"

"The dead are free from all this. Like Henri."

"I'm so sorry, Élise."

"I envy you, 'Marie'."

"Why?"

"I stayed here in 1944 to be with my brother when he died. I knew he was going to die. But it was you who was with him in his last hours."

"He saved me."

"I was told."

"I failed."

"How so?"

"I tried to raise the alarm. I tried to get people to run before the bombers arrived, but I failed."

"Several hundred people heard you, Henri and the soldiers shouting and fled south into the woods and valleys."

Anna looked up.

"You and Henri saved their lives. And now I am glad that you were with him. He was with family. I still have family."

A large grave had been dug to take the dead. Each day the pit swallowed more bodies, mostly unidentifiable, as they were uncovered from the smoking wreckage. No one could bear the thought of taking Henri there, so a quiet spot was found a few hundred yards downstream, beside the river. Pierre and Thaddée dug. Anna, Jim, Céleste and Élise carried him. David knelt and laid wild primroses on his chest.

Jim stood as if to attention. Honouring the people of Vire who had fallen while clenching his teeth to bite back the bitterness.

Thaddée hung his head, cap in hand. Céleste and Pierre clung to each other, no doubt thinking of all the friends and neighbours they had lost in the last two days.

There were no words.

Élise stood motionless over Henri's grave until Anna took her grandma's hand and led her back to the mill.

Only then did Anna fully understand what her young grandma had suffered. Barely eighteen, she had lost her home and all her immediate family in a brutal war. Anna had been even younger when she lost her home and her mum. Her heart ached for Élise.

Vire, Normandy, late June 1944

Élise made a bargain with Anna. Anna would keep out of her way and help the Hamels until Vire was liberated, which would come soon. In return Élise would coach Anna's time travel focus, but only after liberation. Anna understood why. Élise must be part of the Resistance. She and her fellow resistance fighters were going to set this part of Normandy on fire. She would do her utmost to harass the Wehrmacht and help the advancing Allies. But she would never admit to being part of the Resistance and Anna now knew better than to ask.

The cuts on Anna's head and shoulders were healing well, though the flight through Vire and her ordeal in the cellar brought fresh nightmares each time she slept. Jim still had his right arm in a sling, but he was no longer in obvious pain. He was to take a new name,

Henri Couteau. No one liked it but the logic was cold and unassailable. Henri was a Virois, a citizen of Vire, escaped from the bombing and recuperating with friends at the mill. He had papers. He fitted their description because he was the right age, fair haired with blue eyes. He said little because he had choked on phosphor fumes in the attack. Which conveniently obscured Jim's execrable French.

'Henri' felt wretched taking the dead man's name. He felt wretched whenever he looked up at the smoking ruin of Vire. So Anna asked Pierre to find them both something useful they could do while they recovered from their injuries. 'Grind flour', he answered. Seemed obvious, they were in a mill.

It freed Pierre to carry sacks of freshly ground flour to the two surviving boulangeries, one in Martilly to the north and the other on the bombed Rue aux Teintures, at the southern edge of Vire. David helped Anna and 'Henri' at the mill, which is how they discovered Jim's lighter side. Anna's grandad loved kids and he loved messing like a kid.

It started with Jim gurning at David from the other side of a mill stone. Poking his head through the hole in the middle and pulling his cheeks and lips as if they were elastic. At first David just eyed Jim as if he were unhinged, but slowly he began to crack. A twinkle in his eye. A suppressed smile. Then a guffaw that came from the belly and warmed their hearts.

Soon Jim would flick puffs of flour at David or chase him around the mill gear until Céleste came to discover the cause of the commotion. Work got done. Possibly more than before because they engaged with lighter hearts. But time was made for fun and there had been precious little of it till then.

One day Anna found David, Céleste and Pierre all lined up on the little wooden footbridge beside the mill holding sticks and waiting for Jim to say 'go!'

"What are you up to?" asked Anna.

"Poosteeks!" giggled David.

"What? Oh, Pooh sticks! You realise the French don't really do AA Milne, don't you, 'Henri'?"

"They do now," he grinned.

"Now!" yelled David and dropped his stick in.

"Hey!" complained Pierre. "We wait for Henri to say now."

"He did say now."

"But that wasn't the right now."

"Children!" said Céleste and gave Pierre a mock wagging of her finger.

Anna fetched David another stick. "Here, start again."

"Marie can do poosteeks too!" said David bouncing up and down on the bridge, which started to bounce too.

Anna eyed the bridge with suspicion.

"It is safe," said Pierre, shuffling up to make room. "I carry sacks of flour across it every day."

"And every day it sinks a little closer to the water," observed Céleste.

Anna stepped carefully onto the end of the bridge and felt the timbers flex. She pulled a face and David chuckled and started bouncing up and down again. Then Jim bounced with him which made the bridge curve alarmingly. They all clung to the rail and shrieked. Then Céleste put her finger to her lips and made a shushing noise while still laughing. They were reminded that excess mirth could draw unwelcome attention, but that just made it funnier for Jim and David who had a fit of giggles.

Lunch was taken on the riverbank. Anna had a chunk of baguette in one hand and an apple in the other. It almost felt like a holiday. Or it would have done if it weren't for the rumble of distant gunfire. She found herself grinding her teeth, her jaw muscles tense and aching while she listened to it.

Each day the grumble of artillery and the chatter of small arms sounded a fraction nearer. Anna remembered a little from the books she had been reading and the discussions she'd had with Jeanne in the Médiathèque. The Allies were fighting for every house, every field, every hedge across Normandy. The Wehrmacht would not relinquish one millimetre without a fierce fight and some towns were liberated only to be retaken by the occupying soldiers and then liberated all over again, many times over.

Anna was trying to blot this from her mind when Élise made a surprise visit, clutching the feet of a scrawny looking dead chicken.

"Dinner," she said and presented it to Anna.

Anna took hold of the dead thing reluctantly. The only chickens she had encountered were either clucking and laying eggs or thawing in a polythene bag labelled 'Lidl'. Anna didn't have to look at Élise to know she was smirking. Anna did look at Jim, whose eyes had gone into soft focus mode with his mouth slightly open. Ugh! Grandparent in lurve. Anna had seen Jim paying Élise attention before, but he had been too unwell, and the moment had been too sombre. If he kept this up, she'd have to go wipe the dribble off his chin.

Of course, Élise paid Jim no attention at all. However, she did notice David sitting close beside Jim on the riverbank in a buddy huddle.

"Thank you so much, Élise," said Céleste, who diplomatically took the chicken from Anna and led her to the yard to show her how to pluck it. Anna wondered if Céleste knew that 'Marie' was not a local. This was not the only time she had been shown how to perform a simple task. Simple to Céleste and anyone living in rural France in the nineteen-forties. If the Hamels suspected her, they showed no outward sign, they just seemed to accept her. Anna was deeply thankful.

Élise did not stay. Anna was not surprised, but despite the barely concealed jibe, she felt that perhaps she was reaching some understanding with her young grandma. Sharing the same bridge, perhaps, if not yet allowed across to the other side.

Although the Hamels made their guests welcome, Anna was starting to feel hemmed in. She pleaded with Pierre to be allowed to take a sack of flour to one of the boulangeries. Reluctantly he agreed to let her take one to Martilly, on the basis that the route was away from the town centre and further from Wehrmacht activity. The sack was heavy. She found new respect for Pierre by the time she had carried, dragged, and hauled the thing along the riverside towards the little hamlet. She stopped short of the bridge and watched as a convoy of army trucks rattled across. So much for being further from the Wehrmacht. She could just see the faces of the soldiers at the back of the last truck as it trundled up the hill towards the husk that used to be Vire. They looked tired. Drained. They were on the losing side and they knew it.

Anna felt confused. Part of her was elated to see the occupying forces withdrawing from the onslaught of the Allied invasion. Part of her felt relief that the surviving Virois were close to liberation, after so long hiding, rationing, and surviving. But another part of her felt deeply sorry for the rank-and-file soldiers who were now caught between a fanatical dictator and the vengeance of the western world. Knowing the outcome of the war did not help unravel her feelings. Witnessing the suffering of all involved only made her heart break.

She was about to swing the sack onto her shoulder again when she saw a young woman approach an officer who had remained standing on the bridge. She recognised the young French woman. She recognised the German officer. They embraced and Anna's confusion felt all the more profound. If Élise loved Werner Lehman, then how would she ever end up with Jim? If Élise and Jim never got together, then how would Eleanor Partington ever be born? Or Anna?

Evacuation

Vire, Normandy, 5th August 1944

Élise returned early on the Saturday morning. "You must flee," she said sharply. "The Americans are coming."

"But the Americans are coming to free us," said Céleste.

"The Americans are coming to wage a bloody battle with the Wehrmacht," said Élise. "Do you wish to be caught in the middle?"

"Where can we go?" asked Pierre. "No one has food to spare. No one has a bed to offer."

"You must take what you can," persisted Élise. "You saw what happened to the centre of Vire."

There was grim silence. The American soldiers had a job to do. They were here to shoot enemy soldiers and God help anyone who got in their way: friend or foe.

"Lieutenant Lehman has agreed to keep the road south clear for all evacuating Virois," added Élise. "Leave or die."

Pierre scratched his head and looked around the mill. Céleste gripped David's hand and stood watching as Élise left.

"We should help pack," said Jim.

"Give them a moment," said Anna and motioned for him to step outside with her.

They walked down to the mill bridge and stood side by side, watching the clear water splash beneath their feet.

"It's their home," said Anna, "they need some time in it before leaving."

"I'm sorry, of course you're right, Marie."

"My name... is not Marie."

Jim looked up. "I'm not Henri either, but you know that. I expect I shouldn't ask who you really are."

"Mm," Anna nodded. She wanted to say her name. She wanted to say the next time they'd meet she'd be a tiny baby and he'd be in his final year of life. She wanted to say how glad she was to have met her grandfather properly and seen his wonderful smile and how she wished she'd been the small child he had played with on the bridge. But she didn't even know if he would ever get to be her grandfather.

"You like Élise, don't you?" she said instead.

"Mm," he nodded like a shy schoolboy.

Anna had to remind herself he was only nineteen and, despite being an airman at war, he probably had little experience of love. "I think you're a brave man, Pilot Officer Partington. See if you can persuade Élise to think so too."

Jim nodded again, continuing to watch the river waters rush by.

Anna could hear the Hamels starting to collect their things so she returned to see if she could help. They really didn't have much. All their most precious belongings fitted into a handcart and a pair of flour sacks. Anna thought about the mountains of stuff people accumulated in the modern day and wondered how they might cope with a sudden evacuation. Then she thought of the Nailors and Little John, whom she and Rob had met on their way to Nottingham in 1194. All they carried was a sack, a few tools, and the clothes they walked in. Rob had carried the sack. Anna had carried Little John when he was still little enough to be carried. They too had been fleeing from war. Seven and a half centuries later and she was fleeing with the refugees again. No one learns from history, she thought. It broke her heart.

They struggled to the top of the dirt track onto the narrow road called Rue Jean le Houx, that wound its way along the gorge. A loud explosion echoed off the sides of the valley and Anna convulsed, involuntarily. Céleste went to put her arm around Anna, her face drawn with worry.

"I think Marie has the trench sickness," said Pierre.

"Shell shock," explained Jim.

Anna felt her body tremble beyond her control, as if someone was passing a current through it and her limbs were jolting.

More explosions followed interspersed with sounds like someone hitting a large hollow metal object with a hammer. Each blow made her jump and clench her teeth.

"It's a tank battle," explained Jim. "The hammer sounds are American shells bouncing off thick German armour. The explosions are German shells ripping American tanks apart."

"The bridge at Martilly," said Pierre. "That is where the gunfire must be coming from. They are very near, we must hurry."

Another explosion emphasised his point. Another jolt through Anna's spine.

"How the hell are the Allies winning if all tank battles are so unequal?" asked Anna through gritted teeth.

"The Americans have a lot of tanks," Jim said.

"But that must mean..."

"A lot of them are dying."

Anna screwed her eyes tight to shut out the insanity. It was hard to hate the Americans for bombing Vire when she could hear dozens of them losing their lives for it just outside. It was hard to be angry at the cold-hearted Allied war machine when her grandad pilot was carrying a sack of cooking pots over his slowly mending shoulder and leading a small Jewish boy to safety. Politicians and generals had the luxury of winning and losing wars. Regardless of the outcome, everyday people just suffered.

Anna shook her head and helped Pierre push the handcart, gripping the handle tight to stop her hand from shaking. Surely such thoughts served no purpose. And yet a tiny stubborn part of Anna Partington said there was an idea there somewhere. An idea of rebellion. Of taking the selective record of history away from the few and telling the true stories of the many. Hadn't her grandma told her about the power of ideas?

Walking down Rue Jean le Houx they saw hundreds of German soldiers swarming across the hillside to their left, on the edge of Vire. About where Anna had experienced one of her strange melancholy feelings. They were digging holes to take cover in, anticipating the fight to come. The trucks she had seen crossing the bridge the other day were disgorging their down-beaten reinforcements and decoupling wheeled artillery. They expected a fight and they expected it right here in this valley.

Anna and the other refugees crossed the River Vire and followed the road that snaked alongside it, skirting the town to the south. Workshops lined both sides of the river. Some of them had been built to straddle the water and take power from it. One had been hit by a stray bomb and all they could see were twisted girders and piles of bricks teetering on edge. The river was forced to flow over and around random shards of concrete floor that stuck out of the water. Through the trees above they saw heaps of broken stones and timbers where houses once were. Further across the ridge was the promontory where the ruin of the old castle donjon stood, presumably destroyed in another war, long ago. On the opposite side of the valley some of the houses seemed to have escaped the worst of the bombing but there was no sign of their owners. Instead, there was another battery of grey-painted artillery with gunners standing by. Anna wondered if she saw a glint of something shiny in the sunlight. Someone with binoculars? Were they were being observed? The thought made her skin crawl.

As the road climbed, the river flowed through a muddy basin with a broken weir at the near end. Perhaps it had held water in a pool before the air attack. It dawned on Anna that it could be the pool where she watched a pair of boys feeding ducks on her arrival to modern day Vire. On the far sides were grim piles of stones where warehouses and workshops had been. By contrast an elegant three-storey stone chateau stood almost untouched beside them.

"The Hôtel-Dieu survived," said Pierre, noting Anna's stare. "God spared the pensioners who live there, but I doubt they will be spared the bullets."

"Then we should help them leave," said Jim.

Pierre, Céleste and Anna all looked at Jim as if he were mad. Even David looked dubious. "How?" asked Pierre reasonably.

Jim walked to the courtyard entrance then waved at the others to follow. He pointed at an old horse carriage standing idle on the cobbles. "We could take a few in that."

"A horse would be useful," observed Anna.

"We could try the stable block," said Pierre, looking at the thatched building behind them.

They were lucky. There were a pair of chestnut mares inside. They looked bony. Underfed. Anna wondered if they would be capable of walking themselves let alone pull a carriage, but they seemed happy enough to be led into the courtyard and put in the harnesses.

Pierre and Céleste went from door to door, knocking to see who was still there. Some must have left already but a few answered. Nervous, weary faces. Frightened. About twenty said they would come and seemed relieved that they had been remembered at last. There were three who refused to move: they looked resigned.

Fortunately, many could walk and were glad to have the carriage to hang their bags on. Half a dozen were helped or carried into the carriage seats. If the situation weren't so grim it would have looked like an early Saga outing to Bognor, thought Anna. One old dear was smiling at the semi-organised chaos from her seat, looking as if she were about to be taken to the Ritz for tea. The old chap beside her gripped a carpet bag stuffed with his belongings looking anxious.

There was a clatter of automatic gunfire from the west and Anna flinched. "We must go," said Jim and presented an arm to an elderly gent with a walking stick who refused to ride in the carriage. David noticed and offered his shoulder to a lady with a slight limp. She smiled, ruffled his hair, and put her arm around him, gladder of the company than the structural support.

The strange procession left the courtyard of Hôtel-Dieu and turned right, down the remains of Rue aux Teintures. Narrow shattered footbridges with twisted black railings crossed the river. Once they brought the two sides of the busy market street together, but now they looked perilous under heaps of rubble that had tumbled from the crumbling shops and apartments either side. Plastered rooms were exposed like shattered dolls' houses. Brick walls bared the scars where roofs once rested. Holes where joists once lodged now looked like empty tooth sockets in a beaten jaw. One shop at the end of the street was almost intact. It was one of the two boulangeries that Pierre had been taking flour to. He stepped aside to talk to the boulanger then returned shaking his head.

"She won't leave," he said.

"Why not?" asked Anna.

"There are some who will not leave Vire or their farms nearby," explained Pierre. "'What will they eat?' she asked. 'What will you bake with?' I replied. She shrugged and wished us good luck."

Anna swung the sacks back over her shoulder and followed the carriage up the hill out of Vire. Whatever was left of it. She watched as Céleste gently encouraged the scrawny horses up the incline. It seemed utterly incongruous to see horses in the middle of a mechanised war, alongside tanks and warplanes and motorbikes. She remembered Pierre explaining that petrol was rationed like food and that the Wehrmacht took priority over all others. There were three modes of transport in wartime France: walking, cycling and horses. After the steady increase in motor traffic over the last couple of decades, the horse was enjoying a temporary comeback.

At the top of the hill, they saw German soldiers. Céleste motioned for David, Jim, and Anna to walk on the opposite side of the carriage, less visible. A soldier stepped forward and started checking papers at random among the ragged line of refugees. Despite their forged documents, or perhaps because of them, Anna and Jim were starting to sweat. Anna was more worried for little David. Not now, she thought. Not after all this.

A dark grey staff car drew up alongside them, bearing the black and white cross of the Wehrmacht. A young officer stepped out and approached the soldier making spot checks, who saluted. After a moment's discussion the soldier saluted again and withdrew to the side of the road. The officer turned around and waved the refugees on. Anna recognised him; it was Lieutenant Werner Lehman.

She wanted to thank him, but she had learned caution over the last few weeks. Instead, she kept her head down and pulled the sacks up around her as she walked by, taking care to keep the carriage between her and the soldiers.

The road stretched out in the fading sunlight beyond them, rising and falling between the fields and hedgerows. Behind they heard small-arms fire interspersed with the thuds of larger guns. Anna fought to stop herself trembling and clenched her teeth again. It did not feel like liberation to Anna. It felt like defeat.

They reached the little town of Saint-Germain de Tallevende as the shadows merged and dissolved into the gloom of dusk. They were greeted by a pinch-faced man who shook his head and pointed to a country lane that led east across the darkening fields again. Pierre argued politely with the man for a while and gestured to the sad and weary group that leaned against the carriage for support. Eventually they reached a compromise. The refugees would spend the night sleeping on the floor of the inn and share what little food could be spared. In the morning they would walk.

Anna endured a familiar feeling. Just like the other refugees she was not wanted there in Saint-Germain. She remembered that state of rejection and subsistence from her days drifting between institutional beds and the cold pavements of Nottingham. It didn't seem to matter how you became homeless: poverty, war, flood or famine. You always became an embarrassment to those who still had their homes. You were moved on. Not wanted here. Someone else's problem.

Anna felt a deep kinship with the Virois. It made her think of the millions of refugees from many modern-day countries who fled from war. Every man, woman and child who found themselves thrown upon the mercy of a merciless neighbour.

The Bocage, Normandy, 6th August 1944

The next morning it rained. Of course. They left Saint-Germain at dawn and Jim nudged Anna and pointed at a hedgerow on the hill. She couldn't see anything odd to start with. This was the bocage, of course there were hedges. Then her eyes focussed on a series of long dark barrels protruding from under a net full of leaves and branches that hovered just above the hedge. A Wehrmacht gun battery.

The trudge through the rain to the next village felt like an epic march along twisting muddy lanes but was in truth little more than two miles. Even that was too long for some of the elderly who squeezed in alongside those in the carriage. Anna looked at the two horses, bones poking out of their sagging skin, and hoped they weren't going to be told to move on again.

David asked when he would see his parents. Céleste gave him a hug and Jim stepped in to distract him with a game of I Spy.

As they walked, she asked Pierre how it was he had appeared so forgiving of the Allied bombing of Vire.

"I do not forgive," he said. "I do not condemn. The German army invaded four years ago. The Blitzkrieg, the lightning war. We had no idea it would be so fast. In the previous war, armies had dug into their trenches and shelled each other for years, going nowhere. This time they took all northern France in weeks. They had been building their tanks and warplanes and arming their soldiers in preparation. They knew exactly what they were doing, they were going to punish us for the previous war. As Parisiens fled in their hundreds and thousands along country lanes, they sent their dive-bombers to attack."

"What? They bombed unarmed civilian refugees?"

Pierre nodded. "Have you heard a Stuka dive-bomber attack?"

Anna shook her head.

"They put sirens into them. When the pilot points it down at the people he is attacking, the sirens wail louder and louder. It is screaming at them, 'Here is your death, I am coming for you.' And there is nowhere to run or hide. Some were killed by the bombs and bullets." He looked across his shoulder at the carriage. "Some of the elderly died of heart attacks. And some still freeze in panic when they hear an air-raid siren. So much easier to kill them when the next attack comes. Whoever it comes from."

Anna put her hand on his. "I'm so sorry," she whispered.

They approached a sleepy hamlet, a picture of rural peace. Pierre knocked on the door of a house, next to the sign that said La Lande Vaumont and another that pointed to two places called Truttemer Le Grand and Truttemer Le Petit. She wondered how small the Petit version could be compared to this place. Pierre returned with his shoulders slumped. If he had a tail, it would have been curled between his legs. He was about to break the bad news when a middle-aged man with spectacles and a neatly trimmed beard approached them from the lane leading to the Truttemers. He observed the sad and sodden group, introduced himself as Doctor Couppey and asked Pierre if the villagers had offered any help. Pierre shook his head and studied at the puddle by his feet.

"We have no room at the Chateau in Truttemer," said Couppey, "It is full of the wounded from the air attack on Vire. But there is a barn to the south of this village, and we can fetch food for you. Let me take you there."

The barn had a thatched roof supported on sturdy oak frames and bales of straw that the doctor explained could be laid out as beds. It was more comfortable than the inn floor and Doctor Couppey was far more welcoming than the pinch-faced man at Saint-Germain. Anna reminded herself that the man at Saint-Germain must have seen every refugee coming out of Vire as it was the very next town. She had sympathy for his unwelcome message if not his delivery. The doctor returned to the barn within the hour, accompanied by a pair of kitchen orderlies bringing bread and water. He assured them they should be safe there for as long as it took for the fighting in the larger towns to pass them by.

"Good," said Jim. "I need to go back to Vire."

Anna looked at him as if he were mad. "We've only just reached safety."

"I need to find my way back to my squadron at RAF Tangmere in Sussex. The only way I can do that is find Allied soldiers. Last I heard they were advancing on Vire."

"Oh hell," muttered Anna. She could feel her teeth clenching in anticipation. "I'm coming with you."

Vaudeville

The Bocage, Normandy, 6th August 1944

Céleste begged 'Henri' and 'Marie' to stay. David clung to Jim's leg until he was gently prised off. Pierre thanked them and wished them luck. "If you see Élise, tell her we are safe at La Lande Vaumont."

Anna promised she would. She could tell that Jim hoped to find her too: another reason why he wanted to return. Anna wanted to find her grandma for different yet equally selfish reasons. She wanted to make sure Élise survived and made good on her promise to coach Anna. She also wondered how Élise and Jim could ever become an item.

At least the weather was improving. The sun played hide-and-seek between the clouds and the fields smelled of wet grasses. In another time, this would have been a pleasant stroll in the fields of the Bocage. Too bad they were searching for a warzone.

As they walked back towards Saint-Germain, Jim nudged Anna and pointed to a low hill. This time she knew what to look for: leaf strewn nets and gun barrels.

"The Yanks will waltz straight into their line of fire," said Jim.

"And the other guns just north of Saint-Germain," said Anna, "and the guns on the hills around Vire."

"I doubt any spotter planes will have seen them with the camouflage netting over, so we have to warn them."

There was a grumble of distant gunfire which made Anna clench her teeth again. "I suppose that means going towards the gunfire, not away."

"I'm afraid so, old girl. The tank battle we heard was on the north-west of Vire so that's where we must go."

"Less of the old girl. I'm only a year older than you." Now. He'd be far older the next time they met.

"Sorry, just a turn of phrase."

They walked in silence along the track to Saint-Germain. There they found the road blocked by an armoured car and German soldiers. There was a stutter of automatic weapons coming from the north-west across the fields.

"Better go cross country," said Jim. "Roads will be buzzing with troops."

Anna wasn't convinced the fields would be safer but didn't have any better ideas so she followed Jim through a gate and around the edge of the nearest field, heading north-west as best they could guess. A warplane roared low across the field and they dived beneath a hedge like rabbits till it passed.

A mile or so further on they reached the edge of a stream. "This must lead back into Vire," said Jim. "We can follow it a while and cross before we get to the town."

Past the next field it was joined by another stream and the waters tumbled through a rocky cascade then broadened out into a fast-flowing river that wove through the trees of the wood ahead of them.

"I hope there's a bridge," said Anna as they followed it into the wood. "You wouldn't want to carry the old girl across that."

Jim looked suitably embarrassed. He was about to say something contrite when a series of explosions erupted from over the hill on their left.

Anna cowered against a pine trunk and shuddered with each shot. She heard shouts from behind her and shrank down among a crop of ferns, trembling. Jim hid too. A patrol of German soldiers passed, searching the wood, so they lay beneath the foliage until they disappeared, up stream.

"Jolly good job we were in the shadow of the trees," whispered Jim.

The explosions subsided. Anna's trembling subdued. The two of them slipped away up the dark wooded hillside, relieved at their escape. The early evening sun caught the tops of the trees, setting them alight with a warm glow, which made the gloom at ground level even more of a contrast. At the edge of the wood, they stopped and blinked, shielding their eyes against the low sun. There were blackened metal carcasses strewn around the fields ahead of them. About half a dozen huge hulks near them, all bearing the black crosses of the Wehrmacht. Further off were twice as many smaller olive-green tanks with white stars. All were belching black smoke.

"Bloody hell. Canned carnage," muttered Jim.

A shout came from one of the burning green tanks across the field, followed by a harrowing scream. Anna recognised that scream. It was just like those who burned in the phosphor bomb attack on Vire. She ran towards the scream.

"HEY, MARIE! STOP!" yelled Jim then ran after her.

A young lad of about seventeen or eighteen lay half-in, half-out of the hatch on the front of the burning tank, pulling on his legs. Anna put a foot on the tracked wheel and jumped up onto the armoured front. She covered her mouth and leaned into the smoking hatch to search for whatever trapped the lad's legs. Her arm brushed the side of the hatch and she recoiled with a yelp. It was hot enough to fry breakfast. Looking down she saw the soles of her boots smoking.

"JIM! HELP!"

Jim jumped up beside her, grabbed the hatch cover for balance before she could warn him, shouted, and recoiled. Anna gripped his shirt and stopped him from falling off. He nodded thanks and leaned into the hatch, avoiding the sides. Anna lifted the lad's shoulders off the scorching metal. Jim pulled, grunted, shoved, and finally lifted his legs out. Between them they half staggered, half fell off the tank and into the long grass.

"Quick, we need to get him away," said Jim.

They carried the young man to the edge of the field and laid him down in the shade of a hedge where he groaned. There was another cry from the turret of the same tank. Jim got up and ran to find whoever was suffering. He got within twenty metres of the tank then disappeared in an ear-splitting fireball.

The reasoning part of Anna's mind was running after her grandad, to see if he was alive. The unreasoning beast lay on the ground convulsed in shock. Anna let out a ragged breath and risked lifting her head, which rang like a struck bell. She caught a motion from her left, then a line of light green uniformed soldiers came loping across the field, crouching to minimise the targets they presented. One spotted her and approached, levelling the muzzle of his carbine at her.

"Who the hell are you?" he demanded in an east coast American accent. He dripped sweat from under his helmet and his jacket was covered in dirt and bits of leaves from his crawl through the hedges, most likely on his belly for the last part until the tank battle had stopped. There were three stripes on his shoulder, so Anna figured he was a sergeant.

Anna clenched her teeth to stop them chattering and tried to answer, but whatever came out was unintelligible.

"Can't understand you, kid," he shook his head then waved to another soldier. "Hey, Hank, got a local here. You have some French, so tell her to get the hell outta here."

Anna objected to being called a kid even more than she objected to being called an old girl. It was just what she needed to jolt her back into her normal lippy state. "I'm not a sodding kid and I'm not going to be sent away like one."

That brought east-coast up short, and Hank stood back as if he'd seen a land-mine. "Woah there, gal, thought you were a French local."

"I have a wounded soldier here and there's an RAF officer over there who needs our help," she pointed towards the smoking ruin of the exploded tank.

East-coast turned to Hank, "Call stretcher bearers." He helped Anna to her feet, and they crossed the field to find Jim lying motionless before the blown-out wreck. The sergeant knelt and felt Jim's neck. "Still gotta pulse."

Anna blew out the breath she'd been holding in and knelt to hold Jim's red-raw hand. Hank returned with two pairs of medics who lifted Jim and the injured tank man onto stretchers, then into the back of a truck with a red cross on the side.

"Guess that tank guy wouldn't have made it without you two," said east-coast. "We owe you one."

"I have vital intelligence about German gun positions," said Anna, "I need to talk to your senior officer before you all walk into a trap."

East-coast lifted his helmet to scratch his head, "No kiddin'! Hank? Take this ki..." he caught Anna's narrowed eye and corrected himself, "young lady back to find the Major-General." Hank's eyebrows disappeared up inside his helmet in surprise. "On the double! Lives at stake!"

"This way, miss," beckoned Hank and they jogged off along the lane towards a farmhouse.

A jeep roared up the lane towards them flanked by bikers and followed by trucks. Hank stood into the middle of the lane and waved his hands frantically. The jeep driver skidded to a stop just a few metres from Hank who stood sharply to attention and saluted. Anna thought that was a strange reaction for someone who was about to be mown down by a military convoy.

A middle-aged man wearing a middle-aged crisis bomber jacket and a helmet with two stars on it leaned out of the jeep. To be fair he wore the jacket well. He had a craggy face that said don't mess with me. "What the hell, private!"

"Major-General, Sir! I have orders to take this young woman to see you, Sir. She has intelligence."

"More intelligence than you showed by standing in front of a speeding jeep. Who's she?"

"She has seen where the German artillery positions are," said Anna.

"How do we know we can trust you?" asked the Major-General.

"Because she just saved one of ours from a brewed-up tank, Sir," said Hank. "And her friend near got killed trying to save another. Don't think they'd try that if they weren't on our side."

The Major-General nodded. "Can you read a map?"

"Of course," said Anna. It was on the tip of her tongue to ask if he could drive, seeing as he had to be chauffeured everywhere, but bit her tongue. She approached the jeep as he grabbed a rolled-up map from the guy in the seat behind him and spread it out on the bonnet.

"We're here," he pointed to a hamlet to the west of Vire called Saint-Martin Tallevende. "Yesterday our armour was all shot to hell over here," he pointed to the bridge at Martilly, where the boulangerie she took the flour to had been, and hopefully still was. "Just had the rest of it shot to hell over there," he pointed to the field with the smoking metal wrecks. "Gimme some good news."

Anna searched the map for the names of the places she had been. "There are gun batteries on these two hills outside Saint-Germain de Tallevende, here and here," she pointed. "There's another on this hill just opposite the old castle south of Vire. And there were hundreds of German soldiers digging in on this hill the other side of the valley, close to here," she pointed again.

"They got big guns too?"

Anna nodded, "At least six, maybe more by now."

"Damn!" He shook his head. "Can't get tanks through this wood and down that slope. Most of them brewed-up anyway unless we wait for the rest of the division."

Anna looked at the sun starting to sink lower behind the farm and considered the dark wooded valley she had just climbed out of. If this were a film, then the cavalry would arrive and save the day. It was horrifyingly real, and the metal cavalry were all smoking wrecks in the field beyond. Cavalry. A picture came to Anna's mind of Gandalf the White sitting on a pure white stallion next to the Riders of Rohan at the top edge of a steep valley. Then she remembered them charging down the hill while the orcs were blinded by the rising sun. This wasn't Middle Earth. The sun was setting, not rising. But...

"The woods on this side are in shadow," said Anna. "The Germans are looking into the sun."

The Major-General took his helmet off, scratched his head and regarded Anna, then he looked at the setting sun, then at the map again. "Get in," he thumbed at the spare seat in the back of the jeep. Anna hopped up and sat beside the surprised looking officer with the maps. The Major-General jumped back in the front, beside the driver and reached behind to hand his helmet to Anna. "Put this on. Don't want no civilian advisors getting their heads shot off."

"Thanks," said Anna, almost as surprised at the officer beside her.

"Gerow," he said offering a firm hand to shake. "Major-General Leonard Gerow, 5th Corps."

"Marie Couteau," said Anna.

Gerow gave Anna a shrewd look, "I guess I'll find out your real name some other time ma'am, when you ain't undercover no more."

Anna shrugged and put the helmet with two stars on her head. It was big. She had to lift the lip to see out.

Gerow grinned, "Welcome to the US army."

They parked the jeep and trucks as far into the edge of the wood as they could go then walked the ridge until they caught a glimpse of the other side of the valley through a clearing. Gerow scanned the scene with his binoculars. Anna remembered being watched by the German emplacement from above.

"Well, here we are," declared Gerow, "the original Vaudeville." Anna looked just as puzzled as his aides, so he explained. "We're lookin' at the valley in front of Vire. Olivier Basselin wrote a bunch of medieval drinking songs he called the Vauxdevire, or Valleys of Vire. Likely it got changed to Vaudeville."

There was more to Leonard Gerow than met the eye, thought Anna. He had some historical knowledge of the region he was waging war in. "Can you see the German encampment?" she asked.

"Yeah. Some of it. Well dug in, just like you said. Can't see their big guns yet."

"I think they must have put camouflage netting over them. They have at Saint Germain and nearby."

"Uh huh. Wait... yeah I got 'em now. Thanks a million. You stay here with Lieutenant Hutton. Our boys are gonna see how near they can get through the shadow of these woods before the shootin' starts."

"We saw a patrol down by the river," said Anna.

"Thanks again, I'll send scouts ahead of the two battalions. Hutton?"

"Sir?" answered the lieutenant.

"Guard Mademoiselle Couteau with your life."

"Yes sir!"

Vaux de Vire, Normandy, 6th August 1944

Anna's mind tumbled. She objected to being told to stay out of the fight but was equally relieved. She was no soldier, but she had just been giving military advice which might save American lives while taking German lives. Jim had found the Allies, but he nearly got himself killed: Anna could only hope that the medics would revive him. And Élise was nowhere to be seen. What a mess.

She watched as hundreds of GIs stalked into the woods and down the slope before her. They looked grim. Determined. Many just looked too young, even younger than her. Were they afraid? Of course, they must be. But they had a business-like air about them, a job to be done, and she sensed they believed it would be. At a cost.

Anna wondered what it must be like. They knew that some of them were about to die, but they didn't know which of them. It was a gamble. A game of roulette. Hopefully, most would be lucky, but some would not. The last of the soldiers faded into the gloom of the trees below and an eerie silence fell. No voices, no shuffling of feet, not even a chirp of birdsong.

The minutes stretched out. Anna found herself holding her breath. When would they be seen? When would the shooting begin? When would the dying start again?

A violent burst of machine gun fire ripped through the peace and tore chunks out of some trees below, followed by shouts and a stutter of return fire. Anna jerked with each shot and clutched her sides. Then the artillery on the hill opened up with a series of crumps and explosions which lit the woods momentarily. She crouched by the side of the jeep and clutched Gerow's helmet down over her head.

"It's okay, miss," said Lieutenant Hutton beside her. "They ain't aiming up here."

It was meant well, but Anna's faith in military aim had been seriously undermined. She leaned into the wheel arch and trembled.

The shooting seemed to go on for an age. The sun sank behind them and the moon rose in front of them, lighting the hill that the German soldiers held, grimly fighting each bush, each wall, each foxhole. Below her she could hear shouts and screams. One young lad was calling for his mum. She shut her eyes tight and stuffed her fingers in her ears, but you can't unhear something like that.

It must have been the middle of the night by the time the shooting stopped, and the big guns fell silent. The constellations were crystal clear in the velvet sky and a strange calm settled. Hutton knelt beside Anna and gently prised her clenched fingers off the wheel arch.

"Gotta go now miss," he said and helped her into the jeep. "Gets easier after a while."

Anna nodded and clutched her sides again. How selfish was she? These guys had no choice. They were conscripted and sent to fight for Uncle Sam in a foreign land against people they'd never met. They went from one battle to the next to the next and never knew which might be their last. It was time for her to get a grip on herself. Easier said than done.

Hutton drove them at an alarming angle, weaving their way through the trees down the steep slope. Several times she thought they would roll over but, somehow, he managed to swing the jeep back into the slope and get them to the bottom of the valley. They crossed a temporary metal bridge over the river Vire and got out to see the battlefield above. She could see the silhouettes of men standing, arms in the air, at gunpoint, being moved off the hill. The Wehrmacht had fought bravely and lost. The GIs had fought bravely and won. This time.

Anna thought again of the melancholy feeling she'd had while crossing the hill with David. Had she experienced some premonition of the deaths up there? Was it the same as the feeling she'd had in the Porte-Horloge?

Liberty

Vire, Normandy, 8th August 1944

It took two more days for the Americans to take the centre of Vire. Two more days of shooting, suffering, fear and dying before the last hill was overthrown and the last guns were silenced. It had taken over a week for Gerow's men to gain control and the toll had been heavy. And this was just one town, there were many more to go before the Nazis would finally be driven out of France.

Gerow made a point of finding Anna and shaking her hand before they moved out. "I wanna thank you Mademoiselle. There's a good many of our boys who may yet see home again because of the intel you gave us."

And a good many German boys who won't, thought Anna. Had she done the right thing? Her grandma's warning before she left Pagham echoed around her head: 'Take great care what you do in the past. All acts have consequences. Don't kill anyone.' She hadn't pulled a trigger, but she may as well have. Anna was starting to realise that doing the right thing was far more complex than she had ever thought. The thought she clung to was that the Nazis' organisation was evil. Individual German soldiers may not be, but that was the master they served, willingly or not.

"You look like you could do with a rest," said Gerow, snapping her out of her reflection.

"Mm. Not as much as your boys. I guess that'll be a way off yet."

"Next stop Paris," joked Gerow, fully aware of how many French towns they'd have to fight for before they got there.

"How did you know about Vaudeville, Sir?" asked Anna.

"Now you're on vacation from the US Army, you can call me Leonard. My surname is Gerow, it comes from the French name Giraud. Guess I oughta know a thing or two 'bout France."

"Good luck. Hope you all make it to Paris."

He winked and turned to his lieutenant, "Remember to look out for the hidden batteries at Saint-Germain de Tallevende, just like the lady said. Get these wagons rolling!"

"Sir!" Lieutenant Hutton snapped a smart salute and started barking orders to the troops nearby.

Anna's preconceptions about brash Yanks had mellowed considerably in the last couple of days, though she would never forget or forgive those who authorised the bombing of Vire and so many other French towns. She vowed to find out who made those decisions, American and British. She doubted it was any of their men in the field.

Watching the American trucks and jeeps roll out, she found herself lost and purposeless. She walked down the dusty track towards the stark ruins of what was once a town called Vire. A few American trucks remained. A small party of troops had been ordered to drag bodies from the rubble and take them to the burial pits, American, German and French. If Gerow had family from France and so did Anna, then she wondered if some of the German soldiers who fought here did too?

One man in the light olive-green uniform of the US army was standing in front of the Porte-Horloge, taking a photograph with a clunky contraption that must have been the latest technology in 1944. He saw Anna staring at him and waved.

"Hi! I got myself plenty of evidence to show the top brass back home," he said.

"Evidence?" asked Anna, puzzled.

"Well, damn! Just look," he gestured at the scarred and pitted remains of Rue Saulnerie. Barely a single wall still stood. The bookshop was a pile of stones and charred timbers. The stretcher team prised a beam up to pull another body clear. "Just look what the Nazis did to this place!"

"The Nazis?"

"Sure, who else?"

"The Nazis occupied Vire. The Nazis sent a little boy's mother and father to the gas chambers. The Nazis shot my great grandmother for shaking her fist at them and made my great grandfather a slave in Essen. But it was the Allies who fire-bombed my grandfather to death in Essen. It was the Allies who bombed this town flat. It was the Allies who came straight back and incinerated every survivor with phosphor bombs. It was the Allies who killed my great uncle Henri just over there and nearly killed me."

The photographer staggered back under Anna's onslaught, tripped over a broken window frame, and landed on his backside. "'scuse me Ma'am, but at least we liberated this place," he managed, sitting up again.

"This is liberty? And where are all the Virois you just liberated?"

"Er..."

"I'll tell you where they are, they're all DEAD! Go tell that to the top brass at home, and make sure you tell them who dropped the bombs that killed them." Anna found herself leaning over the man, her face in his. She stood up. He was trembling. She turned on the spot and stalked away. A few yards down the tattered remains of the street, she realised she was trembling too, not with fear but with rage.

Perhaps she shouldn't have yelled at the photographer, he wasn't the one who dropped the bombs. But a lie was a dangerous thing, especially on the lips of the victors. Maybe, just maybe the man might report the truth.

Anna found Élise at the top of the hill overlooking the donjon and the other ruins of Vire. She was singing softly to herself.

"I will return soon,

Let us have patience...

Wait for me my love,

In a beautiful corner of France,

Where we had so many care-free days..."

Élise stopped and looked up as Anna approached her.

"My mum... your daughter, used to sing that song to me," said Anna. "And I sang it to myself. Literally to myself," thinking of when she returned to Blackheath and sang to five-year-old Anna.

"It is popular here now," said Élise. There are many of us who wait for those they love.

"It's good to hear it in English, though that's weird because I know you're singing in French. How does that work?"

Élise shrugged. "It works."

"Will you wait for Werner?"

Élise closed her eyes. She seemed calm, almost rested compared to the stressed fighter of the Resistance who had, until now, walked the knife edge between compassionate liaison and undercover warfare. "He is gone," she said simply.

"Where?"

"He probably died somewhere in Vire. Perhaps here, on this hill, where they made their last stand. There are no records in the future, and I have searched for him."

Anna sat beside her grandma. "I'm sorry."

"You think me foolish. For loving one of our enemy."

"No. No, I don't. He was a good man. He protected us when Jim was leading the elderly out of Vire."

Élise opened her eyes and looked at Anna. "The airman?"

"Yes. He nearly got himself killed trying to save a young American tank crew. I was told he's making a good recovery at the field hospital near Saint Sever. They'll send him back to England soon."

"Will he live?"

"I hope so." *If he doesn't then I won't exist,* she wanted to add, but couldn't. Her grandma obviously wasn't ready for that.

"The Barron boy was fond of him," recalled Élise.

"Very. Jim is good with children."

Élise nodded, as if making a mental note. "Vire is liberated."

"What's left of it."

"Hm. Those who survived will return."

As if on cue, an elderly couple walked hand-in-hand to the edge of the hill a few yards from where they sat. They surveyed the grim scene before them, and the man put his arm around the woman to comfort them both. The man shook his head. The woman wiped a tear from her eye.

"It doesn't feel like victory, does it?" said Anna.

"You have seen Vire in your time, have you not?" asked Élise.

"Yes."

"And it thrives, does it not?"

"Yes. Yes, it does."

"And there are no swastikas or occupying forces? No rationing, no hiding, no suspicion or fear?"

"No. Vire is free."

"Then it is victory. But like many things worth having, it will take time."

Anna observed her young grandma. She seemed remarkably wise for her young years. Anna thought about the time she herself had already spent without Rob and wondered if she would ever see him again.

"You need to take a few days," said Élise. "Back in your own time. To recover from all this."

"I do? Yes... I suppose I do, but..."

"I will be here. I made a promise and I intend to keep it."

"You'll wait for me to return?"

"How long I have to wait depends on how accurate you are. So, I shall give you your first lesson before you go."

"A lesson?"

"Yes. Judging by the way you arrived, just as my fight was at its most intense, without any papers and no clue about the dangers of occupation, you make no preparations. No attempt to understand the time you are travelling to. You just... arrive!"

Anna clenched her fist and frowned. She didn't like her grandma's blunt assessment, but she couldn't disagree with it.

"Now you know what to expect when you return to 1944," continued Élise, "But we will be going to February 1417, so I want you to read all you can about that time. I don't want you blundering around medieval Normandy in the same way you blundered through our liberation."

Anna gritted her teeth. Her grandma could be exceedingly condescending. "And why are we going to February 1417?"

"Because that is when you will meet the most knowledgeable person in our family of time travellers. Your great, great and many more greats grandmother, Eleanor Couteau."

"She will teach me?"

"She will teach us both. I have already learned much from her."

"Then I'll read all I can find out."

"Good."

"How will I avoid keeping you waiting?" Anna asked sourly.

"Observation."

"Yes?"

"Look at me, what I am wearing. Look at the angle of the sun, the length of the shadows, the elderly couple over there."

Anna observed the elegant cut of her grandma's dark red culottes, her yellow blouse and the long grey cloak lying folded neatly on her lap. She observed the early evening sun and the shadow thrown by the shattered oak tree behind her. She observed the elderly couple who clung to each other as there was little of Vire left to cling to. An image. A snapshot of time. She committed it to her memory. "Okay."

"Good. Now you know the exact moment to return to. If you do this properly then I will not have more than an hour or so to wait. If, on the other hand, you make another mess of it I could be here for days or weeks."

Anna scowled. "How can I forget your supercilious expression, Grandma? I'll be back in a minute." And she closed her eyes, turned her mind's eye upwards and watched the sun race into the horizon. The stars emerged, the days ran forward, the seasons and the years. The machines arrived. The debris cleared. The walls climbed up and Vire reconstructed itself in time-lapse. Anna counted the passing of the summers and then started to slow the chasing of the seasons, searching, observing, looking for the morning she left in 2022.

Vire, Normandy, 6th June 2022

Anna found herself standing on the same hill overlooking the donjon and the roofscape of Vire in the early morning sunshine. Beside her was the memorial plaque dedicated to the US 5th Corps who stormed this last hill on 8th August 1944. She knelt and brushed her fingers gently down the list of names, silently adding those she knew: Henri, Étienne and Estelle Couteau, and Werner Lehman. Then she rose and walked down the hill (no gun emplacements), across the pool with the ducks (full of water, not mud or rubble) and up the road past the Hôtel de Ville (no air raid siren or swastikas).

At the top of the road was the roundabout with the flowers and flags. To her left was the Porte-Horloge standing proudly apart from its modern neighbours. The Café Central was full of locals taking their morning coffee.

A car drew up and parked in the square. A couple in their sixties got out, one to take a wheelchair from the boot, the other to help a little white haired old man from the back seat. He wore a smart dark suit with a row of brightly polished medals with coloured ribbons and a US military cap. Several of the locals rose to greet him, putting their arms around him and kissing him on both cheeks then shaking him firmly by the hand. The little old man shone like his medals and stood a few inches taller. One of Gerow's boys? Anna stood hugging her sides and smiled while a tear rolled softly down her cheek.

"Hey! Anna!" called a familiar voice. She turned and saw Jeanne Rajaonarison from the Médiathèque walking across the square waving. "You're back! Good timing, you're just in time for the D-Day commemoration."

Anna's voice failed her. The ordeals of the last weeks threatened to overwhelm her. She threw her arms around Jeanne and hugged her tight. Jeanne, surprised, pulled gently back and saw Anna's cheeks wet with tears, her eyes red raw.

"Oh Anna! What is the matter? What happened?"

"I found out what happened to my relatives here... seventy-eight years ago. I found out what really happened to your town and its people."

Jeanne studied Anna's face, trying to understand the strength of her emotions for events of the last century. "Sit down Anna. I'll get us some coffees."

Anna sat at one of the tables outside the Café Central while Jeanne spoke to the waiter. She watched the white-haired old man, who must have been in his late nineties, sitting surrounded by the Virois. People of all ages he had helped to liberate when he was only a lad.

Jeanne returned with two coffees and a box of tissues. "Here. Tell me what you found."

Anna looked at her friend and wondered how much to say. One thing she had learned in 1944 was discretion. Another was the value of friendship. She was so tired of evasion and deceit. She was exhausted by bottling her emotions. "If I were to show you something... something extraordinary, would you keep it to yourself?"

Anna's Quest

Vire, Normandy, June 2022

Anna made sure Jeanne was sitting back safely on the sofa in her flat. She didn't want her falling over like Angela Briars. Jeanne looked just as sceptical as Angela had and more than a little worried, as if Anna had some condition that may need specialist therapy.

"Don't worry, I'm fine and I'll come straight back to you," Anna reassured her, "Just sit tight and wait."

Jeanne nodded, looking as if she wanted to phone for help. Anna looked carefully at the shadow thrown by the sun and noted just how far across the floor it reached, just touching the leg of the coffee table. Then she rolled her eyes when she noticed the clock on the wall: ten forty-four AM. She wouldn't need to watch the shadow this time, though it helped. She closed her eyes and looked down within her mind's eye. Somehow it always seemed easier looking down into the past than up into the future. She watched the shadows stretch out and the apartment go dark, and she stopped there, in the middle of the night before 6th June. She got up to fetch a glass of water from the kitchenette then returned to Jeanne's living room and sat down on the chair opposite the sofa again. Anna closed her eyes, searched upwards and watched the dawn light creep into the room and followed the shadows back to that point in the middle of the morning where the shadow was just short of the coffee table again, then looked up at the clock: ten forty-five AM. When she opened her eyes, she saw Jeanne, mouth open, clenching a cushion to her chest.

"Ta-da!" Anna mocked herself softly. "And here I am back again."

"Putain de salopard!" whispered Jeanne.

"Here, have a glass of water," said Anna handing it to Jeanne.

Jeanne eyed it with deep suspicion, but recognised her own glass and took it, sniffed it, found nothing satanic or foul and had a tentative sip.

"It just travelled through time with me," said Anna. "Not through an enchantment or a secret sewer."

Jeanne pointed a trembling finger at Anna, "You... you just... disappeared."

"Yeah, I do that."

"And reappeared with this."

"Yep."

Jeanne got up and went to her kitchenette where she counted her glasses then returned and stood in front of Anna, looking at her accusingly. "Is this a trick? Did you come into my apartment and take the glass and hide it?"

"Nope."

"And how did you fill it with water?"

"From your tap. In your kitchenette at about midnight last night."

"But..."

"I didn't break in, no."

"You travelled back in time."

"Bingo. That's a 'yes' by the way."

"So... when you said you were going away to research for a while, you were actually going back in time. Seventy-eight years. To when Vire was occupied and liberated."

"Yes."

"Which is why you were crying when you saw the war veteran."

Anna nodded and looked down at her lap. She could feel her eyes burning again.

Jeanne sat down on the sofa in silence. Anna was beginning to wonder if she had done the right thing, whether she could trust Jeanne or not, then Jeanne came over and sat on the edge of Anna's chair and put her arm around her, hugging her tight. "My God, what did you see?" she whispered.

Anna took a deep breath and started with her arrival at the train station, and her walk up the hill to Chateau Jeannin.

It was late when Anna finished her story. Jeanne took Anna to a crêperie because they were both ravenous and, after they had each taken a glass of smooth red wine, Jeanne began asking all the questions that had been queuing up in her mind.

Anna did her best to answer. Yes, she had seen random past events since she was small, but it was only after she fled a rapist and fell that she was physically jolted into the past and discovered her ability to time travel. No, she didn't understand how that worked, which was why she had travelled to 1944 to find her young grandma, Élise, and eventually persuaded her to start teaching Anna. Yes, she was going to go back to find Élise again and learn more.

"What do you intend to do with your knowledge?" asked Jeanne.

Anna picked at the wax on the side of the candle on the table. She wanted to say that she was going to use her ability for good. She wanted to say that she would carefully research and pick the times in history where she could go and do most to protect people who had been as vulnerable as she had been, when living on the streets of Nottingham. Instead, she told the truth. "I started out wanting to find my family. But most of all I want to find out if the man I love is still alive and, if he is, I want to go back and be with him."

Jeanne looked as if she were about to be told the best love story in history and Anna didn't know if she could possibly deliver. "What is his name?" asked Jeanne, "and what is he like?"

Anna carried on picking at the candle and feeding the pieces of wax back into the flame for a while. "Rob Ahmed."

"Rob Ahmed," repeated Jeanne, beaming. "Don't tell me, he's dark, brown eyes and unassuming."

"And cantankerous. Don't forget the cantankerous."

Jeanne laughed, "How could I forget! And where and when did you last see him?"

"That's complicated."

"I am learning not to be surprised."

"I last saw him alive in Sherwood Forest in 1215."

Jeanne's eyes narrowed, as if the cogs were turning.

"I last saw him dead in a cemetery cave in Nottingham in 2019," continued Anna. She heaved a deep breath, "I buried him there. With his golden arrow."

"A golden arrow? Like in the movie we watched? You... you fell in love with Robin Hood?"

Anna nodded and picked some more wax off the candle.

Jeanne squealed out loud and the entire crêperie turned their heads to stare. Anna tried to sink into her chair. "My God! You fell in love with Robin Hood and you're on a quest to find him again. Do you understand how amazing that is?"

"I miss him," said Anna in a small voice.

Jeanne shook her head in wonder.

"I know I could travel back to 1215 to look for him," said Anna, "but I'm afraid he won't be alive there anymore. I'm afraid there won't be any evidence that he was there at all: he's supposed to be a legend, a myth. I want to find out if it's possible to die in one time and carry on living in another. I must find that out before I go back and search for him because I can't face losing him all over again."

Jeanne clasped Anna's hands, stopping her from picking at the candle and making her look up. "That is beautiful. How can I help you?"

Anna shrugged, unsure. "Well, you could help me find out about Vire in 1417." Jeanne looked puzzled. "That's when my grandma Élise wants to take me for my next lessons. And to meet my ancestor who knows loads more about time travel. Élise said I should do more research before I arrive in the past, rather than just... arriving."

"I think I can help you with that," smiled Jeanne.

After dinner Jeanne led Anna to the big public space in front of the donjon. There was a brass band playing in the bandstand and flags strung around. At three minutes past eight in the evening they all stopped. The crowd stood in silence. The late evening sunshine caught the tops of the trees alight, and Anna clenched Jeanne's hand while she remembered her flight from the Hôtel de Ville to the cellar under Henri's bookshop. She remembered the sound of the bombs exploding, the screaming, and Henri holding her tight. Finally, she remembered the charred bodies and the lost child standing on a heap of rubble.

The silence was broken by a lone bugle call. The band started to play again, and people began to talk and smile and laugh again. Life went on.

After the light faded, the donjon was lit up together with the tower of Notre Dame and the clock tower of the Porte-Horloge. There was whoosh and a bang and Anna flinched, then looked up to see a shower of golden sparks. The next firework did not make her jump so much, but she still felt the percussion through her spine. Jeanne looked at Anna, worried, then understanding came and she put her arm around Anna. Each bang got easier. By the end of the show Anna was smiling and applauding with the rest of the crowd. But as the fireworks faded from her retina, the price of liberation paid by the Virois burned in her heart.

Médiathèque, Vire, June 2022

Anna had her head in the white history book of Vire of 1944 when Jeanne arrived carrying a pile of books and a printed list of online articles about medieval France.

"I thought you were going to 1417?" asked Jeanne.

"I am. But I was looking for the photos taken by the American military, just after liberation and I think I've found them, but I can't fully understand the captions because they're in French. And I'm a language dunce."

Jeanne put the pile down and looked at the captions. "It says 'Official US commentary: The devastation suffered in Vire after Allied bombing.'"

"Yes!" Anna punched the air. Jeanne looked at her blankly. "A small victory for the truth." Jeanne still looked blank. "I met the military photographer. He was going to say it was all caused by the German occupiers. I told him... well, I think I shouted and swore at him a bit, but I told him to print the truth. And he did."

Jeanne's eyes widened. "So... you changed history."

"A little bit. Not much. But the truth is important."

"The first casualty of war."

"The first and last."

"I don't know what to say. What you do... it is... powerful. As well as dangerous."

"Mm," Anna nodded, looking at the photos. "By the way, what does putain de salopard mean?"

Jeanne's cheeks reddened and she looked away. "Ah..."

"It's what you said when I time travelled in your apartment and came back again."

Jeanne nodded. "I know. I was in shock, you understand?"

"Of course."

Jeanne muttered the translation to Anna under her breath, embarrassed.

"My Grandma Élise was right. I really should learn to swear in French. Far more satisfying. Can you teach me more?"

The medieval books were helpful, and the article references were excellent. Who held Vire, who they fought, what they ate, what they wore? Their faiths, superstitions, music, and literature. Anna read and inwardly digested until she was sated. She took a break for coffee then went back to digest more.

"You know 1417 is in the middle of the Hundred Years War, don't you?" said Jeanne.

"Uh huh."

"So, aren't you just a little afraid that you'll get caught in the fighting?"

"Wouldn't be the first time," answered Anna, trying to sound casual.

"I know Vire wasn't attacked until 1418, but that doesn't mean it will be peaceful in 1417. There could be any number of raids or uprisings or chevauchées."

"What is a chevauchée? Something to do with horses?"

"Think of it like a fifteenth century Blitzkrieg with armoured cavalry instead of tanks," said Jeanne. "The English used it to intimidate as many people as possible across as big an area as possible."

"Something else for us English to be proud of," said Anna sarcastically, shaking her head. "Why did they do it? Sport?"

"There was an element of that," said Jeanne. "They considered it a measure of their military prowess to see how destructive they could be. The idea was to stop taxes being paid to the French Duchy and Crown, and to frighten the locals so that they asked their Dukes and King to come out and protect them."

"I presume they did come out to fight?"

"Usually. The provocation often resulted in a pitched battle that would decide the fate of the area."

"I bet they didn't want to give up their land or taxes. Lukewarm about what happened to their people though."

Jeanne smiled, "You sound as if you've read about the behaviour of Dukes and Kings before."

"I've seen it first-hand," said Anna, "and I've seen what war can do to ordinary people."

Jeanne regarded Anna thoughtfully. "I've been doing a little research of my own after you told me what happened to you in 1944. I found Monsieur and Madame Barron. They were taken to Dachau. They did not survive. I am so sorry."

Anna nodded. She had prepared herself for that. "What about David?"

"I could not find any record of a David Barron; it is likely they hid those records deliberately to protect him. However, I found a David Hamel, adopted son of Pierre and Céleste Hamel. He died peacefully in 2012. But he is survived by his son Ben Hamel, who lives in Saint Sever. I called him this morning and explained I knew someone whose family knew his father in 1944. He said he would be delighted to talk if you would."

Anna's mouth opened and closed soundlessly before her brain would engage. "Yes," she croaked and cleared her throat. "Yes, I would."

EVERYDAY SPIRITS

Saint Sever, June 2022

Ben Hamel lived in a small apartment over a flower shop on the high street in Saint Sever. He welcomed Anna and Jeanne with a warm smile and invited them to sit with him for coffee and éclairs. Anna had been nervous the whole way over, but Ben's easy manner and the chocolate éclair did much to relax her. Anna suspected he was in his early fifties and wondered if there was a Madame Hamel. She looked around at the photos on his mantelpiece and side tables. The usual collection of family groups and individuals of all ages. Ben saw Anna looking at them and went to pick up one of a small elderly man with the same easy smile as Ben.

"This is my father, David," he said handing it to Anna. "I understand that one of your family knew him as a small boy in Vire."

Anna looked carefully at the old man's face. It was the smile and the glitter of the eyes that gave him away: the same she saw when David was playing with her own grandad. "Yes," she gently brushed the photo with her fingertips. "My grandad, Jim Partington, was a pilot. He was shot down, captured, escaped and protected by Pierre and Céleste in the mill house by the river, just off Rue Jean le Houx."

"I know it well," nodded Ben.

"That was where Jim met David. They became mates. They played on the little bridge by the mill. They would bounce on it until it almost broke and shriek with laughter. And Pierre would join in and Céleste would shush them in case the soldiers heard. When the Americans came, they all had to flee in case they were caught in the shooting. David helped Jim and the Hamels to take twenty pensioners from the Hôtel-Dieu to safety in a barn in La Lande Vaumont. David would offer his shoulder for some of the elderly ladies to lean on. He was a little gentlemen, so Jim said." Anna added, trying not to give a first-hand account.

Ben glowed in the warmth of Anna's account. He asked many questions about David's time with the Hamels and then he asked the question that Anna had been dreading. "Did your grandfather find out how David came to be with the Hamels?" He saw Anna's stricken look. "It is alright. I know what happened to David's parents. It is just that I know so little about how he managed to avoid being on that train with them."

Anna took a deep breath and told Ben about the game of hide and seek. The soldier who 'looked' for him in the loft. The soldier (perhaps the same one) who sent him away. And the woman who found him and took him to the Hamels.

"Did he say who that woman was?" asked Ben "My dad always wanted to thank her for what she did."

Anna shook her head and looked out the window. "I'm sure that anyone would have helped a little lost lad."

"Not at that time. Not when they could have been shot for hiding a Jew, no matter their age. I believe she was a courageous woman, just as courageous as the Hamels and your grandfather."

Anna continued to look at the flowers in the windowsill on the other side of the street in case her eyes betrayed her. "No one knows how they will act until they have to. And not everyone gets to find out what happens next. I'm sure the woman would be glad to know that David grew up and had a family."

Jeanne drove Anna back to Vire, occasionally glancing over to see her lost in her thoughts. "You must be proud of the part you played, Anna. It is no small thing you did."

"It was small compared to what the Hamels did. They risked their lives every day they had David and Jim in their house."

"As did you," said Jeanne. "But they couldn't leave. You chose to stay."

Vire, Normandy, June 2022

Jeanne came with Anna to the hill opposite the donjon one warm summer evening when Anna felt she was ready. The light was fading. The memorial was now in shadow. A few bright stars were starting to show beyond the rooftops.

Anna had a long green woollen smock over grey leggings and carried her oversized overcoat under her arm. Unsurprisingly she was starting to sweat, but she remembered Élise saying they were going to February 1417. It would be cold. The smock and leggings had been chosen to try and blend in with fifteenth century attire, but Anna made no apology for the overcoat. They had been through a lot together.

"Good luck with your quest," smiled Jeanne and gave Anna a big hug.

"Thank you. You don't know how much it means for me to have shared my secrets with you."

Jeanne waved away Anna's thanks. "Learn lots. Go get your guy!" she beamed.

Anna nodded and stood back. She closed her eyes and cast her mind downwards into history, watching as the days and seasons rolled back. A firm picture of the scene she was aiming for fixed in her mind...

Chevauchée

Vire, Normandy, August 1944

"You are late," declared Élise. "But not as late as I expected."

"Ooh, look at you. So free with the compliments today."

"I do not appreciate sarcasm."

Anna rolled her eyes. "Sorry, Grandma. I appreciate you keeping your promise to me."

"You are family. But I prefer you call me Élise, not Grandma."

"I suppose it could be confusing."

"Might give us away should the wrong person be listening," Élise beckoned for Anna to follow her down the hill, towards the river. As they walked, she pointed at Anna's overcoat, "What is that thing under your arm?"

"My overcoat."

"It is disgusting. And it is too modern."

"It's been with me to the thirteenth century and back three times and no one paid it any attention. It comes with me."

"No."

"Yes, or I'll freeze, and I'll blame you."

Now Élise rolled her eyes. "I shall disown you. I expect you counted years when coming to 1944?"

"I did."

"But you did not count when going to the middle ages."

"No," agreed Anna sourly, "I just arrived."

"Exactly. Not at all precise. So now, I will teach you 'the kingfisher.'"

"The kingfisher," Anna echoed flatly, beginning to suspect Élise was taking the Michael. Thinking of which, Anna still had lingering questions about the saint of that name. It was the one part of her story she had taken care to omit when confiding in Jeanne.

"When you go back in time, your mind's eye looks down, does it not?" asked Élise.

"Yerse..."

"As if you stand on the edge of a pool of time, searching for just the right fish and judging just the right depth to dive?"

"Perhaps." Anna had to admit that the analogy made some sense to her. Or maybe it was just because they were standing next to the muddy basin that would one day be a duck pool again.

"It is a technique that allows us to move swiftly to the right moment, even if that moment is many centuries away. First, I need a focus. That focus is Eleanor Couteau. Because I have met her, it is easier for me to picture her and concentrate my search upon her, though it sounds as if you have focussed on ancestors without understanding you were doing so." Anna nodded in agreement with Élise. That would explain why Anna had arrived at such specific moments in the history of Nottingham and met relatives almost every time. "Next, I picture the context: the season, the landscape, the buildings, the clothes. Finally, I look for an event."

"An event?"

"A specific event in time. In this case we are searching for the return of a Norman raiding party to the castle. It pins our search to February 1417, when Eleanor is approaching the height of her skill and a full year before Vire is taken by the English. We do not want to get involved in that."

"You want me to picture all that?"

"No, I shall picture it. You will observe and learn."

"Okay. I'm agog."

Élise raised a beautifully manicured eyebrow.

"I'm ready," clarified Anna.

"Hold my hand. And close your eyes."

Anna did as she was asked. Her inner sight became aware of Élise's presence, and she allowed herself to be guided. She did indeed feel as if they were a pair of kingfishers, perched on the edge of a deep, deep pool of time. Anna grew aware of the shapes and shadows that passed below her: the ghosts of the past. A person swam into view. A woman, perhaps in her mid-thirties, tall, dark hair, brilliant green eyes, and a long flowing cloak of dark purple. Eleanor Couteau? She looked familiar: more than a passing resemblance to Anna's mother Eleanor.

The woman stood at the edge of a river, the Vire? Weak winter sunshine cast spidery shadows through skeletal trees and across the banks. A light frost lingered on the ground. Women wearing cloaks and woollen wraps heaved wicker baskets full of multi-coloured linens to the river's edge. Some already knelt to scrub their clothes against boards in the flowing waters.

Above them Anna could see the donjon, in full glory with conical tiled roofs and flags depicting the Little Cats fluttering on a stiff breeze. Along the ridge to the right her attention was caught by riders bearing a matching motif, yellow cats on red, and they were galloping towards the castle.

"We are here," said Élise.

And as her grandma announced their arrival Anna saw a copse of bare young trees materialise around her and felt the cold breeze bite against her cheeks. She swung her oversized overcoat on and turned up the collar, immediately feeling more comfortable.

"Let me introduce you to Madame Couteau," said Élise, and stepped to the edge of the small stand of trees, about thirty metres from the women at the river.

Anna saw the long purple cloak again, it stood out against the other cloaks and wraps. Madame Couteau was almost a head taller than most of the other women and would have drawn attention regardless of what she wore. Especially as she seemed to have a stretch of bank all to herself. Were the others showing deference to her or keeping away from her? Perhaps it was the woman's companion, a hefty young man with a tonsure, holding a crossbow. A short bow, quiver and sword were slung across his back. He would make most people stand away. The woman looked up as they stepped into view, studying Élise and Anna in turn. She approached them and beckoned her companion to follow.

"Good day to you, Mademoiselle Couteau," she said, recognising Élise. "Who have you brought to see me?" She had a commanding alto voice that carried crystal clear.

"A relative of ours," explained Élise, "She will go by the name of Marie Couteau."

"I will?" asked Anna, already feeling the need to avoid being overpowered by her two powerful ancestors.

At that there was a twitch of Eleanor's lips. Perhaps she was amused to see that Anna was not a doormat. Perhaps she was pleased. "Maybe I will get to know another name in time," she said. "But you may have chosen a dangerous moment to arrive."

There was a trumpet call from the donjon walls above them and Eleanor looked up sharply. More riders traversed the ridge towards the castle and Anna could see people scattering before them. Close by there was a shout and a scream. Armoured knights on horseback burst from the trees to the east and galloped along the riverbank, lances lowered.

"Into the copse!" commanded Eleanor.

All four of them took what scant cover they could and watched as nearly a tonne of man, horse and armour slammed into the nearest woman and smashed her body into the icy waters of the Vire like chaff. She was lucky. Two more women were impaled on the rider's lance, splitting their chests, and splattering his polished leg plates bright red. He released his grip on the lance and drew a long blade that glinted in the low sunshine. The other women were yelling and running from the rider, but he spurred his horse and caught them easily. One was decapitated with a casual swipe; another had the top of her body parted from her legs by a vicious back swing. Then he lifted his leg across and dismounted at a run, dispelling any doubts Anna may have had about the agility of knights in plate armour. The horse shortened its stride, strutting alongside him wearing a fine cloth over its armour. 'A caparison', remembered Anna in a random recollection of her research. The caparison cloth had two large blue squares with yellow fleur-de-lis and two large red squares bearing three Little Cats each and she thought she remembered these too.

The knight seized a woman and threw her to the ground. She was young, pretty, and blonde. Anna knew exactly what would happen next, so she pulled the short bow off the shoulder of Eleanor's hulking companion and plucked an arrow from his quiver. As the knight held the young woman at sword point, he pulled his helmet off revealing long dark tresses and unbuckled the shiny metal cuisses that covered his thighs. He motioned for his prey to spread her legs just as Anna placed her legs for balance. He pulled his undercoat up just as Anna pulled on the bow string and loosed. The man jerked and gaped in horror at the arrow that protruded from his groin. He turned his tressed head to look for his attacker and a second arrow pierced his throat. He collapsed, gagging and gurgling, choking in his own blood. The young woman scrambled to her feet and fled.

Anna's heart thumped. That was the second 'noble' she had felled with an arrow through the throat. It felt easier this time, almost satisfying. And she hated herself for it.

She was starting to feel that strange disturbing melancholy she experienced at the Porte-Horloge when a strong hand gripped her elbow and dragged her away through the copse of trees.

"You can shoot," said Eleanor as they ran.

"I learned from the best," said Anna.

Eleanor glanced at Anna out of the corner of her eye. "Only shoot to defend yourself. Never intercede."

"He would have raped her."

"Do you know who you killed?"

"No." That melancholic aura ran cold fingers down her spine.

"Gerard of Gisborne, champion to the Duke of Gloucester and cousin of Sir Warren Fitzwalter."

Anna tripped and fell flat on her face. Eleanor and her hulking companion stopped to drag her to her feet and urge her into a run again, pushing through spindly branches and driving deeper into mature woodland beyond. Anna's mind did somersaults. She knew from the research with Jeanne that Duke Humphrey of Gloucester led the assault on Vire in 1418. Anna and Élise had arrived a year late and landed themselves in the middle of a chevauchée. But worse than that she recognised the name of the dead man's cousin. It bore a horrifying resemblance to her father's: Harvey Warren Fitzwalter. Surely that could not be a coincidence.

They were running uphill now, among mature pines and beech trees. Eleanor threw questioning looks at Anna, as if she were trying to understand her reaction to the name of the man she had killed. Anna didn't have enough breath to say anything, all she could do was keep pace with the others. Eventually they emerged into an open field that glittered with frost. Ahead was a modest cottage with rough rendered walls and a thatched roof. They slowed to a jog and then a walk. Eleanor pushed the oak door, stood aside, and waved them in.

"You are welcome to my abode," she said, "so long as you promise to stop shooting nobles and changing history." She gave Anna a sharp yet not unfriendly look.

A small patch of sunlight pierced the dark interior and lit an oak table laid with fine cutlery and glasses, which seemed wholly out of character with the simplicity of the cottage. Eleanor threw shutters open revealing benches either side of the table and she invited Élise and Anna to sit.

"Fetch our guests some water and pottage, Benoît," Eleanor asked her companion. He nodded and loped over to the hearth where he grasped a silver jug, and a black iron pot that had been hanging over a smouldering fire. He brought them to the table and filled the glasses with water, then he picked up some fine pewter bowls and filled them with a thick vegetable stew. There was something about his frown and his deliberate movements that made Anna think he might not be quite like the rest of them. "Please introduce yourself, Benoît," said Eleanor, noticing how Anna studied him.

The big lad stopped and bowed to Anna and Élise in turn. "My name is Benoît. I am proud to serve Madame Couteau. How may I be of service, Mademoiselles?"

Élise smiled and nodded to Benoît and he smiled back. They seemed to know each other already.

"I'm very pleased to meet you, Benoît," said Anna leaning forward to shake his hand. "Thank you for the pottage. And I'm sorry I took your bow."

Benoît smiled a broad uncomplicated smile and carried on shaking Anna's hand until she gently withdrew it. "You shoot well," he said and gave a little clap. His voice was incongruously high, almost as if it had not quite broken.

"It would be well if Marie did not shoot first and ask questions afterwards," said Élise tartly.

"I wouldn't have had to shoot if we hadn't arrived late," retorted Anna.

Élise gave Anna a look that could tarnish plate armour. Anna returned it with a look that could burn the blood off a sword.

"You are here," said Eleanor in a soothing voice. "I suspect that a year here or there when arriving from the twentieth century can be tricky. Especially as I am frequently at the river to wash my clothes, whether it be 1417 or 1418."

Élise looked murderous. Anna felt smug.

"I am guessing that Élise brought you to me for instruction on the art of walking between times, Marie."

"I'd be so grateful, Madame Couteau."

"Please call me Eleanor," she noticed a strange look in Anna's face. "You are happy to call me Eleanor?"

"Yes, of course, it's just that you have the same name as... my mother."

"That is good, is it not?"

"The last time I saw her she was dying."

Chivalry

Saint-Martin de Tallevende, Normandy, February 1418

Eleanor warned them to stay away from Vire over the coming days. "The Duke of Gloucester has taken the outer walls by surprise. The Normans still hold the donjon, but they will not hold it for much longer. Not while the goddons brutalise our people."

"The goddons?" asked Anna.

"The English invaders, they are so foul mouthed," explained Eleanor. "'God damned this' and 'God damned that', so we call them the goddamns, or goddons." She noticed Anna looking uncomfortable. "You were born in England, were you not?"

Anna nodded and looked away.

"I do not hate the English, only those who arrogantly assume that Normandy is theirs and believe they have the right to slaughter its people."

Anna noticed Benoît sitting close by watching her, a slight frown on his forehead. "A glass of water for Marie?" he asked. "A glass of wine?"

Anna smiled. "No thanks, Benoît, I'm fine."

"Please would you cut us some more firewood, Benoît?" asked Eleanor. "I shall send Marie on later to help you bring it in."

Benoît stood, looking relieved to be doing something useful and pleased that Anna would come to help. Élise had gone for a long walk that afternoon to 'clear her head'. More likely avoid the shame of messing up the year of their arrival, thought Anna.

"I think Benoît likes you," noted Eleanor with a wry smile, after he had left for the woods. "He certainly admires your skill with a bow. You said you learned from the best. Who were they?"

Robin Hood and the folk of Sherwood Forest was what Anna wanted to say. "A dear friend." She looked away again in case her eyes betrayed her.

Eleanor observed Anna for a few moments before she spoke again. "Here is what I think. Please correct me. Judging by the coat you carry I suspect you were born sometime in the twentieth or twenty-first century. You discovered your gift to walk between times and yet your own mother, Eleanor, had not taught you how to use or focus your gift." She paused, allowing Anna to contradict any of those opening statements. She did not. "I suspect that you went in search of someone who might teach you and the first person you found was Élise. Élise does not suffer fools. Because she brought you here, I deduce that you are no fool. And yet shooting an English noble so closely related to the Fitzwalters and Gisbornes shows exceptional recklessness. Especially if, by some accident of fate, you might be related to one of those families." Eleanor gave Anna a questioning stare. "I saw the look on your face when I told you who that man was. Are you related?"

"It's possible," mumbled Anna. How many Fitzwalters could there be, she wondered?

"Then you were indeed reckless."

"He would have raped that woman," growled Anna.

"Have you been raped?"

Anna's eyes burned more fiercely, and she cuffed away a tear. Eleanor came to sit beside Anna on the bench and put her arm around her. "You punished your rapist?"

Anna nodded.

"Did you kill him?"

"No. I scared him. Almost as much as he scared me."

"Good. You have retaken control. I do not know much about the twenty-first century, but I suspect that punishment for rape is no more likely to happen than in the fifteenth. In the fourteenth, it became a lesser crime. No longer a crime against the person, but a crime against the husband. It seems women are to be considered their property."

Anna looked at Eleanor. "Do you have a husband?"

"No. I shall never be someone's property. Though I have had love affairs and for that I am given names: 'harlot' and 'witch' are favoured. If you have knowledge of the fifteenth-century then you will understand that it is exceedingly dangerous to be called a witch."

"So, that's why you have Benoît to protect you."

"Yes. You see he is a gentle soul really, but he puts the fear of God into those who would call me witch to my face."

"Is he a monk?"

"The tonsure? He was brought up in a monastery, but he found it hard to read or write, so they encouraged him to follow another path. I promised him food and lodging in return for my protection. He still prays morning and night, and he still cuts his hair as a tonsure because he is comforted by his routines."

Anna wondered if Benoît may have been diagnosed with learning difficulties in the twenty-first century. She thought about Rob and his dyslexia. If Benoît had the wrong upbringing, just like Rob, it was likely he would have suffered anyway.

"I suspect you did not come to me to learn how to punish rapists, Marie?"

"No."

"I would like to know why you came. I think it would be polite for you to be honest with your new teacher. Before we start."

Anna cut straight to the most important thing on her mind. "I want to know if a body can die in one time and continue living in another."

Eleanor regarded Anna, thinking. "You have lost someone you love. Perhaps the friend who taught you to shoot a bow?"

"Yes," she whispered.

"Normally, I would say that if you die, you die."

"Normally?" Anna couldn't keep the hope from her voice.

"Did your loved one have the gift too?"

"A little. I had to lead him. Now I wonder if I killed him."

"Hmm, I doubt that you did anything of the sort. I once heard a story of someone who seemed to die and yet lived. One of us. However, you must understand that this was hearsay. It is likely your friend has passed on."

"But there's a chance he hasn't?"

"Perhaps. I must read certain scripts at the monastery of Mont Saint-Michel before I can be clearer, but I have heard of one who appeared to die."

"What do you mean, 'appeared to die'?"

"As I say, I must read the scripts because I do not remember the details. I do not wish to get your hopes up only to bring them down again. I promise I shall find out for you. But you must promise to listen carefully to my lessons. And stop shooting nobles... even if they are not noble, just rapists."

"I promise."

"Good. Go help Benoît carry the firewood."

Anna found Benoît at the edge of the wood with two neat piles of cut branches stacked on sack cloths and ropes tied around them. Benoît beamed as he saw Anna and pointed to the smaller stack.

"That's less than half the size of yours, Benoît. Share them out equally, I can pull my weight."

"Please try first," he suggested.

Anna wrapped a length of rope around her arm and tugged. The sack cloth and wood pile only moved a few inches before she turned bright pink with the effort. Benoît gently touched her shoulder to stop her from doing injury to herself, lifted some of the wood off her pile and tucked it under one arm as if he were carrying sticks. Then he wrapped the rope from the larger pile around his arm and over his shoulder. He leaned into the rope and the huge pile was dragged forward through a combination of technique and brute force.

Anna took the rope over her shoulder too and leaned into it just like Benoît. It was easier this time, but she still had to stop every few metres to get her breath back and shake out her aching arms. Benoît had dragged his stack all the way across the field to the cottage and was on his way back again to help. Anna didn't want to look the weak helpless female, so she put her full weight into it and got the pile sliding across the tops of the frosty ruts, skimming rather than wedging between them.

Benoît didn't stop her, he stood back and smiled like a proud dad who'd taught their daughter to ride a bike for the first time. "Thank you, Marie."

Élise reappeared from her walk. She had been sensible enough to go west, away from the trouble in Vire, and she returned carrying a dead chicken. "I believe you know what to do with this now," she said handing it to Anna.

Anna took it without a smart retort (which felt harder than dragging wood) and went over to a corner of the neat yard to pluck it. A few minutes later she returned and asked for a knife so she could prepare it for the pot. Élise produced a large business-like knife from her pocket.

"Keep that for doing your nails?" asked Anna, all restraint gone by now.

Benoît sniggered. Élise scowled.

"Ah wonderful!" said Eleanor, emerging from the cottage. We shall dine well this evening. "But we must start our lessons first. I understand that Élise has begun to tell you about the kingfisher."

It was on the tip of Anna's tongue to say it was more of a shabby seagull than a kingfisher but, to her credit, bit her lip and nodded.

"I shall return to that," said Eleanor, "it is a most difficult technique," she looked at Élise who seemed slightly mollified. "We live in dangerous times, so the first thing I shall show you is how to side-step. I am sure that Élise will not mind me teaching it again, it never hurts to practise. Marie, what do you think this side-step might be?"

"It sounds like something you'd do in a fight, to avoid getting hit."

"Very good. 'Time travel' is a phrase you twentieth and twenty-first century people use. We prefer to call it 'walking between times' and so beginning with a step is a good way to start walking."

Eleanor showed them how to cast themselves just a few minutes back in time, take a step away and then travel forward to the same moment. To the observer it seemed as if Eleanor had disappeared and reappeared instantly a metre away. If she did this fast enough, it could make the difference between being struck down with a sword and living to seek help, or wrong foot your opponent. She invited Anna and Élise to practise. Then they repeated it while walking a few paces, then at a jog, and again running.

"The speed at which you run is not as important as the speed at which you move between times," emphasised Eleanor. "Find your focus and move towards it as quick as you can. If you feel in danger, you should have a focus that you can move to should you need."

Anna was still taking far longer to shift between times than Élise. "What do you mean by focus here? When we arrived, we were searching for you."

"Who can you always rely on to be there?" asked Eleanor.

"Me," said Anna, a little too quickly, then looked down at her feet.

"Yes. No matter how good your friends may be, they cannot be everywhere, and they cannot be with you at all times."

It would be good to have someone there when it really mattered though, thought Anna. Her father had left her when she was only a baby. Her mother had died when she was barely an adult. Rob had died in her arms in the cemetery cave in Nottingham... or had he? She wanted to process the startling promise of hope that Eleanor had hinted at but realised it would do her no good until she had a better mastery of her gift.

"Marie?" Eleanor had been trying to get her attention.

"Sorry, I... never mind. I focus on me. A few minutes in the past."

It was sound advice and she improved dramatically. By the end of the afternoon, they had Benoît pretending to attack them with a stick and Anna started moving even faster than Élise, disappearing and reappearing behind him in the blink of an eye. She would tap him on the shoulder, vanish and re-emerge behind him again as he spun round to find her. Benoît thought it huge fun and the two of them started giggling like children playing grandmother's footsteps.

The light faded, and Eleanor ushered them all back into the cottage. Benoît held the door open for them.

"Very chivalrous, thank you Benoît," smiled Anna.

The reaction from Benoît and Eleanor was stony cold, as if she had called Benoît a goddon.

"I believe that chivalry has a different meaning in the fifteenth century," said Élise.

"To be chivalrous here means that you show skill at arms and are sufficiently merciless to deploy that skill on a chevauchée," Eleanor explained.

"I know what a chevauchée is," said Anna, starting to feel mortified.

"Indeed," said Eleanor. "You just blunted one by killing the most chivalrous noble in the Duke of Gloucester's army. You saw only too clearly what Gerard of Gisborne was doing. He was showing off. He was demonstrating his consummate horsemanship and swordsmanship to his fellow knights at the expense of those who could not fight back. That is a display of chivalry in fifteenth century Normandy."

"I am so sorry Benoît, I didn't mean to..." Anna was flustered and started again. "I wanted to praise you. The word means the complete opposite in my time. It means that you are courteous, selfless, pure of heart and protect those who cannot protect themselves."

Benoît blushed.

"Benoît is all of those things and more to me," said Eleanor, putting her hand on his broad shoulder. He went a deeper shade of crimson and smiled sheepishly. "If that is what it means in the twenty-first century then you were right to call him so. But you have just learned another important lesson. Just because your gift allows you to understand other dialects and languages... yes, I know that is another question you have, ...it does not mean that you will always understand people from other times."

Anna nodded, absorbing her wisdom. "So, why can I understand other languages? My French is rubbish and I know it's different to the kind of French you're speaking. What's going on?"

"Let us make supper first," suggested Eleanor patiently. "When we are comfortable, I may talk to you about the spirit..."

Peas in the Water

Saint-Martin de Tallevende, Normandy, February 1418

Supper was surprisingly civilised for a fifteenth century peasant cottage in rural Normandy. Élise and Anna shelled peas while Benoît had laid the oak table with a fine linen cloth and set out silver cutlery, engraved pewter plates and beautiful cut glasses for wine. The final flourish was a small brass candle holder with a wreath of snowdrops wrapped lovingly around the base.

"Wow!" said Anna.

"I think Benoît wanted to impress you," said Eleanor, over her shoulder as she spooned the cuts of chicken and the sauce into bowls.

"I'm impressed. Thank you Benoît."

Even Élise permitted a thin smile. Benoît beamed.

Eleanor served the bowls to the table and Anna was about to sit down when Élise caught her gently by the wrist and motioned for her to remain standing. Eleanor, Élise and Benoît clasped their hands together and closed their eyes.

"By the grace of God, we welcome our guests this evening," began Benoît, "And for what we are about to receive, may our Lord make us truly thankful, Amen."

"Amen," echoed Eleanor and Élise.

Anna mouthed an amen feeling foolish and self-conscious.

"Chicken with prunes," announced Eleanor.

Anna suspected it would sound more enticing in French.

"One of my favourites," said Élise, "thank you so much."

"Enjoy," said Eleanor simply.

Anna realised Eleanor was probably saying 'bon appetit' but of course she was hearing it in a form that would make more sense to her. She was suspicious of anything with prunes in, but one taste took away all doubt. "This is delicious!" she announced and tucked in as if it might be the last meal that week. The habits of sleeping rough did not leave after one square meal and a roof over her head.

Eleanor and Élise exchanged looks. Benoît chuckled and followed Anna's lead, attacking his food with gusto.

"More?" asked Eleanor as Anna mopped her bowl.

Anna looked up and saw that Eleanor and Élise had barely started. "I'm sorry, I'll wait," she said, embarrassed.

"I suspect you are not used to regular meals?"

"I am now, but..."

"...it was not always so," Eleanor finished for her. "I have seen enough hunger and poverty. I am so sorry that you have endured it. Even in the twenty-first century."

"How does it work?" asked Anna, seeking to change the subject. "You speak in old French, and I hear in modern English. I speak in modern English, and you hear in old French. What's happening?"

"You may remember I need to talk about the spirit first," said Eleanor. "Don't look so uncomfortable. I know that you come from a godless time and we pray to God as a matter of course in ours. You may be interested in a more... scientific explanation, from Archimedes. You have heard of him?"

"The eureka man from ancient Greece," said Anna.

"He was from Syracuse, in Sicily. A city-state founded by the Greeks and taken by the Romans. Sadly, he died directing the city's defence, despite orders to spare him. I met him. He swore he never ran naked through the streets shouting eureka."

"Shame."

"I was disappointed too," smiled Eleanor. "But many anecdotes are embellishments of a truth. Archimedes became most excited when he discovered how to measure the volume and density of a complicated item by displacing water. He used a scale submerged in water to take accurate measurements. But he assured me he did not jump naked out of a bath."

"Did he believe there was such a thing as the spirit?"

"He observed the displacement of water caused by my spirit."

"…"

"Yes, I know," nodded Eleanor. "It sounds improbable. And I understand that in your time any discussion of the spirit is discouraged or derided."

"What do you mean by spirit?" asked Anna, carefully.

"An excellent question," smiled Eleanor. "We are quick to connect the word with ghosts and the supernatural. We also think of the Holy Spirit, God's gift to us. Perhaps you might think of it differently in your own time. Perhaps you might think of it as a force that comes from within our minds and stirs us to act."

"Surely you're just describing thought?"

"Yes and no. You have a phrase: 'force of will'?" Anna nodded, so Eleanor continued. "A person may be tempted to an act of negligence or evil but, through force of will, they may choose to act for good. They overcome their own thoughts or constraints and demonstrate who they really are by how they act."

Anna thought about Werner Lehman. He had been an officer of the Wehrmacht, Hitler's army occupying Northern France. He had orders to find and deport Jews. He knew he would be shot if he did not act on those orders, yet he warned the Jews through Élise, who was sitting next to her and quietly grieving his loss. Werner's force of will made him act differently. Perhaps his acts were not wholly good, because he did not denounce the Nazis or seek to stop what they did. Yet he sought out a small window of opportunity to do some good which others could not have done. Élise had stayed through the gruelling attacks on Vire despite being able to leave. She chose to be there for Werner, for Henri and for the Virois. "I understand," said Anna and placed her hand on her grandma's out of view, beneath the table. She gave it a gentle squeeze which Élise returned in silence.

"You have a particularly strong force of will, Marie," said Eleanor. "You overcome the flowing waters of time and dare to swim upstream."

"That I don't understand."

"I sought Archimedes because he had written a script on the displacement of time. No, it is not widely known. His experiments with water and calculations of volume and density had led him to think about their applications to other media and one of them was time. He had a theory that a particularly strong spirit, or force of will, might cause time to quicken or slow by displacing it, pushing against it. He was delighted that I found him. Apparently, I was not the first and likely not the last of my kind to do so. He said that was a proof of itself. He began by asking me to push against the water in a cup on his table, just like this."

Eleanor filled a glass almost to the brim from the jug of water. Then she closed her eyes. The surface of the water in the glass appeared to form a well, like the little whirlpool that forms over a plughole yet without any apparent rotation. The water at the sides lifted to the brim and threatened to overflow. Then Eleanor opened her eyes and the water dropped with a light 'splop'.

"Perhaps you understand why people might call me a witch," she observed.

Anna was gobsmacked. "That... that was your... mind?"

"My spirit. Or force of will."

"People in my time might call that telekinesis. Moving things with your mind. It's supposed to be impossible."

"I sense that your mind is not closed though, Marie?"

"How can it be? Unless you're an expert conjurer."

"I shall ignore that because you know better, being able to 'conjure' yourself from one time to another yourself."

"So, you believe that I'm moving through time through force of will?"

"Archimedes would say that you displace it with your spirit. After he tested my spirit with the water, he asked me to slow time for the two of us. I took him by the hand. He seemed pleased about that, but by force of his own will he concentrated on the science." Anna smiled at that. Eleanor, like Élise, was probably quite diverting to the opposite sex. "I walked us both back in time to the day before I arrived. Archimedes went to observe himself taking a stroll along the coast of Ortygia island. He was so excited he wanted to run up and shake his own hand, but I dissuaded him. It is not always wise to meet yourself."

"Why not?" asked Anna, then remembered how it would have freaked her out if she had seen herself in Brightmoor Street when running from the rapist.

"I suspect you have," said Eleanor.

"Twice. But I only made myself seen to me when I was five. My five-year-old self didn't recognise me grown up, so I didn't scare myself."

"Exactly. Imagine what would happen if you were so scared you attacked yourself."

Anna tried not to. "Why did Archimedes think you were displacing time, rather than moving through it?"

"He believed that we did both. If we think of this glass of water as a moment in time then he thought that a person like us could enter that moment, pushing the waters of time out around us." Eleanor dropped a pea into the glass which bobbed. "The level of the water rises a little because of the pea, just as a moment in time is pushed and reshaped by the presence of the person who can walk between times. Most people do not even see into the water. You not only see, but you push your way into it with your spirit. Your will.

"What happens if there are too many peas?" asked Anna.

Eleanor smiled again, clearly impressed by her young student. She dropped a spoonful of peas into the glass, and it overflowed. "We lose time."

"What? You mean time actually slows down?"

"The moment is lost. We cannot remember it. If one person too many pushes into that moment, then someone is pushed out of it. They cannot experience it or remember it. Have you ever had that sensation where you feel you have lost time?"

Anna opened her mouth to say yes and then stopped. "Are you saying that too many time travellers have entered that moment? That I forgot what happened because there were too many of us and I literally wasn't there?"

"Yes. That is what I am saying, or rather, that is what Archimedes said. I do not know if he is right. As far as I know, no one has proved him right, but I have yet to meet anyone who can offer a better explanation."

"But that would mean there are lots of us. Going everywhen. All the time!"

"There have never been many of us. Our existence is not widely known, deliberately so. But a moment in time is always close to the brim." She scooped the peas out of the glass and refilled it. Then she picked up the peas and started dropping them in, one at a time. The first one made the water flush with the rim. The second pushed the meniscus of the water higher than the rim and the third pushed it higher still. The fourth one caused a drop of water to run down the outside of the glass. "There you go. Pushed out of the moment by the travellers. It did not take many, did it?"

Anna sat in thoughtful silence for a while, absorbing what Eleanor had said. "Assuming what you... what Archimedes says is true, how do I understand what you're saying? How did you understand what he was saying?"

"It is your spirit, Marie. This is even more important than your ability to walk through time because you are opening your mind to others to understand and be understood. You make your thoughts understood to others through your will, and by your will you become more receptive to their thoughts. Much of what we say is gesture, expression, the background of what is happening around us. We only need to open our thoughts to others so we can hear them clearly."

"But why does the written word stay the same?"

"Because it has no will of its own."

"And why do I still struggle with French in my own time?"

"Because you are not using your will!"

"..."

"Yes, you should try it. Carefully, mind you. You do not want to make people suspicious of you. As I said before, there is a reason why there are few of us and we keep our existence secret." Eleanor's mood changed, as if the conversation had become too serious. "Enough of such things for one evening. Perhaps Benoît may sing for us?"

Benoît proved to have a beautiful falsetto voice. He started with some lively folk songs and, as the others settled themselves into fur wraps and throws, he followed with some wistful ballads that soothed them. Anna recognised one of the songs from around the hearth in Ruth and Little John's cottage in the Shire Wood. Her thoughts turned once again to Rob. This time with hope as well as sadness and longing. Perhaps he may yet live. Perhaps, through sheer force of will, he was still in medieval Nottingham. That would sound like Rob, thought Anna. Alive through sheer bloody mindedness!

They woke with the dawn light. Élise went to fetch water from the nearby well. After spending a few moments staring at the water in a glass and wondering whether she could push it without touching it, Anna helped Benoît mop the cottage floors. Eleanor was busy cutting herbs and grinding powders on the table and she was interrupted by a knock on the door. She opened it to find a young woman in a tattered shawl, almost in tears.

"Come in, my dear, and sit down. Benoît, please fetch her some pottage."

"Please help me, Madame Couteau," the woman pleaded. "My Laurent was attacked by one of the goddons. We bound his wounds, but he started a fever and I fear for his life."

"Likely the wound is infected," Eleanor's knowledge was not common for the time. "Take this powder, mix it with clean water. It must be clean you mind, and add a spoonful, just so," she handed a small spoon to the woman. "Two doses morning and evening. You must keep him wrapped up, even though he will sweat. Come back to me in three days and tell me how the fever is progressing."

"Thank you, Madame. I..."

"Please take it as a gift."

The young woman kissed Eleanor's hand and wept freely. She took the powder and spoon and hurried off to her man.

"Sometimes my customers pay," said Eleanor. "But I did not want her to worry about that at a time such as this."

"You have customers?" asked Anna.

"I have to make a living, just like anyone else. It helps pay for the fine cutlery and glasses."

"You are a doctor?" Anna realised that the word may be mistaken in medieval times, even with her will to be understood. "A healer?"

"Not really. I use my ability to learn a little from other times and apply it when I can. That is why I prepare these powders and herbs. I know enough to help with many common ailments, but I would not pretend to advise on anything serious."

Anna suspected Eleanor was being modest. "Dying of an infection sounds pretty serious to me."

"Alas, yes, it is often the simple things that take us away. That is why I seek to help as I can. But I have no answer for the Black Death."

Anna shuddered. Most people knew of the Black Death or the Bubonic Plague. "I thought that finished in the last century, the mid-thirteen-hundreds?"

"And it came again many times. The most recent was in the year 1400. It will not be the last."

Anna thought of the Coronavirus pandemic of 2020 and the recurring waves since. "A plague doesn't die, it just changes and comes back."

"Just so. After almost seventy years of war, plague and famine, the number of Virois have halved. I believe it is the same in much of France and England."

"Halved!" Anna was shocked.

"The goddons plunder our towns and villages. They kill our people. Our men take up arms to defend us and neglect the fields which feed us. It is hardly surprising that we should be so vulnerable to plague."

Vulnerable. That was a phrase Anna encountered too often. "Is it possible to feel the presence of death?" asked Anna.

Eleanor frowned and studied Anna's face for a moment before replying. "Where have you encountered such a feeling?"

"At the Porte-Horloge in Vire in my own time and again in 1944. Also, at the forest of Saint-Sever."

"Describe to me exactly what you felt."

"Like... sadness. Emptiness. The absence of life and happiness. I touched the stones of the Porte-Horloge, and I felt as if something were draining my life away."

"Do not ever linger close to that place again."

"Why? What was it?"

"It is likely a death you caused. Not just that death but the absence of the lives that would have followed. It could be your mournghast."

Witches, Witch-hunters and Mournghasts

Saint-Martin de Tallevende, Normandy, February 1418

"What the hell is a mournghast?" asked Anna, fearing the answer.

"Just as we may push into a moment in time, adding another life to it, the absence of a life that should have been there can pull at that moment. It is exactly as you say, an emptiness."

"Why would it be my mournghast?"

"Because the family of the deceased will be sensitive to the mournghast, and especially the person who took that life. Your gift, your spirit, makes you even more sensitive. You took the life of Gerard of Gisborne near the Porte."

Anna looked at her feet feeling a mix of dread and guilt. "And I killed Guy of Gisborne in Nottingham in 1215. I guess they're related."

"There is only one family of that name in Normandy that I know of. It is possible that one or more of Guy's descendants would have been living in the castles at Vire or Saint-Sever had you not taken his life in 1215. The strength of the mournghast may be even greater by your own time, in the twenty-first century, because of the additional loss of Gerard in the same family. More descendants who never were. And judging by the strength of your reaction, it seems more than likely you are related to them."

Anna looked at Eleanor, eyes pleading her for help. "What can I do?" she whispered.

"Repent."

Anna's expression changed from pleading to non-plussed. "How would that help? Remember, I'm godless."

"Your time may know relatively few who believe, but I think you are a little quick to judge yourself." Anna looked seriously puzzled now so Eleanor went on. "Élise has told me much of what you did in 1944. You have done many selfless things, Marie. Or should I say Anna?"

Anna studied her hands which were fidgeting. She picked up a snowdrop from the candle decoration and spun it around between her forefinger and thumb. "I was christened Mary Ann Fitzwalter." Eleanor's eyebrows raised at the mention of Fitzwalter. "I choose to call myself Anna, from my middle name, and Partington from my mother. I may have been christened but it doesn't make me a Christian."

"I do not say you should be. But I think you believe in something more than just yourself. Do you not?"

"I... I believe in good and bad. I believe most people can choose to be good... if they apply their will."

"Good, you do believe in the spirit of good. That is enough. Appeal to that spirit and seek forgiveness."

"Forgiveness? Gerard Gisborne took five lives right in front of us and was going to rape a girl. I lost count how many deaths Guy of Gisborne was responsible for in Nottingham, and he was about to kill my Rob!" Anna realised her voice had risen and she had crushed the snowdrop under her palm against the table. She controlled her voice with an effort, "Why should I ask forgiveness of people like that?"

Eleanor looked at Anna and waited for her temper to ebb. "Does it follow that Gerard's son or daughter would have been disposed to acts of evil because he was?"

"Knowing that family, yes!"

"But do you know them? And is it inevitable?"

Anna peeled the squashed flower off her palm. "Perhaps not. Bloody likely though! And what about all the lives they would have taken if I'd let them live?"

"I wish I were able to give you an easy answer, Anna. But are you the right person to decide who lives and dies?"

She looked up at Eleanor. "Okay, I get what you're saying. But I just can't bring myself to... repent."

"Think on it," said Eleanor. "By force of will you sought to understand another view. Yet you still fail to realise how important that is." Eleanor stood and put her hand on Anna's shoulder. "Just promise you will stay away from those places where you felt the mournghast."

"What would happen if I stayed too long?" asked Anna, remembering her terrifying dreams at the Porte-Horloge after the air attack, and how long it took her to recover.

"Have you seen a whirlpool?"

"Yes."

"You saw how it draws everything in, how it sucks at the water and all that floats on it. Swallowing. Drowning."

Anna looked Eleanor in the eye, remembering that very feeling.

"It may drown you, Anna. Worse, it may drown all the good in you and leave only evil."

Many others came to Eleanor's door that day. They all asked for medicines and advice to heal those who had suffered at the hands of the Duke of Gloucester and his goddons. Anna and Élise helped in whatever ways they could while Benoît carried on with the daily chores.

There was little time for Eleanor to teach that day, but Anna had more than enough to think on.

The following day the four of them took the risk of travelling to visit Eleanor's patients around the edges of Vire. Laurent, the man with the fever had already started to improve. Several needed broken bones setting, and splints applied. Others just needed a shoulder to cry on.

Their homes were often worse than hovels with up to a dozen sharing one squalid room. Some were already eyeing the rats with hunger because the goddons had taken anything worth eating for themselves.

All the time they kept a wary eye on the castle and made sure of a quick exit should they need it. A few were able to pay. Most could not and Eleanor waived away promises saying it was not expected. However, one of the elderly women was stubborn.

"You give me medicine and I will give you money. I will not take charity from you, Madame Couteau."

"If you wish, but it is not necessary. We are all suffering from the invaders."

"All the more reason for you to be paid then."

"Thank you, Madame." Eleanor inclined her head and left with the others.

"She was insistent," said Anna, "and a bit sharp."

"She was frightened. And proud."

Anna understood proud. She had seen that. She had been that. "I can see she was frightened of the English, but why should she be frightened of you?"

"I am a witch," said Eleanor sourly.

"She doesn't believe that, does she?"

"Oh yes she does. I am an educated woman living with a strange man for my protection in a remote cottage. I have knowledge of medicines that few others nearby have. That much would be enough to brand me a witch. But there are rumours. Rumours that I can do strange things. The rumours rarely agree what things, but they do agree that these things are unnatural and so I am not to be trusted."

Anna stifled a snort. "She thinks you'll turn her into a toad?"

"Or worse," said Eleanor, her face serious.

"Welcome to the fifteenth century," said Élise.

"Now if someone said you could turn me into a toad, I'd believe them," taunted Anna.

"If only I could," Élise replied deadpan.

"Mademoiselles!" said Eleanor.

"Turn to toad. Heh, heh!" Benoît sniggered.

The sun was setting behind the cottage as they walked across the field towards it. Anna was exhausted in the same way as when taking coins to the poor of Nottingham, that Rob had taken from the rich. So much poverty. So much misery. Anna knew that she would be angry soon, having lived that bitter existence herself. But just now she was drained.

Something whipped past her ear followed by a whack on the oak door ahead. An arrow shaft quivered, fletches fluttering, head buried in the door. They turned as one and saw four riders about fifty metres behind them, following them across the field.

"Let me talk. Remember your training," murmured Eleanor.

Benoît went to pull his sword from its scabbard over his shoulder, but another arrow struck the hard ground at his feet and he stopped.

"Stay where you be!" called one of the riders in a commanding high-born voice. Sure enough, he had a breastplate polished to a shine. They're always the ones, thought Anna bitterly to herself. The horsemen approached until their mounts stood a few paces away, scuffing the ground with their hooves. "Name yourselves," demanded the man with the shining breast plate.

"I am Madame Couteau, sir," answered Eleanor calmly. "These are my daughters, Élise and Marie. This is my nephew, Benoît."

Benoît smiled and bowed. Élise curtseyed while keeping a beady eye on the riders. Anna scowled.

"Explain your business in Vire this day," the noble ordered, as if he now had a right to know everyone's business. It reminded Anna of having to produce her papers in Nazi-occupied Vire. Then it struck her that Vire was occupied now. By the English.

"We offered some care to our neighbours," said Eleanor.

"One of my men saw you by the river when my cousin was murdered," he accused.

"I was there, washing my clothes, sir. I am sorry for your loss."

The man narrowed his eyes, appearing to weigh Eleanor's words. "What did you see, Madame Couteau?"

"A fine display of chivalry." Anna could just detect a hint of sarcasm in Eleanor's voice, but she was putting on a good display of polite co-operation.

"Gisborne was our finest. You saw who murdered him?"

"I saw that he was struck down with arrows. I did not see the archer," she lied smoothly.

"If he is lucky, we will only hang the murderer," stated the man with the breastplate. "And anyone who seeks to protect him will be hung too." Just like a man to assume the murderer must be a man, thought Anna.

"I wish you luck, sir," said Eleanor, wishing nothing of the sort.

He stared at Eleanor and each of them in turn, lingering longest on Anna, who returned his scorn with her own. He had fair hair that flopped across his grey eyes. A long nose for the eyes to look down, high cheek bones and a beard that was cut to a point. It was a familiar face to Anna. She had been patronised by one just like it.

He gave Anna a look calculated to intimidate then turned his horse around and led the other riders away. Anna was not intimidated, she was incensed.

"That was Sir Warren Fitzwalter," said Eleanor quietly when the men were out of earshot. "Likely an ancestor of yours," she added looking at Anna.

"Just like my father, only Sir Warren showed more interest in me," said Anna acidly.

"I advise you to keep away from both of them," said Eleanor. "Sir Warren is a renowned witch-hunter from a family of witch-hunters. It is likely your father is one too."

Anna looked at Eleanor, trying to digest her news. "What exactly do you mean by 'witch-hunter'?"

"He finds and burns witches," she said bluntly. "There is often a farce they call a trial between the finding and the burning. No one has ever been exonerated."

"But... nobody can turn people into toads... right?"

"I explained that there are many excuses for calling a woman a witch. I happen to fulfil most of them, including the rumours of strange practices. They fear me. And if they really knew what I can do then they would have even more reason to fear me. And you."

"Me? I'm just a beginner."

"You are a natural, Anna Partington. I have never encountered such raw force of will. The Fitzwalters have particular reason to fear you."

Anna was silenced. A rare event. She looked at Élise expecting to see envy or indignation, but she saw neither. Élise shrugged, "I would not have brought you to Eleanor if I had not seen your potential. I took days to learn the side-step, but you mastered it in hours. I was trained to see and then to walk through time by my mother. You just saw... and walked."

"And soon you will run," added Eleanor, "so I must resume your training before you run into dire trouble. Before you run into that witch-hunter again. Or start another mournghast."

Annex

Saint-Martin de Tallevende, Normandy, February 1418

Eleanor started teaching again that evening. She stressed the importance of focus that Élise had begun to explain and made clear how they should focus on people they had never met nor have any relation to. Research was key, and that was something which Anna enjoyed and excelled at. Eleanor told how she had researched many scripts on Archimedes before walking through time to find him, but even she had had a false start and needed to check her facts again before finding him.

"When did people start walking through time?" asked Anna, eyeing the water in her glass.

"We do not know for sure," said Eleanor. Anna could tell she had asked another good question by the pursing of Eleanor's lips and the nod. "But we have evidence they have been doing it for at least five millennia."

"Five thousand years! What evidence?"

"Menhirs."

Anna frowned. "A menhir is a standing stone, right? A stone that someone stood on end in the middle of nowhere."

"It was not in the middle of nowhere when the stones were placed. They were often on high ground near to thriving encampments which have since disappeared, so now the stones look as if they were placed in the middle of nowhere."

"How do you know?"

"I walked through time to find the people who placed them. I found that their travellers were treated as shamans who were venerated as wise women and men."

"Wise because they had knowledge beyond their own time?"

"Just so."

"But why did they place the stones?"

"To remind them when and where they left."

"What? Wait, so the standing stones are a kind of way-finder for time travellers?"

"Yes. The stone casts a shadow. The length and position of the shadow changes with the time of day and year. The markings they carved on the stones, or on the ground around them, would signify which year to that traveller. Larger groupings of stones were used by communities of people who walked through time and some of those groupings were sophisticated. Even if the markings eroded over the centuries, they could tell the year by the positions of the stars against the stones."

"Bloody hell! So, Stonehenge is a time traveller's crossroads."

"I do not know about Stonehenge. Avebury is the site of the largest community of time walkers in England. And Carnac in Brittany is the largest that I know anywhere. But I have not met anyone who claims to understand Stonehenge. Yet."

Anna leaned back from the table, her mind boggling. It seemed the more she discovered, the more questions she had. "Can we go to Carnac?"

"Perhaps. But first you have much to learn, and I am taking you to a friend for safety tomorrow."

"Who? Where? Are you coming too?"

Eleanor smiled, "Father Barnabé at the Abbey of Hambye. It is about a day's ride from here which means it is safe from Fitzwalter and the goddons. For a while. I shall come with you, but Élise has offered to stay here with Benoît for a few days to check on our patients. They will come to join us."

The Bocage, Normandy, February 1418

The grey stallion snorted and shook his mane, then turned his head to give Anna the evil eye.

"Grip with your thighs," advised Eleanor. "Be firm. Make sure he knows who is in charge."

"He is. And he knows it," muttered Anna trying to outstare the horse and failing miserably. Anna prided herself on her blistering stares, but she had never taken on a horse before, let alone ridden one. Eleanor's friends at the nearby farm only pointed her at the horse and expected her to get on with it. It was Eleanor who explained how to mount and make the horse move. Anna made a mental note to add horse riding lessons to her time travel preparations and hoped there might be further instructions on how to stop...

"Fitzwalter did not warm to you," observed Eleanor.

"He doesn't strike me as the warm and fuzzy type."

"Fuzzy?"

"In this context, 'easy going.'"

"You enjoy a little sarcasm, Anna. Be careful it does not get you into trouble."

"I always end up in trouble. The trick is trying to get out of it again."

"Indeed. I think Fitzwalter sensed something in you, Anna."

"More than just my talent for getting into trouble and my winning smile?"

"Hmm. I think he could sense your force of will," she said darkly.

"How can anyone sense that?"

"You would be surprised. There is a reason why Fitzwalter and his family are witch-hunters. They can sense our spirit."

"The Fitzwalters sense someone's force of will?"

"Specifically, they and all witch-hunting families can sense when someone is about to walk between times. They have a latent ability to see and walk too, though they abhor the thought of doing so. To them it is a violation of nature. They see us as heretics, yet they share the same gift as us."

"That's... senseless. And sad. Like one family divided by the very thing they share." Anna thought about her father, Harvey. She usually tried not to. He used to turn up sporadically and try to ingratiate himself briefly before disappearing again with some lame excuse.

"Tell me about your father," asked Eleanor, as if reading her mind.

"The last time I saw him was when my mum was told she would die of cancer. He brought flowers, made a fuss then left me to carry on doing all the shopping, cleaning and caring."

"He left your mother before, when you were young?"

"I was two."

"So, you do not feel you know him."

"No."

"Has he ever looked at you like Sir Fitzwalter did or been hostile towards you? Have you ever sensed anything strange about him?"

"No... and no," answered Anna. The absence of hostility was not the same thing as the presence of love. "He never stayed long enough for me to sense anything, other than he doesn't give a monkey's."

"But he did come to see you."

"I suppose."

"Please say if I am asking too many questions, but do you know why he left?"

"I don't mind. It's a long time since I talked to anyone about my parents. Mum rarely said anything about it, and she'd often clam up if I asked. But I remember her once saying they were too alike. Seemed a weird thing to say since they'd split up, but what you were saying just then almost made some sense of it. As if whatever made them alike also drove them apart."

"Your mother would have carried the same potential as Élise. And you. If your father is descended from Sir Fitzwalter then he too has that potential. The potential to see and to walk between times. But the Fitzwalters have dedicated themselves to burning every last time walker from God's creation."

"It's a miracle they ever married."

"Not quite, it has happened before though it is rare, and I have never known it last. You are the miracle, Anna."

L'Abbaye d'Hambye, Normandy, February 1418

It was a miracle Anna made it to the abbey without falling off. The horse whinnied as she led it to the stables, and she had the uncomfortable feeling it was laughing at her. Father Barnabé greeted them and took them into a long stone refectory hall for supper. Barnabé was tall, lean, and walked with a slight stoop. He had no finery, just a plain brown habit like all the other monks.

"You understand that you will be sleeping in the annex," he said apologetically.

"That is all we ask, Father, and we thank you for your kindness," said Eleanor.

Anna wasn't sure what that meant but decided it couldn't be that bad if Eleanor was happy with it. She was relieved not to be sharing a dormitory with a bunch of hairy monks. She suspected they'd be relieved as well, if only for the removal of temptation when it came to Eleanor. Just like her young grandma, she seemed to turn heads, including some tonsured ones in the refectory.

The supper was unexpectedly fine: cuts of roast pork served with a rich apple and camembert sauce. Anna made a superhuman effort to eat slowly, noticed the young monks further down the table tucking in then lost all self-control. Father Barnabé raised a polite eyebrow and Eleanor concealed a smile. Anna wiped her mouth with the sleeve of her oversized overcoat and was relieved to see the young monks doing likewise with their habits.

"I understand the English have taken Vire," said Father Barnabé, as if he were making casual conversation about the weather. Anna supposed that seventy years into the Hundred Years War was going to take the edge off news like that.

"The Duke of Gloucester is leading King Henry's attack to the west," said Eleanor. "Take care, he may come this way before long."

"We have endured before," said Father Barnabé, sounding tired. "We will endure again, should it be God's will. In their bid to annex all Normandy to England, I hope they do not seek to repopulate Vire."

"Repopulate?" asked Anna, looking up from the cup of water she had been staring at.

"If the population resists, they will force them out," he explained. "Then bring English people in their stead, just like Harfleur, Cherbourg and Caen."

Anna's jaw dropped. "No! That... that's evil. That's trying to wipe the French people out, as if they never existed."

Father Barnabé looked at Anna patiently. "It has happened before. It will happen again."

"Yes. It will," said Anna miserably, thinking how the Israeli government systematically resettled much of the West Bank, forcing the Palestinians into ever smaller strips of barren land. She wondered if they had ever stopped to compare this with what happened to David Barron's parents and the millions like them. It mortified her to think that her English ancestors did such things to the French in Normandy. Many people can't imagine what it's like to be made homeless. Anna could.

The annex was small, bare and exceedingly cold. But it did have a hearth which Anna helped Eleanor to light, and it also had a pile of woollen throws and blankets that they heaped over themselves to get warm. More than many in Vire might manage tonight, thought Anna.

"Thank you," she said sleepily, pulling a blanket up around her chin.

"What for?" asked Eleanor.

"For taking me in. For feeding and protecting me. For taking me here to teach me. And for taking an interest."

Eleanor smiled and patted her through a thick wodge of wool. "My pleasure."

Anna slept well that night, despite the cold.

They fell into an easy rhythm over the next few days, rising with the dawn, practical lessons in travelling backwards and forwards in time followed by discussions of the differences between them in the evenings, after supper.

"Does Father Barnabé know?" asked Anna on the way to the refectory one evening.

"Father Barnabé knows better than to ask," said Eleanor.

"If he doesn't know then he can't give us away," said Anna, remembering the hard lessons learned in Nazi-occupied Vire. "Pretty tolerant for a church man. I didn't think they liked 'witches,' even if they only suspected them."

"He believes we are all here for a purpose."

"Even the goddons?"

"We are all related, are we not?"

Anna thought about that. Her mum, the historical researcher, had once described the Hundred Years War as starting out a family feud and ending as all-out professional war. Anna hadn't understood at the time but now it was painfully clear. Not only were the kings and queens all intermarried, hence the claims and counter claims on Normandy, but the people were too. Ever since the invasion of William the Conqueror (Anna preferred 'the Bastard' now), there had been ordinary French people settling in England. And ever since English kings had invaded France, ordinary English people had come to live in Normandy. Her own ancestors had done both. She was as much French as English by blood. Anna had rarely dwelled on the fact that she was a quarter French by Élise until she had come to meet some of her French relatives. Relatives who took a genuine interest in Anna.

They were almost at the door to the refectory when there was a shout from the stables.

"Benoît!" called Eleanor and ran to him.

Anna ran after her, not understanding the tone of panic. They had been expecting him and Élise to arrive around now. When she reached the stables, she saw Benoît dismounting and pulling a limp heap of blood-soaked linen from the back of the horse.

"Élise!" shouted Anna and rushed to help.

Écorcheurs

L'Abbaye d'Hambye, Normandy, February 1418

Élise had been caught by surprise. No chance for her to side-step away, explained Benoît. Her wounds were terrible, though she still drew ragged breaths. They carried her into the annex where Father Barnabé helped build a big fire in the hearth. Eleanor sent Anna and Benoît to fetch water and clean cloths.

"Who did this?" asked Anna as they hurried to the well.

"Écorcheurs," said Benoît. She could tell he was shaken. Anyone who scared someone as big as Benoît must be terrifying.

"I don't understand, who or what are écorcheurs?"

"Flayers. They flay the skin from your body. They attacked us."

Anna could see Benoît a little more clearly in the dim light coming from the refectory, by the well. An angry scar crossed his cheek, and his hand was bound tightly in red stained rags.

"Benoît! You're hurt too," and she took his hand in hers to start washing away the caked blood, then pulled a handkerchief from her overcoat pocket to re-bind the livid wound.

He stood watching her, his eyes starting to well up. "I am sorry," he said.

"Why?"

"I was frightened. I ran."

"You protected Élise, you brought her here to safety," Anna gave the big man a hug. She could feel him trembling, still in shock from their ordeal. "Here, take this bucket to the annex. I'll get the clean cloths."

Eleanor washed Élise and used an ointment to disinfect the deep cuts that slashed her back and thighs. Then she took a needle and thread and started to sew the ripped flesh back together. Anna sat by Élise's side, held her hand and stroked her hair. There was not so much as a whimper, though Anna could tell Élise was awake and painfully aware of all that was happening to her. Benoît sat in a corner with Father Barnabé and prayed.

It was almost dawn by the time Eleanor had finished sewing the wounds and covering them with fresh bandages. Anna could see a faint blue glow to the eastern sky through a gap in the tiny window shutter. Benoît and Barnabé had fallen asleep while leaning against each other, hands still clasped from prayer.

"She will live," declared Eleanor.

"Thank God," breathed Anna. "And thank you."

"She is family," shrugged Eleanor.

"Our family," nodded Anna, grim faced. "Where do the écorcheurs come from and who do they serve?"

"They were once paid soldiers, but now they are mercenaries who kill and terrorise for anyone or no one. Sometimes it is just for the thrill of killing," she sat back and breathed a long sigh. "Benoît is a mighty man to have fought them off long enough to rescue Élise and bring her here."

"He was trembling," and the thought made her tremble too. "Could they have been working for Gloucester and Fitzwalter?"

"Perhaps. It is the sort of thing they might do, especially if they wanted to terrorise the Virois into leaving Vire."

"So they can resettle it with English."

Eleanor nodded. Anna could see how drained she looked. Élise's eyes were closed and her breathing was calmer, deeper. "She is sleeping," said Eleanor, "we should too."

Anna tried but the nightmares she had at the Porte-Horloge returned. Images of armoured warriors skewering helpless women and children on their lances now reinforced by what she witnessed of Gisborne's 'chivalry' at the riverside. And there were new scenes of desperate blood-soaked men wearing the skins of their victims, brandishing cruel blades that were made to rip and tear. She sat forward, hugging her sides. Daylight now pushed through the gap in the shutters. She rose, threw her oversized overcoat around her, and walked out into the new day.

Pale sunlight caressed her and melted the frost on the grass. Underneath a beech tree she saw the violet bud of a crocus peeping from a clutch of sap green stems. She walked along a dirt path, past the imposing frontage of the abbey church and up into the woods. Pigeons called and sparrows chirped. A rustle of leaves betrayed a fleeing roe deer. The path led her through the woods to the edge of an open escarpment that looked south-east, over the rolling hedgerows and fields and the track they had followed from Vire.

Anna had come here to learn. She wanted to learn if there was a way for her to return to Rob. What she had found was profoundly troubling: that her family were both the victims and the persecutors of vicious hatred and violence. She wanted revenge. But no, thought Anna, what good can come of revenge? Rob had taught her that it only led to more misery and he steadfastly refused to kill anymore. It was Anna who had taken Guy of Gisborne's life in Nottingham to stop him from murdering Rob. It was Anna who had shot down Gerard of Gisborne at the river in Vire when he was about to rape a young woman. Did she feel better for it? The young woman had escaped, though who knows how long she would survive the écorcheurs. Rob had escaped from Guy of Gisborne only to die in her arms. She could see the pointlessness of revenge, and yet...

For those fleeting moments Anna had felt in charge. She was no victim at the moments she loosed her arrows. It was the consequences of those arrows that now haunted her, and those consequences had a real manifestation and name: mournghasts. She remembered how Eleanor had warned her away from the mournghasts saying how they could drain all the good from her.

Had Rob found the same? Had he seen how the consequence of revenge could drain all good intentions from him and leave only bitter thoughts?

Anna sat down to watch a brother monk herding cows across the field below her. One of them tried to break away but he stretched his arms wide and shouted until it re-joined the herd. No staffs or whips, just firm direction, and encouragement. That reminded her of Eleanor's advice about horse riding. 'Be firm. Make sure he knows who is in charge,' she had said. Then she thought about the arrogant authority in Fitzwalter's voice, how he seemed to expect everyone to obey. She felt angry again. Enraged that he and men like him should bully their way through other people's lives. Incensed that he might even consider hiring the écorcheurs to chase the Virois out of Vire, terrorise Benoît, and flay the skin from Élise.

Élise slept through that day and the following night. Mercifully the wicked wounds were beginning to heal by the next morning as she regained consciousness and whispered that she was thirsty. Anna helped her roll from lying on her front to her side and propped her with blankets. The stitched wounds ran all the way from her thighs to the back of her neck and Anna was reminded of the old scar she had seen on her grandma's neck in Pagham. Now she knew it was one of many. She held a cup of cool water to Élise's lips.

"Thank you," she croaked.

"Thank Eleanor. She was the one who cleaned your wounds and stitched them together." Eleanor was outside with Benoît while Anna watched over their patient.

"I will. But I am thanking you. My granddaughter." Anna looked away and bit her lip. It was the first time young Élise had properly acknowledged their family bond. "The écorcheurs have gifted me some spectacular scars. Perhaps it will make me more interesting?"

Anna shook her head and screwed her eyes tight shut. What had those savages done to her beautiful grandma? "I wish I hadn't brought you here," she said.

"We may walk through time, but we cannot undo what we have done."

"I want to make the écorcheurs regret what they have done to you."

"The écorcheurs barely understand what they do. But Fitzwalter does."

Anna opened her eyes wide, staring at Élise. "What?"

"One of them whispered in my ear, 'Sir Fitzwalter sends his regards to your sister'. I think he meant you."

"Oh God!" Anna pressed her lips to Élise's forehead and held her as tight as she dared without pressing on the myriad wounds on her back. "I'm so sorry, I'm so sorry. I swear I'll have him for this."

"I could try stopping you," said Élise, softly, "But I doubt I would overcome your will."

Eleanor returned and knelt beside Élise, while Benoît hovered awkwardly at the doorway. "You are awake," she said.

"It was Fitzwalter who had the écorcheurs do this to her," said Anna rising to her feet.

"And I expect you will seek revenge?" said Eleanor, matter of fact.

"I want to do something better than that."

Eleanor looked up; eyebrows raised in surprise. "Yes?"

"I want to make him apologise and promise to stay away from us. All of us: the Virois, the Couteaus and all time-travellers."

The three of them looked at Anna as if she had grown an extra head, then Eleanor barked with laughter. "I have no doubt you would do it too, Anna Partington! And I would dearly like to be there if he does. Do you happen to know how you might achieve this incredible feat?"

There was a knock on the door which saved Anna from answering that question. Father Barnabé stepped inside and smiled with relief to see Élise propped up drinking water.

"Praise be to God," he said. "I am so sorry to be the bearer of more bad news, but the Duke of Gloucester now marches an army our way. He intends to take the Abbey then move on to attack Coutances. We can take care of Élise, but I believe the rest of you should flee."

"I don't want to flee, I want revenge for what Fitzwalter did to Élise," said Anna, a cold fury rising from within her. "If I were a knight, I would challenge him to a duel."

"Perhaps it is as well you are not," said Eleanor.

"He expects to be challenged by strong men," argued Anna, "but he doesn't expect to be challenged by a woman."

"He would crush you!" warned Eleanor.

Anna hung her head, understanding the truth of it. "But he would suffer even more if I were to win," argued Anna defiantly. "I don't want to kill him. I want to make him give in. Just think of the embarrassment and shame in that! He wouldn't dare show his face to Gloucester or any of us again."

"I would not count on that," warned Father Barnabé. "Chivalry is not the same thing as honour."

"He would never duel a woman," said Eleanor. "He can have your head cut from your shoulders for insolence. He can have his men tie you to a stake and burn you. He can even ignore you if he chooses, but he will never face you in an honourable duel."

That lit the flame. "I will not be ignored," Anna thumped the table with her fist. "I would rather he burned me than ignored me."

"Be careful what you wish for," said Father Barnabé. "Even if he were to agree to a duel, how would you defeat him? Do you have any skill at arms?"

"I can shoot a bow," said Anna, defiantly.

"That you can," said Eleanor, "but he would never agree to that. The bow is a peasant's weapon. He would insist on the sword."

"I suppose I better learn to fence," said Anna, beginning to see the gaping holes in her own plan. One more thing on the preparation list: learn the history, learn to ride a horse, learn to fence. Easy really. Assuming you had all the time in the world.

"I will not allow you to fight him," said Eleanor.

Anna raised an eyebrow, "Really?"

"No," she said shaking her head firmly. "Even if you were to learn, he would still overpower you and kill you."

Anna nodded, beginning to understand that bending the laws of time did not extend to the enhancement of her own physical strength. "Guess I'll have to wing it," said Anna.

"I do not understand," said Eleanor, "please explain 'wing it'?"

"Make it up as I go along. Just... arrive," she said, looking at Élise.

Élise tried to shrug then winced as it stretched her stitches. "It is what she is good at."

L'Abbaye d'Hambye, Normandy, March 1418

The sun had real warmth the next morning. Blossoms were creeping across the wispy boughs in the wood above the Abbey. Spring was on its way and so was Sir Fitzwalter's vanguard. A score of riders weaved along the path from the south-east. They carried two flags; one Anna recognised from the cloth that covered the barding on Gisborne's horse. The other was yellow with two red chevrons divided by a horizontal red stripe.

"The flags of Gloucester and Fitzwalter," said Eleanor. "It seems that Fitzwalter rides in advance of the Duke's army."

"Perhaps we can confront them?" asked Anna, dubiously. "There are not so many of them."

Eleanor looked at Anna and shook her head. "Force of will does not overcome brute force. Twenty armed knights are more than enough to slaughter every soul in this abbey."

Father Barnabé stepped forward to greet the knights as they entered the main courtyard. "Welcome to Hambye's Abbey, sirs. May we offer you food and lodging?"

"You will bring us food and you will take these horses to feed and water them," commanded Fitzwalter, as if the offer had not been heard. He dismounted and waved at his fellow knights to do likewise.

Father Barnabé beckoned a handful of the younger monks to take their horses away to the stables. It seemed he wanted to present a scene of old men and women, less of an apparent threat to the knights. It didn't work.

"You harbour witches," accused Fitzwalter.

"I give shelter to these women who sought the sanctuary of the abbey," answered Barnabé. "I do not believe them to be witches."

"Far from me to challenge the beliefs of a man of God, but I believe they be witches."

"We are all on sacred soil, sir," said Barnabé, quietly but firmly. "The women are here under God's protection, just as you and your men are here under God's invitation."

"I believe them to be witches," repeated Fitzwalter, holding Father Barnabé's eye.

"And you have proof of this?"

Fitzwalter's cheek muscle twitched. His eyes narrowed. "I know it," he said stubbornly.

"These women stand on holy soil," answered Barnabé calmly, "yet they do not burn or scream out as you would expect of a witch or demon. I believe them to be ordinary women and they are under God's protection. You may not harm them, and you may not take them against God's will," Barnabé paused for a moment to observe Fitzwalter, standing tall in front of him. "And I represent God's will here in Hambye's Abbey... sir."

There was an uncomfortable murmur from the knights. Fitzwalter scowled. He may have been bold enough to order everyone around, but it seemed he drew the line at challenging God so openly in front of his men. "This time, I shall respect God's will," he allowed. "But only this time." He turned to look directly at Anna, pointing his finger like a sword, "You have one month while I must prepare the way for my Duke to Coutances. One month before I return to find you and, as God is my witness, I will kill you and your coven of witches, no matter where you hide."

Anna was furious. "Why? Because you're afraid us?"

"Why should I be afraid of a woman?" Fitzwalter spat the word.

"A woman shows a little intelligence and strength of will and you call her a witch and have her burned rather than allow her to challenge you," said Anna, "You sent the écouchers to skin Élise because you were too scared to confront us yourself."

"One month, woman. It does not matter where you hide, I will find you."

"One month and I may have a sword in my hand."

There was a moment of stunned silence broken by callous braying laughter from Fitzwalter. The other knights joined in and laughed heartily, taunting the slight young woman who stood defiantly before them.

"What's the matter?" asked Anna. "Lost your nerve? Too scared to take on a woman so you resort to mocking me instead?"

Fitzwalter stopped laughing abruptly and a few moments later his entourage caught the change of mood and shut up. "You are as insolent as you are abhorrent in the eyes of the Lord. Woman."

"Then you'll fight me?"

"No. I will flay the skin from you, witch. I will drive you back to hell, or wherever it was you came from."

"Lenton Boulevard, via Bognor. Pretty much the same thing."

He tilted his head as if wondering if she had uttered a curse on him.

"Please," interceded Father Barnabé, "As I have said, these are women, not witches. Let me take you and your good men for refreshments."

Fitzwalter held Anna's glare then allowed himself to be led towards the refectory.

"We must go," said Eleanor.

Anna clenched her fists as she watched Fitzwalter walk away. He was arrogant, bullying, and abusive, just like Guy and Gerrard of Gisborne. And she had killed them both.

Mont Saint-Michel

Normandy, March 1418

"Flee to Mont Saint-Michel," urged Father Barnabé, after he had shown Fitzwalter and his knights to the refectory. "No one has taken it by force, you should be safe there."

Both Eleanor and Anna could have fled to another time to escape, but Élise was too ill to go anywhere. Anna would not abandon her grandma and Eleanor proved to be as stubborn as Anna. Eleanor wanted to use the library at Mont Saint-Michel, to see if she could answer Anna's questions about what happened to Rob. She added that she planned to return to the people of Vire, and she would not let some small-minded man bully her away from those who needed her care. Anna wondered if it were more than that: that her ancestor and teacher would not be driven from her home, either in space or time.

Élise asked to be left at the abbey saying the journey would pull her stitches but there was no way that any of them would agree to leave her behind. Barnabé loaned them a small cart and had it lined with blankets to cushion the jolts from rutted tracks on the journey to the coast. She was jarred by each rut and pothole but remained stoic throughout.

Anna sat with Élise while Eleanor rode the dappled grey horse that pulled the cart and Benoît walked beside. There was a cold breeze, but there was a little warmth in the sun that lit the fields. Anna was still angry and scowled as she tried to brace her grandma against the next rut in the track.

Élise grimaced and gripped Anna's arm. "Will you have a sword in your hand?" she croaked.

"Hmm?"

"That is what you said to Fitzwalter. If he comes to find us in a month from now."

"When," said Eleanor firmly, over her shoulder. "He is a witchfinder. He will come to find us; I have no doubt."

Anna held Élise's hand and stared out across the hedgerows. Small signs of spring were creeping across the countryside. Hints of colour, a haze of new growth just breaking the surface of the soil. "I learned to use a bow," she said grimly. "I can learn to use a sword."

"Better that you learn to hide," said Eleanor.

"And what will Élise do while I'm hiding?" asked Anna, remembering how her grandma had stayed in occupied Vire to be with her brother. "And that's exactly what he wants. He wants us to run and hide ourselves away forever. I want to learn how to defend myself, so I don't have to keep hiding."

"I have met a few of the brothers from Mont Saint-Michel," said Eleanor. "One of them, Florian, is a master of the sword."

"How can a monk be a swordsman?" asked Anna.

"Just because you are a man of God does not mean that you cannot die by the sword. He teaches the brothers how to defend themselves. Mont Saint-Michel has been attacked but never taken, just as Father Barnabé said. If you insist, then I can ask Brother Florian to teach you. But it is better I teach you to how to hide."

"Looks like I'll be busy learning from two teachers," said Anna.

"A month is not long enough to become a master of the sword. It is good that one of those teachers knows how to make the most of your time," said Eleanor.

Anna felt as if she were about to become Hermione Granger carrying her time-turner around Hogwarts.

They crested a hill at the end of a long and difficult journey and Anna saw two things that took her breath away. The sun shone across the sea, catching the ripples with diamonds of light that made the whole bay shimmer. In the middle of the bay was a lone island. A vertical tree-lined rock on which some madmen had erected houses, walls and, at the very top, a chapel with a tower that dared the sky. Anna had seen photos of Mont Saint-Michel and wondered if they had been enhanced or altered to make it look more dramatic. Now she knew they must be false because they failed to capture the drama of reality.

"I can see why Mont Saint-Michel has never been taken," said Anna. "Who would wade through the sea to climb that?"

Fortunately, they did not have to wade. Eleanor took them to a croft that clung to the edge of the beach and knocked on the door. A greying man with a weathered face answered and, after some negotiation, agreed to ferry them to the mount's sea gate in his rickety rowboat. Anna hoped it wouldn't sink before she helped lift Élise from the boat at the mount.

A grim-faced monk in a black habit met them at the gate.

"Sanctuary," was all that Eleanor said to him. He looked at Élise being carried between Benoît and Anna, nodded and beckoned them to follow. He led them on a climb up the steep cobbled lane that wound itself around the rock like a helter-skelter. Benoît cradled Élise in his huge arms like a father carrying a precious child. Close to the top, as Anna struggled for breath and the seagulls circled the chapel tower overhead, the monk stopped and pointed to an unremarkable door in a stone wall. Eleanor was about to approach it when the door was flung open and a wild-haired man in a shabby black habit stepped out. His eyes lit up and he beamed like an idiot.

"Madame Couteau! Benoît! What brings to you Mont Saint-Michel, my friends?"

"We seek your hospitality and sanctuary, Father Amos," said Eleanor. "For us and for our family," she looked at Anna and Élise, hugged to Benoît's chest.

"Please, come inside," he beckoned, full of concern. "What happened to her?"

"The écouchers."

He gasped, "My God, it is lucky that she yet lives."

Father Amos led them along a narrow corridor and up winding stairs to a couple of dark rooms. He burst into the first one and flung the shutters open. Sunlight transformed the dark cavern into a bright haven. Benoît laid Élise reverently on a pile of furs and Father Amos scurried off, calling over his shoulder that he would return with food and ointments for the patient.

"Sanctuary," breathed Eleanor, with relief.

"Sanctuary," echoed Benoît.

In a strange way this gothic folly, which drew the stares of all who passed within thirty kilometres or more, felt as secret and safe as the hidden village in Sherwood Forest. What it lacked in secrecy, it more than made up for in impregnability. Anna sank to her knees and clasped Élise's hand.

Mont Saint-Michel, Normandy, March 1418

The next day Anna, Eleanor and Benoît followed the ebullient Father Amos up steep stone steps towards the buildings that clung to the top of the rock. Below them Anna could see fortified stone walls facing the coast to the south-east and vertiginous rocks facing seaward to the north. You would have to be mad to attack the place. You would also have to be as eccentric as Father Amos to live here permanently, thought Anna.

The tide had gone out and a narrow mud strip was revealed temporarily joining Mont Saint-Michel to the shore. Anna could see folk walking that strip far below. The ones approaching seemed to be carrying baskets. Perhaps that was how this fortified island was kept fed, wondered Anna. Looking north-east across the bay she saw a few sails, so perhaps they fished as well. Then an extraordinary sight, nearer to the mount, caught her attention. People appeared to be walking on the water.

"Father Amos," called Anna, pointing at the mirage, "what's happening there?"

"Ooh!" he bounced up and down and clapped his hands, "the mussel pickers are out today. We shall have mussels for supper!"

"But... they look as if..."

"Yes, yes, like Jesus, walking on the water. What a sight eh? What a sight!"

"The seabed is very flat and shallow here," explained Eleanor. "At the right time you can walk from here to the Cotentin Peninsula over there, with the water just lapping your ankles or knees."

"Oh yes!" added Father Amos, "and at the wrong time the tide will carry you far out to sea," he giggled like a schoolboy enjoying a prank.

"You have to know the tides and pick your time," said Eleanor. "The locals know. Fortunately, the goddons do not."

Amos took them to a long refectory hall, like the one at L'Abbaye D'Hambye, but this one had seagulls flying past the arched windows and a sheer drop below. They stood behind the benches and waited for a stern looking elderly monk to raise his hands and say grace. At least Anna understood to wait by now and respected their prayers even if she didn't really understand the point of them.

The food was simple: sticks of fresh bread and a cheese that seemed like camembert. It was delicious and Anna struggled to eat at a polite pace, so she picked off small pieces and swallowed a little at a time. She was staring at the watered-down ale in her cup when a slight man in his early forties seemed to step silently out of nowhere and took the bench opposite. He smiled and bowed his head to her.

"I am Brother Florian. I understand you wish to be my new pupil?"

Anna gulped her mouthful, brushed the crumbs off her fingers on her overcoat and reached her hand out to shake. "Marie Couteau. Thank you so much. You're a life saver!"

He raised an eyebrow. "It is possible you may have to take a life to save one. Do you think you can you do that, Mademoiselle Couteau?"

Anna looked down at the table then carefully held Brother Florian's eye. "Yes. Unfortunately, I know I can."

He returned her stare steadily, considering. His blue eyes and gentle features gave little away. "Do you plan to take another?"

"No. Not if I can help it."

"Then I shall be pleased to start teaching you. Outside, in the cloister as soon as you are ready. Madame Couteau will take you for a somewhat different lesson after noon."

When Anna arrived, she found Brother Florian sat benignly on the cloister wall in the early sunshine, hands in his lap. He seemed a most unlikely sword master to her, though she wasn't quite sure what a sword master should look like. Pointy beard? Monocle and scar?

"Should I have a sword?" she asked reasonably.

"Not yet," said Brother Florian, "Today I shall teach you to stand and to walk."

"Er... here I am. Standing and walking." Anna did a little turn on the spot then put her arms out. "Ta da!"

Florian smiled indulgently, as if to a small child. "How would you stand if you did have a sword in your hand?" he asked.

Anna scratched her head. "I'm not sure. Like this?" she struck a pose like the photo of a classical fencer she had seen, her right hand out in front of her holding an imaginary blade and her left arm curled behind her like a balancing tail. Florian looked blankly at her. She put her feet a little apart and bent her knees, "Or this?"

"Why would you stand like that?" he asked, genuinely puzzled.

"Because that's how I've seen it done before?"

He shook his head and stood up. Then he dropped into a half crouch, one foot a good metre behind the other and both hands together in front of him, as if in prayer. It looked natural, comfortable, and balanced. "You try," he said.

Anna did her best to copy Brother Florian, carefully placing her feet and flexing her knees slightly. She curled her body forward a little and put her hands together. "Why am I using both hands?"

"To hold the sword. It is heavy."

"Ah," she was starting to realise that the image she had in her head was of fencing, rather than sword fighting. That came much later, for duelling and sport. She was going to be given a business-like medieval blade designed to hack through plate armour. "Will I have to work out?"

"Work out what?"

"Um, train, get fit... muscular?"

"You will become stronger when you start to work with the sword, but you do not have to be especially strong. Not if you learn the correct technique."

That made sense. She remembered how Rob had helped her to stand and pull on a taut bowstring. She did not need to be musclebound, though that would have helped. It was far more about the way in which she pulled and aimed. With an effort she drew her thoughts away from Rob and focussed on the lesson. It seemed she would have to learn to use a sword if she were to get as far as finding Rob. If she ever could. Florian gently corrected her stance, asked her to relax then drop into it again. After a few tries she felt as if she were getting closer, but it felt awkward.

Later he showed her how to move, stepping forward and backward, side to side, but always keeping a distance between her feet and her centre of gravity low, between them. The morning passed almost without her noticing except for aching limbs which were straining to work in unfamiliar ways.

"Good," smiled Brother Florian. "You work hard. I respect that. Tomorrow morning, after we break our fast, I shall teach you to lunge."

"No sword?"

"Not yet. You need to learn how to move so that you can forget how you are doing it. There will be much more to learn with the sword. I do not wish to confuse you with too much at once."

"You're not what I expected," said Anna.

"What did you expect?"

"I don't know. Not a gentle encouraging Benedictine monk, I guess."

He grinned. "I suspect that whoever you defend yourself against will not be expecting a young woman like you."

"No, they won't. But young women like me can still die by the sword, just like monks."

Eleanor gave a lesson in the afternoon showing Anna how to walk in and out of a point in time without stopping.

"You may find you have the wrong time. You may find you have an unpleasant reception there, which is much the same. Therefore, you must assess your surroundings quickly and return to where you were without stopping. Without allowing anyone to harm you."

Eleanor directed her to a point in time only a few years in the past. No aggressors, but it was sleeting sideways against the precipitous slopes of Mont Saint-Michel, so there was plenty of incentive not to linger.

The first time Anna tried she was completely thrown off balance by the wind and found herself teetering on one foot, on the edge of the vertiginous slope with the waves crashing against the rocks below. It took her a minute or so to compose herself, think when she had to return to and walk back through time.

"Needs some work," said Eleanor, while Anna brushed tiny hailstones off her oversized overcoat and shivered.

"You could have warned me it was sleeting."

"No, I could not. That is the point of the exercise."

The next time Anna travelled there, she knew what to expect and kept moving, straight back to March 1418.

"Not bad, but you knew what to expect. Now I want you to go forward to the year 1423."

"Why?"

"Just go. And make sure you come straight back!"

Anna counted five years forward as she scanned through the coming seasons. She materialised momentarily into bright sunshine and a hail of arrows that clattered against the rocks below her. There was a plume of smoke from the shore followed immediately by a loud bang and an ear-splitting crash as a cannon ball ripped through the house to her right. She was gone again in seconds.

"Putain de salopard!" exclaimed Anna.

"Language!" chided Eleanor.

"I nearly had my head blown off by a cannon."

"And so you came straight back. Much better."

Anna gave Eleanor a stare that could stop cannon balls, but she seemed to shrug it off as if it were a light breeze. The lesson continued in a similar vein until Eleanor was satisfied that Anna could bounce her way in and out of a moment in time without the opportunity for hailstones or arrows to find her.

At the end of the day Anna found Élise and dropped down beside her, puffing her cheeks and blowing. "Bloody hell!"

"Yes, I am recovering a little, thank you for asking," said Élise, rolling her eyes.

"I'm so sorry Élise, how's your back?"

"Like someone sliced it open, strip by strip and sewed it back up again."

"Of course. Can I get you anything?"

"A new body? If not, I would like to be propped up outside, where I can see you training. It is so boring in here."

"You just enjoy watching me suffer, don't you?"

"Of course."

Anna laughed. "Fair enough. But it's only day one and I'm already fed up with people telling me how to walk. I don't need you to be telling me as well."

"I promise I will not comment. Just watch."

"You won't need to say anything, your expression will say it all."

Anna spent a full week being taught how to walk again by Florian and Eleanor. It was frustrating and challenging in equal measure, but she understood the need to master the basics. She helped Élise out into the shelter of the cloister each morning and made sure she was wrapped up warm. Anna had been concerned that her very presence would put her off, but she found she soon forgot Élise was there when working. Élise was as good as her word and kept quiet, content to watch and enjoy the fresh air. When Anna came to help her back to her room, Élise was often dozing, peacefully recuperating from her wounds. It was only then that Anna was reminded how young Élise was, still in her teens and looking both small and vulnerable. Asleep she did not seem to be the self-possessed young madam that Anna first met. Anna felt protective of her, as if she were a younger sister.

The first couple of evenings after supper, Anna just lay down beside Élise and fell asleep too. She spent at least five hours each with her teachers and supper was late in the evening. But as the week progressed, she grew accustomed to the work and sought out a diversion once lessons had finished. At first, she would wander the spiralling tracks around the mount and look out at the tiny distant lights across the bay. Fires lit in the hearths along the coast. One evening she heard singing from the chapel on top of the mount and went to the door to listen. About thirty monks gathered at the far end of the nave and sang without accompaniment and in perfect harmony. No conductor. No sheet music. Only their memories and years of practice to rely on.

It was beautiful.

Anna didn't think to listen to classical or choral music, it all seemed too dry and unreachable to her. But this felt different. Their voices were utterly right for the space in which they sang. The notes reverberated between the stone walls and arched columns as if singers and chapel were all one perfect musical instrument. She snuck into the back of the nave and sat down on the rearmost pew. For a while she watched, then she closed her eyes and let the voices wash over and around her. She wasn't asleep when they finished, just resting her eyes you understand.

"I hope you enjoyed evensong," said Florian.

Anna started then realised the other monks were filing out of the chapel. "It was wonderful. I didn't think I liked that sort of music, but it just seemed so... right."

Florian smiled, "You are always welcome to come and listen."

"Thank you." As he turned to go, Anna asked, "Brother Florian? Will you show me how to use the sword next week? I'm worried that time is passing, and I haven't even held one."

"You are doing well, and many sword fights are won with your feet and your head." Anna looked puzzled so he went on, "If you anticipate your adversary and move out of their reach while they try to strike you or move into your own distance when they are not ready, then you have only to make a simple swing of the blade."

"I... think I understand."

"Put your hand out," he said. Puzzled, she put it out, palm down as he showed. Quick as a whip he flipped his hand over hers and gave the top of her hand a tap with his fingers. "Your turn."

Anna placed her hand beneath Florian's then went to tap the top of his hand, but it wasn't there. "Hey! You cheated!"

"No, I simply observed you preparing to move your hand and moved mine out the way. My turn." He waited until Anna was ready then waited a little more. Anna's hand flinched, thinking he was about to tap hers, but nothing happened. Just as she was putting her hand back, he tapped hers on the top again."

"Hey! You did it again."

"Your turn."

She paused. Then she waited a little longer. Then she struck and almost brushed the top of his hand as he pulled it away but not quite.

"Don't watch my hand, watch me," he said.

Anna frowned then did as he said. She put her hand out ready for him to tap it. Waited. Caught a flicker of movement from his shoulder and pulled her hand away. This time he just brushed her knuckles.

"You are learning," he encouraged.

A few more tries each and she was finding his hand as often as he was finding hers.

"I think I can see you preparing to move now," said Anna, "but it's so subtle."

"I think I shall give you a sword tomorrow," he said.

Swords

Mont Saint-Michel, Normandy, March 1418

Anna arrived early the next morning, excited, only to find Florian had brought a pair of wooden swords. "But... you promised a sword."

"I did, and here it is," he said handing her a wooden one, grip first. He saw the disappointment on her face, "You would not thank me if the first thing we did was cut each other with steel blades. These will do us well until you have sufficient control."

Anna nodded and sighed, seeing the wisdom. She dropped into her stance holding the sword with both hands and somehow the position felt easier. More complete.

"Good," he said. "You stand well, but first you should salute me." He brought the blade to his nose, waited for Anna to do the same, then both dropped into the ready stance.

"I doubt Fitzwalter deserves a salute," said Anna sourly.

"Perhaps. But all lives should be saluted, whether or not they are about to be lost." Anna felt rightly rebuked. "Now I want you to keep this gap," he continued, "wherever I go you must stay the same distance away from me." He started moving quickly towards her, so she backed away swiftly, keeping her wooden sword between them. Suddenly he switched to move sideways, and she was momentarily wrong footed, but caught up. By the time he next changed direction, she was looking at his whole body for clues. She caught a slight tensing of the muscles on one side, ready to push in the other direction and she found herself moving with him.

"Good. Well observed," he called, then started circling her before driving her back again. Anna anticipated and kept her distance but felt a whack in the back of her legs and tumbled backwards over the low cloister wall. Florian put his sword aside and reached over to help her up.

"You could have told me I was about to back into a wall," she complained. She looked over at Élise who was tactfully looking in the other direction.

"Would your adversary?"

"Good point. Let's go again."

Eleanor's lessons progressed to techniques for sifting through the past. She showed how Anna could use people's clothing as an indicator of time, observing the intensity of farming or its absence as another clue. She also taught Anna how to dive many centuries back in time then slow her descent, as if she were opening a parachute and watching events unravel in a kind of stop-motion photography. Under her guidance Anna saw the mount deconstruct itself, right back to the bare rock, then moved forward to catch the moment in 708 when Aubert, from the nearby town of Avranches, started building a tiny chapel on the mount.

Anna watched him hacking stones from the steep cliff on the north face and stumble up to the summit to place them. She wanted to help. She wanted to ask him why he had chosen such an insane place to build, but kept back, just out of his line of sight and watched.

When she returned to 1418, she asked Eleanor what possessed the man to start a church on this lonely rock in the sea.

"Saint Michael," said Eleanor, as if that were all the explanation needed.

Anna was intrigued. "Are you suggesting the saint just rolled up one day and said, 'Hey Aubert, you look bored, I demand you build a church on top of that rock and dedicate it to me'?"

"Saint Michael never demands, he suggests. And he did not ask Aubert to dedicate it to him, that was Aubert's idea."

Anna stared at Eleanor, unimpressed. "I expect you're going to tell me you met them both."

"I met Saint Michael."

Anna tried to gauge whether Eleanor was pulling her leg, but she seemed perfectly matter of fact about the alleged encounter. "Where did you meet him? And when?"

"He came to my cottage, two years ago, after Élise first visited me from the twentieth century."

"He came to you, to your home?"

"Yes. He is a gentle soul. He was grateful for a little wine, some pottage, and the chance to sit somewhere quiet."

Anna stifled a snort, "So like, he folded his wings, stashed his golden harp and put his feet up with a cheeky glass of red?"

"You are not treating my answers with the respect they deserve, Mademoiselle Partington."

"I'm sorry but I find it hard to believe in heavenly saints and spirits and stuff like that."

"Well, that is entertaining coming from someone who can walk between times." Anna's cheeks coloured a little at that. "I shall let you make your own mind up," she added then annoyingly changed the subject to sifting the future.

After supper that evening Anna went for a walk around the mount. Some of it was still wooded and as there was still a hint of light in the sky, she felt brave enough to wander. The evenings were cold but without the bite she felt a month ago. Venus and a few of the other bright stars had appeared. She sat down on an outcrop to look at the moon, waxing steadily towards a full silver circle. The light reflected from its face threw faint shadows and a deep shadow beside her revealed what looked to be a cave. Anna could just see a door and went to peer through a little circular hole at head height. Unsurprisingly it was impossible to see anything inside and yet she fancied she sensed something as she touched the door. A coldness. An absence. She recognised that feeling at once and stepped away from the door in the rock. Was this the location of another mournghast? Had she found another victim, another life that would now never be, because of her?

She backed off, down the slope towards the sound of the sea lapping the rocky shore below. Eleanor was right. How could she possibly reject the existence of spirits if she time-travelled and accepted something she'd never previously heard of called a mournghast? And yet...

Florian worked Anna for another week and a half with the wooden swords. He taught her how to block his attacks and respond instinctively.

"Never let your guard down," he said, "Always be ready to block an attack or make one."

He tested Anna's defence and suggested she angle the sword more. "Why?" She often asked why.

"Put it straight up and see what happens," he suggested and took a swing at her upright 'sword' with his. Her blade tipped and his struck Anna on the shoulder.

"Ow!" she rubbed her arm, more irritated than hurt.

"Now tip the blade forward."

She did so, then Florian took another swing. This time his blade slid down hers and hit the guard that protected her hand.

"That is why," he said.

Anna nodded and made sure she kept her blade tilted forward from then on.

"When am I least balanced, least able to defend myself?" he asked.

"When you're attacking me."

"Very good. So, counter-attack almost every time."

"Almost?"

"Do not become predictable. You will notice that I have been teaching you many ways of blocking and many ways to attack. Use different counters each time, but occasionally do nothing."

"Okay…" Anna's voice was full of doubt.

"Think of the fight like a dance, to music." Anna cocked her head to one side. Florian continued the analogy, "There are moves that flow in a rhythm, you may get faster or slower depending on the beat. Sometimes there is a gap in the music, a silence. That is just as important as the sound. It punctuates it, defines it. In a fight there can be furious flurries of activity but there are also pauses or silences. These too are important because they are your opportunity to watch and learn about your adversary. Does he keep moving or does he still himself too? You remember what he does and act on it when you have the opportunity."

"Absence is as important as presence," murmured Anna, deep in thought.

"Exactly so. They balance each other."

"Do you know what's behind the door in the rocks on the wooded south-west slope?"

Brother Florian dropped his guard and stopped to consider the unexpected question. "Why do you wish to know?" Anna made a swift cut to his wrist. "Ow!" he shook his wrist out and brought his guard back up.

"Never drop your guard," smiled Anna.

Florian smiled too, "Just so." He continued to circle Anna, both keeping their guard up and watching each other. "Why do you wish to know about the door in the rock?"

"I found it yesterday evening after supper. I sensed something there."

"What did you sense?"

"An absence."

"There is a tunnel that leads from the crypt, down through the rock to that door. It was blocked off some time ago. I do not know why."

"Who used the tunnel?"

"It was an escape route, in case the monks were cornered, but I doubt it was ever used."

Anna wondered how she could have experienced such a feeling unless it was a kind of premonition.

"I found the scripts I was looking for," announced Eleanor.

"Do they explain how someone can seem to die and not?" asked Anna, eagerly.

Eleanor calmed Anna with a gesture of her palm, "The scripts were not clear. They talked of conflicting desires and parting the spirit from the body, but there was nothing conclusive."

"Conflicting desires? Rob and I... we didn't always agree but... I thought we loved each other."

"It is possible to love someone and desire something different to them, is it not?"

"I suppose. I'm not... I'm no expert," Anna looked at her feet. She had spent so long with the ghosts from the past that she rarely looked up long enough to notice other people, let alone fall in love with them. She realised that she was almost as inexperienced in love as her young grandad, Jim.

"This young man, Rob, is he your first and only love?"

"I had a couple of... well, 'boyfriends' makes it seem more than it was."

"Rob was the first one you were serious about."

Anna nodded. Suddenly she felt desperately tired and sat down on the low wall of the cloister. The same one she had tumbled over when sword fighting with Florian. Morning to evening lessons had distracted her, but now she remembered just how much she missed Rob and how far she was from him. She brushed her cheek and found it was wet.

Eleanor sat beside Anna and put her arm around her. "It seems we must travel to Carnac after all."

"Carnac?"

"Remember me saying it was the largest group of standing stones I know, and so it drew the largest community of people like us?"

"Will they have answers?"

"I do not know, but it is more likely we find will an answer there, than anywhere else."

"But it's only ten days until the month is up. How will we get there and back before Fitzwalter returns to hunt us? What would happen to Élise?"

Eleanor looked at Anna and inclined her head gently with a twitch at the corner of her lips.

"Duh! Of course, we'll travel back in time to the moment we left."

"I shall ask Benoît to organise a boat for us. We shall leave tomorrow morning. I shall warn Florian that your arrival tomorrow may be... a little unpredictable."

That evening Anna went to the chapel again to listen to evensong. It soothed her. She stayed long after the monks left absorbing the calm of the stone arches that rose solemnly either side of her. When she was sure there was no one watching she placed her hands together and knelt to pray.

"Dear God," she started, feeling a fool just as she did in the Nazi cell at Saint-Sever. "Please help me find Rob. I love him. I'm so scared I killed him, though I don't understand how and he's the last person I would ever want to hurt." Then she thought again of the strange incident in the cell and her mother's advice to pray to Saint Michael. "And if Saint Michael is listening, I'd be grateful for his help too."

"Would you now?" said a voice from the pew beside her.

Anna jumped up and banged her head off the pew in front of her. "Wha... OW! Shi... Oh my God you're real," and nearly fell off the pew again as she squirmed around to look at the man, perhaps in his mid-thirties, sitting beside her. The first thing she noticed was his clothes. He was dressed all in white: a loose white shift, baggy white pantaloons, white canvas shoes and a white skull cap that barely contained his long black curly hair. He had delicate brown fingers cradled in his lap. His dark brown eyes held Anna's and a mischievous smile played across his lips. No harp. And no wings, but somehow Anna knew.

"It is you," she said, "Saint Michael."

"Please call me Michael," he said in a rich baritone.

Anna opened her mouth to say something and found herself without words. It was that shocking.

"Yes, I let you out of the cell in Saint-Sever," he grinned, as if that were a great prank.

"What else have you done for me?" Anna started wondering about all sorts of serendipities from the convenient placement of the motorbike outside the cell all the way back to finding Rob.

"I haven't had to do anything, apart from the cell door. You seem very capable."

"Then why are you here now?"

"Because you doubt yourself."

"How do you know?"

"Because you don't believe in me, let alone God, and yet here you are praying to both of us," he beamed.

"And how do you know I don't believe?"

"It's obvious. You only pray when you run out of self-belief and I even heard you apologising that you'd never prayed before in the cell at Saint-Sever. So, that is why I'm here. To help you believe."

"In God?"

"In yourself. In the good that you could do, if only you had the courage to believe you can do it. It is up to you whether you wish to believe in God."

"God exists?"

"Has anyone ever talked to you about the power of ideas?"

Anna remembered what Élise had said to her in Pagham before she embarked on her adventures in Vire. "Yes... they have."

"God is an idea. The most powerful idea that people have ever had. You cannot unthink an idea once you have had it, and every one of us has acknowledged the existence of that idea. Some may dismiss it. Some may be unsure, and others imagine God in many different ways, according to their own culture and history. But no one can deny the existence of the idea. And look at what that idea has achieved!"

"Yeah, arguments, division, hatred, wars..."

"... and unity and shared purpose and comfort and going out of your way to help people you never thought of as your neighbour. And love. Never forget love, that will move mountains."

Anna looked away, down the nave towards the cross on the altar, thinking of her love for Rob. Thinking of the mountains she would need to move to find him.

"You love and miss someone. You mentioned his name, Rob. Hold your love for Rob close and never lose sight of that love. If you act out of love, whether little everyday acts or moving a mountain, you may overcome anything."

Anna looked back at Michael, searching his face for some hint of mischief, and instead found him wholly committed to his idea. "Love can't win a sword fight with a witch-hunter," she said.

"Oh, but it can, because you want to win. You have far more at stake than the witch-hunter. Love is your motivation, and purpose is your sword. Take it up."

Anna shut her eyes for a moment, remembering the purpose she took to Mont Saint-Michel and applied to her training. When she opened them again, he had gone.

Standing Stones

The Coast of Brittany, March 1418

Anna thought the ferry from Portsmouth had been hard going. The small sailboat that bobbed over every ripple was close to making her lose her breakfast.

"Stop leaning over the side or you will be sick," advised Eleanor. "Get into the middle of the boat, where it moves less."

Anna dragged herself onto the bench in the centre, just under the mast where Benoît was tightening the sail. He smiled encouragingly. "Good weather! North-easterly wind, just what we need."

"Great," Anna gave a thumbs up and concentrated on not barfing into the bilges.

"You seemed lost in thought this morning before we left," observed Eleanor.

"Hmm," Anna tried to say as little as possible. The bilges were beckoning.

"Do you wish to share anything?"

"Hmm. Saint Michael."

"He visited you?"

"Hmm. What is he?"

"A lovely man."

"Hmm. But what is he?"

"I would have thought a bright young woman like you would have worked that out by now."

"Hmm?"

"He walks between times. Like us."

"Huh? Saint Michael's a time-traveller?"

"If you wish to put it that way, yes."

"But…"

"Yes?"

"But I thought he was supposed to be a saint?"

"Well, the church decided that. He just told me to call him Michael."

"Hmm. Does that mean he wasn't sent by God?"

"Oh no, quite the opposite. I gained the impression everything he did was motivated by his belief in God."

"Hmm. Why did he come to me?"

"Did he not say?"

"Hmm. Said he came to help me believe in myself."

"Well, there you are. That is exactly why he comes to anyone."

"Huh?"

"Aubert always wanted to build a chapel on the mount. Michael came to give him a nudge. In a few years from now, Michael will appear to Jean d'Arc and encourage her in her fight against the goddons," Eleanor shook her head, "The poor girl will need all the encouragement she can get."

Poor girl indeed. The only thanks Joan of Arc got for liberating France was to be branded a witch and burned. Anna couldn't comprehend why Michael would take an interest her as well as Aubert and Joan of Arc. "Why me?"

"Perhaps you may do something good, out of love. Anna?"

"… bleughhh!"

"Benoît, would you be a dear and help Anna clear that up?"

The voyage around the coast of Brittany took three days with a couple of breaks on the shore for the nights between. No sooner had Anna's head and stomach stopped swilling around than they were on the move again. It was torture. Eleanor continued to give lessons on theory in the confines of the boat, but Anna's seasickness limited how much she took in. By the third day Anna thought she might be getting used to it and started to ask questions again.

"When are we travelling back in time to?"

"Three thousand years before Christ," said Eleanor.

"Wow! There's some scope for getting the wrong year then!"

"Yes, you had better concentrate."

"Me?"

"Consider this part of your training. You will be using both the Kingfisher to locate the community and the slow search when you are near. Do not worry, I shall be with you and will guide you if you stray."

A long strip of land stretched into the sea ahead of them. There were stands of beech trees huddled together with long expanses of wind-swept land between and more sea beyond.

"We are here," announced Eleanor and steered the boat into the shore.

Benoît moored the boat in the shallows, running a long rope to a tree trunk then started to build a camp. He would look after the boat while Eleanor and Anna searched for the Neolithic time-travelling community.

"Might we need Benoît with us?" asked Anna.

"No, the community are mostly gentle people," Eleanor said.

"Mostly?"

"Unless we threaten them. We do not look threatening, but although dear Benoît means no one harm that is not always how people respond."

They walked for a couple of miles through woodland, listening to the woodpeckers hammering the trunks and a lone circling eagle crying overhead. Eventually they arrived at one end of a long clearing which took Anna's breath away. She had never seen so many ancient standing stones. Hundreds of the sentinels stretched into the distance in long converging lines that rose and fell over gentle undulations in the field. Covered in red and green lichens, cracked by centuries of frost and gouged by the relentless pressure of the rain. Some had fallen over, some were missing, yet most of them still stood where they had been placed by human hands so many thousands of years ago. A few goats cropped the tufts of grass that grew longest at the bases of the nearest menhirs.

"Wow! How many of them are there?"

"I am not sure, perhaps thousands. This is just one of many sites, but it is the largest. This is a good place to begin our journey. Take care to note the nearest stone, its shape, the long grooves cut into it, its relationship to the nearest stones on each side and its alignment with the rest of the row." Eleanor took a few steps forward and placed a beautiful ornamental rosewood box in front of the stone. It was only a few inches across, but it was exquisite and unforgettable. "This will help us find the right moment to return," she added.

Eleanor and Anna joined hands and closed their eyes so they could see. They stood like a pair of Kingfishers on the edge of the pool of time peering down through the depths. Eleanor had already described the shaman, Heged, whom she had met before. Small, slight yet wiry with pure wild white hair and large hazel eyes. Anna let herself fall through the millennia searching, searching...

Carnac, Neolithic Coast, Circa 3000 BC

Anna watched the woodland around them change subtly through time from a light mix of deciduous and firs to densely packed pines with an undergrowth of thick ferns. While seasons flickered by in an instant, she felt a much slower change in temperatures from warmer to colder to warmer again. The scent of the air seemed thicker with unfamiliar flora and fauna. The stones before her lost their chips and cracks, becoming smoother, shedding their multi-coloured coats of lichen. Some stood up again. Some re-appeared from wherever the locals had stolen them to. But all through the changes the field remained. The edge of the tree line wandered and wavered, but it never encroached on the stones.

She saw the field expanding, the lines of stones increased from eleven to twelve to fourteen and more. The tree line retreated as the stones marched outward. Had the locals taken so many stones away? Was she seeing them restored in reverse? As this thought occurred, Anna slowed her search, watching for people. There were so few. Occasionally a presence would flutter past as ephemeral as a mayfly and be gone again. How could so many stones have been placed by so few people? Then she saw the lines retreat again, like the serried ranks of soldiers thinned by attrition. Was she seeing the placing of stones in reverse? The number of lines reduced from fourteen to eleven to nine...

Time.

It had taken a small number of travellers a long time to place all these stones. And as she watched some of the sentinels disappear her focus fell upon a slight wiry man with wild white hair who carved strange grooves into the nearest stone.

Anna released Eleanor's hand and knelt in the long grass, allowing the warm breeze to blow over her and clear her head. She felt giddy and disoriented from her longest ever journey into the past. The man noticed them and walked over, leaning stiffly on a gnarled wooden staff yet making quick energetic strides. His light brown skin was wrinkled, and weather beaten but his eyes sparkled.

"Welcome, travellers," he said in an unfamiliar accent.

"Heged, do you remember me?" asked Eleanor.

He smiled, nodded, and beckoned them to follow. Eleanor helped Anna to her feet, and they walked alongside the shaman into the pine forest to the north. Anna was fascinated by the old man. Was he old? He looked as ancient as the standing stones, yet he obviously still had vigour. Given how lifespans had increased over time, she guessed he may only be in his forties, which could be ancient by Neolithic standards. He was tiny, shorter than Anna, and she only came up to Eleanor's shoulder.

Around them the forest chattered. Some of the birdsong was familiar including the soothing hoo-hoo of the wood pigeons, but other calls made her think she was in a tropical rainforest. Screeching and chittering unsettled her but left the shaman unfazed. He extended his staff to halt them unexpectedly. They waited a few moments, wondering why, then there was a rustling in the ferns and a stubby hairy creature erupted from them, across their path, and disappeared into the depths of the forest before Anna could identify it.

"What the hell was that?" she asked.

"Boar," said the shaman.

"How did you know it was coming?"

He smiled and pulled his ear. Obviously, it was necessary to develop a keen sense of hearing and observation if you lived in a Neolithic Forest. If you wanted to avoid being run over. Perhaps he would find it equally challenging to wander through twenty-first century Bognor without being hit by an ice-cream van?

On a gentle rise the trees faded away. There was a flat plateau with a rectangle of standing stones. The four corner stones were taller than the others, and in the centre stood an even larger stone.

"This is their calendar," explained Eleanor.

"How?" asked Anna.

Heged beckoned them over to the central stone and pointed south, towards the sun. Then he pointed to the corner stones, left and right, "Mid-winter sunrise and sunset," he said. Then he turned them around and pointed to the two corner stones on the north side. "Mid-summer sunrise and sunset."

"And the stones between mark the passing of the months from mid-summer to mid-winter," added Eleanor.

"Cool!" smiled Anna, impressed at the knowledge and skill that had gone into setting each stone in just the right place.

Heged led them to another clearing in the forest, almost as large as the one with the stones. The ground had been tilled and planted with crops that flourished in the warm sunshine. About twenty goats roamed a pen made from rough timber fencing and a domesticated pig trotted around outside it with an air of entitled superiority. He reminded Anna of some people she had met. And there were people, a few dozen of them tilling the field or working among the huddle of thatched wooden huts in the centre of the clearing. Was this the largest time-travelling community in Europe, wondered Anna? Were there any other settlements?

They walked into the village under the intrigued gaze of the locals and the pig gave Anna a supercilious snort. The huts crowded around a narrow alleyway where she could not avoid rubbing shoulders with the curious locals. Looking at peoples' faces she thought them oddly familiar. Mediterranean? Middle Eastern? Eleanor had explained they were descended from people who started their farming in far-away lands, many generations before. Could they have travelled from the Middle East to settle here, in northern France? She realised with a jolt that these people looked like Rob. Were Modern Europeans and Brits all descended from Middle Eastern people? When Guy of Gisborne had derided Saracens like Rob, had he been denouncing his own ancestors?

Heged took them into the largest hut which had a tall conical thatch. She ducked under the low brow into a scene that felt both alien and deeply familiar. Oil lamps flickered, filling the space with a strong smell of animal fat, and bathing the underside of the reed roof in a warm glow. From the apex a rope hung down, suspending a blackened earthenware pot over a smouldering fire. Opposite the entrance were fine carved shelves stacked between stones and displayed upon them were the family ornaments, or so Anna supposed. Leather drinking cups, tall vases decorated with fine grooves, a variety of animals lovingly carved from bone and several necklaces made from threaded gemstones or shells. She felt as if she were looking at the family mantlepiece and all that was missing was photos of the kids.

Heged invited them to sit on low benches draped with furs, arranged around the central hearth where cuts of wood were smouldering. The furs stank, but Anna sat. A woman about the same age as Heged came forward, nodded to them both in turn and offered them a cup of warm white liquid. Eleanor took a polite sip and smiled. Anna peered at it suspiciously, sniffed then took a sip. Goat's milk. Yuk!

"Mm, thank you," she managed while trying to hide her grimace.

Anna's eyes were still adjusting from the bright sky outside, but she could tell the woman was putting something into wooden bowls. She handed them to Eleanor and Anna. Dread washed through Anna as she picked a piece of mushy white stuff out with her fingers and put it to her lips. Goat's cheese. Now she understood why the pig felt so superior, it was the goats who had to supply all the local delicacies while he supervised.

"Thank you, Heda," said Eleanor to the woman.

Heda smiled and nodded in return.

"This is Anna. She is one of my family, through many summers."

"We are all one family," said Heda. "Welcome Anna."

Anna wondered what Heda meant by 'all one family'. Was she referring to the village or making a much wider statement about humanity? If they were time travellers who had gone even further into the past, then they might have a unique first-hand knowledge of how people spread across the world from their origins in Africa. A global family.

"Anna seeks one who is dear to her. She would be grateful for your help."

"Tell us your story, Anna," said Heda and sat down on a stool next to Heged to get comfortable. "We all live for stories."

For a moment Anna was floored. Eleanor had done her best to prepare her for the journey, telling her about these people and their way of life, but nothing prepares you for how individuals will act. What surprised her was how easy it was to relate to them, despite the four millennia that separated them. They were settling down in their living room to listen to a good yarn and maybe some juicy gossip. No matter where or when Anna travelled, she continued to see more that united people than divided them. Even in Neolithic Brittany.

"I started to see the past when I was small," she began, hesitantly. "When I grew up, I was attacked. I was scared. I fell and passed out. When I woke up, I found that I could walk between times as well as see. Perhaps the shock helped me to take that step without realising.

"I met a young man called Rob. He could see the past too and I helped him to walk there with me. He hated the time he came from, but he made many friends in the past and he grew to be a part of that time, a very important part. He helped many people who were poor and homeless. But I needed to return to my time. I had so many questions to ask and I needed to find my family to ask them." She turned to Eleanor who smiled encouragement. "When I returned to my time, I found Rob's dead body in my arms. I don't understand what happened to him. I don't know why he died or if it was me who killed him. All I know is I love him, and I want to find out if there is a time when he is still alive, and I can return to him."

Anna looked up from the glowing embers in the hearth. She had been afraid she might cry, but she felt strangely calm and relaxed. Heged and Heda were holding hands and looking at Anna with rapt attention.

"I think I want to have a future with him. Not just visit him before his story ends, but live out a story together. Like you two," Anna said. "If he'll have me."

"Men are trouble," said Heda. "But they warm your back in winter," she added with the same twinkle in her eyes as Heged.

"We have many travellers here," said Heged. "From yesterday. From tomorrow. We have heard many stories. I remember one like yours."

Anna leaned forwards, "Really?"

"You say your man grew to be a part of the time you visited?"

"Yes. He just... fitted there. It was as if he should have been born then, not when I was. The help he gave to the poor became a story itself. A famous story for many..." she remembered how Eleanor had put it in their terms, "many summers after."

"A legend," said Heda.

"Yes, he is," said Anna, fiercely proud of her man.

"And you tried to bring him back to your day?" asked Heda.

"I didn't mean to. I told him I was going back to my time, but I would return to his. This was before I learned so much from Eleanor; before I learned control."

"Tell us more," said Heged, "tell us how you travelled from your man's time."

"I fell asleep," it sounded absurd and lame as she said it. "That's how I used to come home. I would fall asleep and wake up back in the time I came from."

"What did you dream?" he asked, as if he had reached the most serious and important question.

"Dream?"

"You dream, do you not?"

"Yes, of course, but... I try not to take too much notice of what I dream."

"Why not? Your body sleeps but your thoughts carry on. You are thinking about what worries you. What you might do about your worries."

"I suppose that's true. But it's all so jumbled with nonsense."

"It is only nonsense if you do not understand. Can you remember your dream that night? We might help you understand."

"I think I can. Normally I forget dreams but that one was so weird. So strong. We had gone to sleep curled against each other. I dreamed I was holding his hand," she looked again at Heda and Heged hand in hand. "It felt good. I never wanted to let go. But then we argued in my dream. That wasn't weird, we had argued a lot when awake. But we had become two pigeons in an oak tree. I kept saying I wanted to fly to another tree, and he kept saying this was our tree. In the end I turned into an eagle and flew up into the sky, but then I noticed I, the eagle, had two heads and they were pecking at each other. Then I turned into a magpie and flew down and down in a great spiral... and I woke up. And at first, I was content because Rob was with me. But then I could see he wasn't breathing... and my heart broke."

Heda knelt forward from her stool and clasped Anna's hand. "You do know what happened to your man."

"I do?"

"Yes," she said. "Do you not see? You just told us."

"Two pigeons in an oak tree," said Heged. "Two people in love. You wanted to fly to another tree: your home. He wanted to stay in his home. Eagle with two heads pecking each other: two powerful independent spirits who want to be one. Your love is so powerful you took his body home. His desire for his new home was so powerful his spirit refused. You woke as a lone magpie with the precious body you took. But it was empty. His spirit had never left."

"But... is he...?"

"I do not think he is dead," said Heged.

"WHAT!" Anna leaped to her feet.

"I think the body you held was empty. I think it will have returned to his spirit."

"Returned? But I buried him. I buried his body under stones, and I left it in a tomb."

"You buried his empty body. I do not think it is there anymore. I think he has reclaimed it. In his time, in his new home."

Anna was trembling with a mad mix of grief and excitement, "Reclaimed his body? How?"

"We walk between times. I think his body was caught in one time and his spirit in another. I think his spirit drew his body back. I think you should look in the tomb. If his body is not there, then it has returned to his spirit, in his time."

Anna slowly sank to her knees and whispered, "I thought he was dead. I thought I buried him…"

Time Up

Carnac, Neolithic Coast, Circa 3000 BC

Anna would have tried to go straight back to Nottingham in 2019 if Eleanor hadn't calmed her down and made her think.

"Fitzwalter will return," she said. "Lives depend upon us both returning to Mont Saint-Michel. Élise is in no position to protect herself."

Anna hugged Heda and Heged. Heda hugged her back. Heged looked bemused. He led them back through the forest, avoiding rogue boars along the way, and they arrived back at the clearing with the standing stones. Before they left, Anna had another question.

"What were you carving on the stone?" she pointed to the long marks on its edge.

"My name," he said simply.

"Really? So... all these mystic runes we see on ancient stones all over the place, are you writing 'Heged was here'?"

"And Heda, and all the other travellers," he smiled. "It helps us to find our way home."

"Home," repeated Anna, quietly. She still wondered where her home was. She thought she had travelled from medieval Nottingham to 2019 to find it, but now she wondered if she had left it there.

"Take this," said Heged, and handed a tiny, polished stone to Anna.

She held it on her palm and gazed at the swirl of pearly blue-white agate. It was beautiful, like a whorl of cloud.

"Thank you," she didn't know what else to say.

Eleanor asked Anna to take her back to 1418. The day they left. She took a moment to recall what Eleanor had taught her about travelling forwards in time. Like sailing a fast-flowing river with many deltas that could carry her far off course if she did not keep her focus. Anna focussed on Eleanor's ornamental rosewood box at the foot of Heged's stone and dived into the rapids of time.

Coast of Brittany, March 1418

Eleanor reached down to pick up the rosewood box and gave it to Anna. "Here, you should have something to put Heged's gift in."

"But... that's too generous."

"I want you to have it. Use it like I do, like a standing stone you can put in your pocket. I notice you have big pockets," she said looking at Anna's oversized overcoat. "It should fit."

"Thank you."

"We must return to Mont Saint-Michel."

Benoît was delighted to see them return. He gave Anna a big hug which took her by surprise. It was as if she had been gone for days, not an afternoon. While he was packing their supplies back into the boat Anna quietly asked Eleanor if he might have a crush on her. Eleanor laughed.

"He just likes you."

"Are you sure?"

"Benoît really likes men."

"Ah okay," said Anna, "Isn't that a bit risky in the fifteenth century?"

"The church forbids it, and that is the other reason why he was asked to leave the monastery."

"Sounds like he was lucky they just asked him to leave."

"Some clergy are more compassionate than others."

Before they left, they sat into the boat and held hands, all three. Eleanor asked Anna to take them back in time four days. "I want to allow for head winds and get us back a little early if we can," she explained.

Anna realised that she was being asked to take two other people and a laden boat through time. No mean feat. She looked worried, but Eleanor confirmed her faith in Anna's ability, so she closed her eyes and watched the days roll back. She was aware of Eleanor holding her right hand and Benoît clutching her left. Was he nervous? Did this seem like magic to him? She was also aware of the motion of the boat beneath them, gently swaying as the waves lapped. When she had counted three nights come and go, she slowed down their motion and opened her eyes. It was around mid-day before the morning they would have left Mont Saint-Michel. They were all still with her, sitting in the boat. She had done it. Benoît was clutching her hand with his eyes tight shut, so she patted the big man on the shoulder and gently uncurled his fingers. He took a moment to look around then gave Anna another big grin. She laughed.

The first afternoon back in the boat was gruelling for Anna but the next morning was not so bad and by the afternoon she felt strong enough to pay attention to Eleanor's lessons and her surroundings. A familiar sail caught her eye and she pointed it out to the others.

"That is us, sailing for Carnac," said Eleanor.

Anna squinted at the small boat and just made out three figures. The smallest one was huddled against the mast in the middle. That was her alright. "Must be the second day sailing out, I still look sick."

"For your sanity, and everyone else's, I recommend that you avoid crossing your own path, if at all possible," warned Eleanor.

"I've done it before," said Anna, thinking of her encounter with five-year-old Anna.

"Meeting your unaware younger self may not upset you. Think how it may unsettle you if you were to present yourself more obviously when not expecting it. And think how others would react to two of you."

"Yeah, I could see that freaking people out."

"I am not sure what you mean by 'freaking out' but if they did not accept your explanations then you would be seen as a freak and likely tried as a witch then burned to death."

Anna considered Eleanor's advice and decided it was sound. "I suppose telling people she's my twin won't always work."

"No, it will not. Especially if the other you is not aware of the story she should be following," Eleanor's frown lifted as the wind moved around to help them. "With luck we should be back a day early," said Eleanor. "You will do an extra time walk with me in the morning and more swordcraft with Florian in the afternoon. At least he knows. But keep yourself out of sight of anyone else."

"A double session of each by two Annas. Hey, I could go back and do doubles from the beginning of March!"

"I do not advise it for the reasons I just explained. There are some at Mont Saint-Michel who know who we are and accept us..."

"... and some who don't," finished Anna. She was quiet for a while. "My time is running out, isn't it?"

"If Fitzwalter intends to claim us then he will come to Mont Saint-Michel in about ten days from now, maybe less."

"And we can't hide?"

"Not forever. He is a witch-hunter. He can sense who and where we are."

"I won't be ready, will I?"

"I will let Brother Florian be the judge of that," said Eleanor. "You are already more than ready as a time traveller. You took us four thousand years into the past to find a man that had only been described to you and returned us to the precise day we left."

"You were there to guide me."

"I just held your hand. You did the walking. I have never seen someone achieve that on their first attempt."

Benoît beamed at Anna in admiration. She felt embarrassed and proud all at once.

"Good teacher," she muttered, looking at her feet. "But if I time travel to avoid Fitzwalter I might as well shout to the whole of the English army that we are 'witches', so I guess it will be up to Florian to say if I'm ready."

Mont Saint-Michel, Normandy, March 1418

Florian was not fazed by the double session, two Annas in one day seemed par for the course to him. The following morning, she arrived ready to take up her wooden sword and found him sitting on the wall of the cloister with two steel swords that looked sharp and dangerous.

"If we had more time, we would spend another month training with wooden swords," he said.

"But we don't," replied Anna, eyeing the swords with a mix of excitement and dread.

He handed her one. "Take up your stance with this."

It felt both heavier and easier to wield at the same time. She realised instantly that the balance of the wooden swords had been all wrong and the weight of the steel sword was much closer to her grip. She took up her stance and made a few trial blocks. The blade swung satisfyingly into position rather than dragging.

"Good," said Florian. "Now put on these vambraces." He handed her a pair of sleeves of segmented plate to wear over her arms. Then he donned a pair himself.

"Wise idea," said Anna nodding to Florian's protection, "especially with my aim."

"Your aim is perfectly acceptable. But I am a moving target, and I shall attempt to be unpredictable, like your adversary will be. Anyone can miss under those circumstances. Besides, I wish for you to hit my arms, in particular my wrists."

"You do?"

"Yes. Why do you think I want you to do that?"

"To stop you using your sword?"

"Very good. They are also the nearest parts of me that you can reach. I am holding them out to you as I reach for you with my sword, therefore you risk less by cutting at my wrists than you do by cutting my body or head."

Florian worked Anna through her routines for blocks and counters and made her go for his protected wrists each time. At first it seemed impossible. His arms kept moving and the target they presented was so small compared to his body. But Anna was stubborn, so she worked at it all morning until finally she heard a satisfying clink as her blade clipped his plate about half-way up his forearm.

"Good. Try to hit me nearer the wrists next time," he encouraged.

"You'd drop your sword if I cut your forearm," said Anna.

"I'd drop it if you hit me hard enough to go through the plates. My wrists are nearer, and they are less well protected."

Anna focussed her attention on hitting his wrists but as she did so, he clipped her lightly across her own plated wrist. "Hey!" she shouted. It didn't hurt, she was just surprised and indignant.

"Remember to watch all of me, not just the part you want to hit. Read how my body is moving. See where my next attack will come. And if you spend all your time looking exactly where you want to hit, I shall know and defend against it."

There was so much to learn. So many things to do all at the same time, it felt overwhelming. At the end of the morning, she sat on the wall and hung her head, feeling the days tick away to her approaching doom.

"You did well," said Florian and sat beside her.

"Didn't feel like it," muttered Anna.

"I have had many pupils. You learn fast. Tomorrow you will be hitting my forearms regularly. The day after you will be getting closer to my wrists."

"You make it sound like I'm preparing for a test, not a fight."

"A sword fight is a test you pass or fail. I have faith you will pass."

"Really?"

"If I did not, I would be telling you to run far away."

"Fitzwalter has probably been training his whole life. How can I possibly beat him?"

"If you think that, you will lose. If you focus on what you have learned and apply it, you may win."

"It's the 'may' that worries me."

"What do you know about your opponent?"

"He's arrogant."

"Excellent. Use it against him."

"How?"

"What will he be thinking if he is arrogant?"

"That I'm just a woman and he can beat me easily."

"There you are. Use that."

Anna scratched her head. "You're saying I should pretend to be a frightened little woman?"

"Yes. Trick him. Let him be arrogant and overconfident. Then cut his sword from his hands."

Anna smiled. "You've got a bit of a mean streak for a monk."

"I do not suggest you kill him. Just make sure he cannot kill you."

That evening Father Amos bounced over to Anna and asked her how the training was going.

"I think I might last a few seconds before I'm slaughtered by Fitzwalter," she answered warily.

"Excellent!" he beamed. "Brother Florian is a talented sword master."

Anna wasn't sure how excellent being slaughtered was, but she agreed with his assessment of Florian. "How did he come to know so much about swords being a monk? I didn't think that was a regular fixture between matins and compline."

Father Amos laughed, "Oh no! Brother Florian comes from the noble family de Ferrer."

"De Ferrer?" exclaimed Anna, remembering the name from the bailiff of Nottingham who had the spoiled daughter Annabel and the evil Guy of Gisborne as his righthand man. "I had an unpleasant experience of the de Ferrer's," she said, trying not to say too much.

"Some of them do seem to act as if they own all of Northern France," he admitted, "but some are good people. Brother Florian is a very good person, and he has devoted his life to Christ."

Anna wasn't sure if those two statements always followed each other but bit her tongue because both Amos and Florian were good people in her view. "I'm afraid I haven't had many good experiences of nobles."

"It does not matter whether we are high born or low. We must all choose how to live and how to treat others. The gift of wealth may blind some to the plight of others or open their eyes to their suffering. In the same way, the curse of poverty may blind a person to those who seek to help."

"Does Brother Florian help?"

"When he is not giving sword lessons, he works in the fields alongside the local farmers. He helps them to feed themselves and in return they share a little with us when they can." A bell rang out above them, and Father Amos jumped up to leave, "Please excuse me, I must join my brothers at evensong."

Anna sat pondering. She had to admit to disliking and distrusting anyone with money on a matter of principle. She might have had good reason but that did not excuse her assumptions. She could imagine Angela Briars frowning at her for prejudging people. She also realised that if her arrow had struck down de Ferrer, the bailiff of Nottingham in 1215 then Brother Florian might not have been here to teach her life saving skills in 1418.

Anna worked hard over the next week. Eleanor taught her the pitfalls of navigating the future and Florian had her clipping his wrist. But each day she felt the dead weight of dread accumulate in her gut. If she were lucky, she would have another two or three days before Fitzwalter and his mob arrived. If she were very lucky Fitzwalter would forget or decide he had more important things to do. She sensed she would not be lucky. Fitzwalter's arrogance would also ensure he came to claim them. He would never have it said he was afraid of three women.

After checking on Élise, who seemed a little less pale and immobile, Anna took an evening walk around the mount. She saw a couple of early bluebells pushing their way up from beneath the stands of trees. They were beautiful but unsettling as they only served to remind her how little time they had. She found herself in the small clearing by the cave door again. Anna stopped abruptly about ten paces from the door, remembering Eleanor's warnings. After a few moments, her curiosity got the better of her and she approached the cave mouth cautiously, reaching out a hand to touch the door.

She felt the warmth of her fingers drained. She felt a chill crawl slowly up her arm and descend upon her heart. With an effort she pulled her hand away and stood back.

"We all have choices," said a familiar baritone voice from behind.

Anna spun around to see Saint Michael standing in his white robe and pantaloons. "Michael! Sorry, Saint Michael."

"I choose to be Michael," he smiled. "You can choose whether or not to stand by that door all night."

"I'm guessing that wouldn't be a good choice."

"No. But this would," he said taking a sword from behind his back and handing it to her. It was beautiful. The blade caught the moonlight and shimmered a rainbow, drawing her eyes along its edge to the finely wrought crossbar and leather-bound grip.

Anna goggled. "But..."

"Take it," he said, offering it to her, polished pommel first.

She took it gingerly with both hands. After the sword she had been practising with, this felt supremely balanced. It looked as if it should be heavier, but it was not. The weight was exactly where it needed to be. She had little knowledge of swords but even she could tell this was a master work. Not jewelled or ornamental, but exquisitely crafted for a singular purpose. She could just make out an inscription at the base of the blade. Were those Celtic symbols, she wondered?

"I didn't think saints went around handing out swords," she said.

"It is an encouragement," he said. "I offer encouragement to those in need of it. Fergus mac Róich said he never lost a fight with it."

"Who the hell is Fergus mac..."

"Róich. I think you would say Roach. He was the King of Ulster for a while until Conchobar betrayed him, but at least it gave Fergus a reason to join with Queen Medhbh," he looked at Anna's gaping mouth. "Queen Maeve. Hmm, never mind. It is a good sword. And it was eventually passed to Artorius who also claimed he was ever victorious." Michael beamed at his little rhyme.

"Artorius?"

"You may know him as Arthur."

"WHAT? King Arthur! You're telling me this is Excalibur!"

"Excalibur, Escalibor, Callibor. It has had many names. Artorius liked to call it Calliborc, which is interesting because Fergus mac Róich called it Caladbolg when I gave it to him."

Anna looked down at the fabled sword in her hands and felt desperately confused and unworthy. After opening and closing her mouth a few times, she managed a hoarse "Why?"

"Because you will use it to beat Fitzwalter."

"But... why me?"

"Because I hope you will choose to do good. More than Fitzwalter is likely to."

Anna shook her head thinking she would wake up and find it all another strange dream to be unravelled and understood.

"After you win, make sure you return it to Artorius."

Anna just looked at Michael as if he had two heads.

"Don't look at me like that, you will find him in the middle of the sixth century, busy protecting farms and villages near Glastonbury and Avebury."

Anna nodded. It seemed reasonable. Borrow legendary sword, return it to mythical king. Fine. She would fit that in between fighting her father's ancestor and searching for Robin Hood. All in a day's work really.

"Oh! And I would be so grateful if you would see Fergus beforehand, I think he may have need of it one more time."

"Anybody else? Any more mythic kings and queens in need of Excalibur for a furtive fable or a turn on their mantlepiece?"

He looked at Anna blankly. "Are you taking the..."

"Michael, I'm sorry, it's just a lot to take in... thank you."

He smiled. Anna looked down at the sword in her hands in disbelief. When she looked up, he was gone. Again.

Mont Saint-Michel, Normandy, 1st April 1418

Anna was climbing the steps to the cloister, wondering how to explain Excalibur to Florian, when she heard a distant shouting from the sea gate below. She leaned against the wall and peered down, trying to see.

"That looks like a fine sword," said Eleanor walking down the steps towards her.

"It is," said Anna, marvelling at the casual understatement. "Michael lent it to me. What's going on down there?" she pointed at a small knot of monks gathering at the sea gate on the edge of the mount.

"I suspect that is Fitzwalter and his men."

Anna looked up at Eleanor and felt her knees give way. Eleanor caught her and propped her against the wall. "Florian tells me you are ready, Anna. It seems Michael has given you the sword you need. All you need is to remember what to do with it."

"I don't feel well," Anna said, gripping the wall.

"Nerves can be a good thing if you use them to focus your mind."

The voices below were getting nearer. Anna could hear arguing and belligerent demands being made. "I don't feel ready."

"No one ever does. But you are both talented and stubborn. I suspect you will find what you need. Your time for preparation is up."

The Vambrace

Mont Saint-Michel, Normandy, 1st April 1418

Fitzwalter stalked up the steep winding track surrounded by his swagger of armoured knights. Monks chased their heels and called after them, imploring Fitzwalter to stop, but he was having none of it.

"... but they were all wearing the Three Cats and the Fleur de Lis and claiming sanctuary," wailed one of the monks. "I thought they were Norman."

"They are Englishmen!" snapped another.

"I know that now!"

"Bring out the witches," demanded Fitzwalter. "By God I shall have them all burned."

"Please, Sir Fitzwalter," pleaded Father Amos, "we have no witches here."

"I know they are, and I shall prove it to you," insisted Fitzwalter.

Father Amos skittered around in front of Fitzwalter and sought to calm him, "We would never dream of harbouring a witch, sir. Please would you wait and..."

Fitzwalter punched the monk out of the way with a mailed fist leaving Amos's brothers to pick him up and wipe the blood from his jaw.

Anna curled her fingers around the grip of Excalibur and stomped down the hill to meet Fitzwalter. "Don't you dare treat Father Amos like that," she scolded.

"You!" replied Fitzwalter, "I have come to bring you to justice, and I shall treat these monks as I wish."

Father Amos had staggered to his feet and was trying to intercede again when Brother Florian stepped forward. "May I show you to the refectory, sir?" No doubt he hoped to lead them to Anna's familiar training ground in the cloister.

"No, you may not!" said Fitzwalter, drawing his sword. "I see the witch and I see she is armed. I shall bring her to justice." He took up a fighting stance like the one Florian had taught and, after a peremptory salute, he advanced on Anna.

Anna attempted to salute back but found herself having to block an aggressive attack straight away. She stumbled backwards across the steps and onto the rough sloping ground beyond. It may have been her plan to appear frightened and incapable but right at that moment she wasn't acting. She was terrified by the onslaught of thrusts and cuts that followed and barely managed to parry them or duck out of the way.

A brutal backhand swipe almost shook Excalibur from her hands, and she stumbled backwards onto the wooded slope. Her arms ached already, and the fight had barely started. She dodged Fitzwalter's next thrust by skipping sideways then tripped over a tree root and fell backwards. A glint of sunlight on metal was the only warning of the two-handed cut descending on her and she pushed Excalibur up in front of her face through pure trained instinct. The blades rang and forced the pommel against her chest. Fitzwalter disengaged to take another swipe, so she rolled from under him and scrambled to her feet, ducking behind a tree trunk as his renewal hacked out a chunk of lumber.

"Yes! Run and hide, woman," he taunted, "You dare to challenge me?"

Anna was too short of breath to attempt any smart reply, she was fighting for her life. At the edge of her vision, she noticed the knights and monks following to watch. The last thing she wanted was an audience for her death. Three more attacks by Fitzwalter had her tripping backwards again, weaving between the trees to leave less space for him to swing his sword. It was a cruel two-handed blade almost as long as she was tall, and it gave him the advantages of reach and strength. The momentum of a full swing would slice a body in half.

Anna lurched back from another thrust into a small clearing where the ground was not so steep or uneven. She ran a few paces back to put some distance between them and attempt a defence. The knights and monks followed and fanned out around the edges of the space as if defining the arena where Fitzwalter would make his kill.

"This is an island," jeered Fitzwalter, "There is nowhere to run."

Eleanor and Florian joined the group at the edge of the clearing. She saw Florian make a calming motion with his hands, palms down. He wanted her to remember her stance, her blocks, her counters. Then he flicked his finger at the wrist of the opposite hand. Anna nodded, took up her stance with Excalibur held out in readiness and eyed the plate armour vambraces that covered Fitzwalter's arms. They looked impenetrable. His gauntlets grasped the hilt of his sword and his breast plate shone. Naturally. Anna wore nothing more protective than her oversized overcoat. She shrugged it forward to cover her arms and shoulders then leaned in towards Fitzwalter.

"Who did you steal that fine sword from?" said Fitzwalter.

Anna ignored the accusation, watching all parts of his body for clues to where his next attack would come. She noticed a flexing of his left knee and right elbow, suggesting he was coiling for a swing from his right. She angled Excalibur forward and trapped the blow down to the crosspiece, just above her fingers, then made her first counter. Which slid off his armoured vambrace.

But it made him stop.

"So, you have learned something in the last month," he acknowledged, half surprised, half impressed. He took up his stance again, a step further away from her, awarding her a modicum of respect.

Anna was about to allow herself a deep breath when she was assaulted by a flurry of thrusts, cuts, and backswings. She parried each one of them though she had no idea how. The last thrust fell short as she hopped sideways and back, then started to circle around him. Into her view came Benoît, with Élise leaning heavily against him. They stood beside a dark opening in the side of the hill. The door to the cave tunnel. Her mournghast.

She almost missed the parry to the next attack but skipped sideways again, blocking, and countering the following two swings. Each time she made a cut at his wrists and each time Excalibur slid off the plates of armour, finding no purchase. She continued to circle Fitzwalter, refusing to present a stationary target for him. As they turned, she caught another glimpse of Élise. She remembered the state of her back and thighs when Benoît brought her to the abbey. She remembered how she had seen Élise standing proud and beautiful in front of the Wehrmacht soldiers, defying the invaders.

Fitzwalter's expression moved from momentary respect to annoyance and frustration. He lifted his brutish sword with both hands to bring a devastating blow down on Anna. All she saw was an opening.

A leather strap dangled from the underside of his right vambrace. She whipped a carefully aimed cut through the strap while his arms were still rising then danced back out of distance before the downswing fell through empty air. Fitzwalter stepped forward with a backswing that Anna met with Excalibur, and she took another counter which shook the loosened vambrace from his arm.

He hesitated. She struck.

The crowd gasped. He looked down.

His gauntlet lay at his feet in the grass beside the vambrace. A stream of bright red liquid ran from a stump where his right hand had been and pooled between the gauntlet and vambrace. To his credit he hefted his great sword with his left hand and took up his stance again, but he wavered, searching for his balance. Anna took a carefully judged swing with Excalibur and knocked his sword from his remaining hand.

He stood, swaying, clutching his bloody stump with his empty hand. "It seems you have me at your mercy," he admitted, "even though you are only a woman."

"You only have mercy because I am a woman."

He lifted his eyes to meet Anna's stony glare. "I yield," he said simply.

"Eleanor and Élise go free."

"You all go free."

"And you leave France."

He gritted his teeth. "Yes." There was a flash of anger in his eyes as Anna stepped back and dropped Excalibur to the ground at her side. He turned away from her. "Don't just stand there, cauterise and bind me!" he growled at the nearest of his knights.

The knight tore a strip of cloth from his own tabard and wrapped it tightly around Fitzwalter's stump. Another ran to seek a torch.

Anna felt a hand on her shoulder. "That was well done," said Florian, "I am proud of my pupil."

"As am I," added Eleanor.

Anna allowed herself to breathe out at last and bask in the praise of her tutors. She was about to reply when she heard a yelp of pain. The knights were cauterising the wound to stop Fitzwalter from bleeding to death. Then they re-bound it with fresh cloths. A part of her felt guilty at the loss of his hand. But only a small part.

"Thank you," she said to Eleanor and Florian.

Anna was about to go to Élise and Benoît when she glimpsed Fitzwalter snatch a blade from one his knights and lurch towards Benoît, who still had his arm around Élise. Before Anna could cry out, he stabbed the blade deep into Benoît's chest then left the way he had come, stalking furiously down the hill to the sea gate.

"NO!" she shrieked and ran to Benoît. He was gasping and choking, dying as he still clung to Élise who held him tight. "Benoît, no, please, no!"

Benoît gurgled, clutched at Anna's hand then closed his eyes and went still, head propped against the cave mouth door. For a moment Anna was in shock as was everyone around them. Anna placed one hand on the door while holding Benoît's limp hand with the other. She felt all warmth and mercy drain from her, flowing out through that door. It was as if a dark void had swallowed everything beyond, and all mercy was flowing from her, just as the blood had flowed from Fitzwalter's arm. Fitzwalter.

He would pay.

Anna stood, crossed the clearing at a run and snatched up Excalibur from the ground where she had dropped it. She slalomed through the trees and burst onto the track ahead of Fitzwalter. He stopped abruptly and looked at her.

"I dare you," he said. "Break the terms of our agreement, for I have not."

"You killed Benoît!"

"The oaf had no part in our agreement."

"You said we all go free."

"All witches."

Anna screamed at him and raised Excalibur. The blade caught the sunlight and a glint strayed across his face and breastplate. With a supreme effort of will she stopped. "No. You don't get away with this," and she flickered out of his sight.

"Thank you," Anna said to Eleanor and Florian, daring to relax after the duel.

She was about to go to Élise and Benoît when she glimpsed Fitzwalter snatch a blade from one his knights and lurch over to Benoît, who still had his arm around Élise. Before Anna could cry out, she saw herself emerge from the trees beside the cave door carrying Excalibur.

"STOP!" second Anna yelled in Fitzwalter's face, pushing Benoît and Élise to one side.

All heads turned as one to look at her and silence stilled the clearing.

"What..." Fitzwalter looked from second Anna to first Anna and back again. "What sorcery is this? What foul tricks do you play? WITCH!" he pointed with the blade in his remaining hand, "Seize her! Seize them both, they are WITCHES!"

First Anna had slipped quietly into the trees out of view. By the time the heads turned to look for her she had disappeared. For most of them it seemed as if she had been standing at the edge of the clearing being congratulated one moment only to appear in front of Fitzwalter at the cave door the next.

"You were about to kill Benoît," second Anna pointed at his blade. "You would break our agreement."

Fitzwalter looked across the clearing and back again, trying to work out if he had been dreaming her other self. "You break our agreement through sorcery."

"I won our fight fairly. I'm here to stop you from killing Benoît. Put down that sword!"

Fitzwalter stood shaking his head, "No, no, no."

"I believe that Sir Fitzwalter is understandably distraught at the loss of his hand," soothed Father Amos. "Please, good knights, take him back to the boat at the sea gate and see that he is looked after."

The knights stepped in to take their leader. Over their shoulders Fitzwalter skewered second Anna with a scowl of pure hatred. She returned it with eyes of righteous rage. As Fitzwalter was led away, she let out a ragged sigh and slumped against the cave door.

"Thank you," said Élise, propped up by Benoît who looked more puzzled than all the others put together.

Anna looked around the edge of the clearing for her other self. Was she still two or one? Had the other Anna ceased to exist? Had she had simply slipped off to avoid being seen? She was aware she was still leaning against the door and jerked away from it. Slowly she put out her hand and brushed the wooden panels with her fingertips. Nothing. Just an oak door.

"My mournghast..." she whispered to Élise. "It's gone."

The Two of Us

Mont Saint-Michel, Normandy, 1st April 1418

"There were two of us," said Anna, "of me, I mean. Where did the other me go?"

"How long did it take you to run after Fitzwalter?" asked Eleanor. "Assuming that is what you did."

"You didn't see me? I was standing right next to you!"

"I was indeed. And as soon as I saw the other you over by the cave door protecting Élise and Benoît, I noticed you slip away into the trees."

"But Fitzwalter had killed Benoît, right in front of us. I picked up the sword and ran after him, down the hill. I nearly killed him."

"Nearly. But I suspect you stopped yourself."

"Yes. I decided to side-step in time, to the moment before he killed Benoît. I decided to stop him... not kill him."

"A good decision. Extraordinarily dangerous, but it turned out well. Because you saw what your other self was doing and hid."

"So... You don't remember me running after Fitzwalter?"

"No."

Élise was sitting on an outcrop next to Eleanor. Brother Florian was talking to Father Amos and the other monks. Florian and Amos glanced over in Anna's direction and smiled then looked away. A polite conspiracy of feigned ignorance. Poor Benoît sat beside Élise, scratching his head, and looking confused. A well of emotion overtook Anna and she threw her arms around him.

"Oh Benoît!" she said, "I'm so happy you're here."

He looked even more confused but hugged her back. Élise allowed herself a smile and shook her head.

"You have created a fork in the river of time," said Eleanor.

Anna released the befuddled Benoît and looked up at her. "What do you mean?"

"Time now flows down two separate rivers. On this river Benoît lives and you have chosen well."

"On the other river?"

"It is best not to follow it," warned Eleanor.

"What happened to the other me?"

"Now she is you," Eleanor regarded Anna who looked as befuddled as Benoît and attempted to explain. "That is why I asked how long it took for you to run after Fitzwalter. Once that time elapsed there could only be one of you at the same moment."

"But... there were two of me sailing the coast. Two of me when I went to see my five-year-old self. Two of me when I confronted my rapist..." Anna closed her eyes and willed the thought of that monster away.

"And after each event you became one, following this river of time. What do you think happened to the Anna that was sword fighting while you were learning about the future with me?"

Anna's head felt as if it might explode. "I... don't know."

"She became you."

"Just in this river? Or does she still exist in another river?"

"As I said, it is best not to follow other rivers. For that way lies madness."

Anna felt as if she were having a lecture on parallel universes from a medieval time-traveller. Her mind was so boggled, she was on the verge of screaming.

"I'm famished," announced Élise, out of the blue. "Take me to the refectory."

Anna stared at her young grandma for a moment then burst out laughing. "Come on! I bet I can eat twice as much as you."

"Twice as fast, perhaps."

EVERYDAY SPIRITS

Vire, Normandy, May 1418

It took another month for Élise to recover from her horrendous injuries enough to travel. Anna was a little overcome to part with Father Amos and Brother Florian. Florian just smiled and reminded Anna to use her new skills to protect lives, not take them. He was fascinated by her sword, but Anna thought it best to keep its identity a secret and made up a story about meeting someone on the coast of Brittany who loaned it to her. He smiled again, obviously not buying any of it, but embraced her and waved them all off in the little ferry boat.

Eleanor's cottage seemed tiny after the lofty halls of Mont Saint-Michel, but comforting. They had been lucky. The next day they all ventured into Vire and found a scene that was both familiar to Anna and heart breaking. Farms were empty, their livestock slaughtered or gone. The shanty town of lean-tos and hovels was now a charred smear on the side of the hill. The only walls that still stood were the castle and donjon, and they were festooned in the Duke of Gloucester's colours.

"What happened?" asked Anna.

"The chevauchée," said Eleanor. "The English seek to draw the French nobles into battle through provocation."

"And ordinary people suffer. Again," said Anna, feeling her blood rise. If she ever saw Fitzwalter again, it wouldn't be his other hand she'd cut off.

"Pardon me, Madame," said a familiar young woman, as they stood among the ruins of Vire. "My man, Laurent. He recovered. I wanted to say thank you."

Eleanor smiled, "That is good news. Where do you live now?"

"In the woods. Made ourselves a shelter there. Done it before, the last time the goddons came and did this," she waved a hand at the husk that had been Vire. "We will wait till they go. Rebuild. Maybe a little nicer than before."

Anna was astounded by her pragmatism and resilience.

"Come to my cottage this evening," said Eleanor. "Bring Laurent. I would like you both to join us for supper."

"Thank you, Madame," she said looking nervous.

"Eleanor. Please call me Eleanor."

The young woman walked off in the direction of the wooded valley. "She still thinks you're a witch, doesn't she?" said Anna.

"Yes, but hopefully she is learning that I am friendly witch."

Surprisingly, the young couple turned up at the cottage as the sun was sinking behind it. They were ravenously hungry but did their best to eat politely. Unlike Anna. By the end of the evening, they had relaxed enough to share a story and a song, yet they still shook Eleanor's hand before leaving. No embrace or kiss.

"I think you will both be leaving soon too," said Eleanor, looking at Anna and her young grandma. "Though I am not asking you to."

"I don't know how to begin to thank you," said Anna.

"You have. You fought Fitzwilliam, protected me and Élise. And now I know the gift of the Couteau family is in your capable hands."

The next morning Anna and Élise gathered what little they had taken to the fifteenth century and prepared to travel to the twentieth. Anna was almost in tears, and she wasn't sure why.

"Do not say goodbye to us," said Eleanor. "Say 'see you again', for we do not know where this river will take us and when we may next meet. And I suspect we may."

Anna hugged Benoît who almost crushed her in his enthusiasm. Then she hugged Eleanor. "I hope we do," she whispered, and as she did, she thought of when she last held her mum.

Élise embraced both but made sure they didn't press her back. She stepped back and turned to Anna. "We shall walk to the hill overlooking the donjon, where we left. Then I would like you to walk me back to 1944."

"Are you sure?" asked Anna.

"Yes, quite sure."

That was praise enough for Anna. She had earned her grandma's trust.

Vire, Normandy, August 1944

Anna needed a focus for 1944. She chose the elderly couple returning to survey the devastation. She closed her eyes and held hands with Élise, then dived into the river of time. Vire rebuilt itself on the hill opposite, expanded down the slope and up the other side of the valley. Industry grew into the valley, by the river where Eleanor had been found washing her linen. The farms receded and the trees retreated in deference to the domain of people. As they came closer to their moment, she slowed their ascent through time. Vire vanished in the violent cataclysm of the Allied bombing attack, and she slowed her search further until they reached a point when the early evening sun threw a shadow of the shattered oak tree behind her. The elderly couple clung to each other to see how little there was of the Vire they knew. This was the image Anna had held in her mind. The snapshot of time.

"Is this really where and when you want to be?" asked Anna.

Élise stood looking at the shattered stumps of her home. "No," she answered eventually. "I admire the young couple who dined with us last night, their strength to come back and start again, just like that elderly couple over there. But I am not a patient person." Anna smiled at that but kept quiet. "I believe I am ready to start a new adventure in another country. Perhaps England will take me."

"After what the English did to fifteenth century Normandy?"

"That is history," said Élise.

"A history we just lived."

"Yes. But now the English are our allies."

"Hmm. Look at what your allies did to Vire," Anna pointed at the scene of devastation.

Élise shrugged. "I have no patience to rebuild. I know that the Nazis bombed England but not as badly as here. I will see what I can offer there."

"Would you like company for the journey?"

"Thank you, but no. You have your own journeys to take. Besides, I know at least one Englishman."

"Who?"

"The airman of course."

Anna laughed. "Yes, of course. Jim Partington. I think he might be pleased to see you." And I'll be relieved if you do, thought Anna privately.

"Yes, he will," said Élise with supreme confidence. "I noticed him looking at me."

"Might be tricky getting there," warned Anna. "England isn't famous for accepting refugees. Even a little hostile."

"I have contacts from my work with the Allies," said Élise, openly admitting her covert resistance work for the first time. "I believe they owe me an invitation."

"I look forward to seeing you again, Élise. Thank you."

"Oh! So formal," and she pulled Anna in for an embrace, careful to mind her back, then kissed her on both cheeks. "So proud of you."

Eventually they let go and Anna closed her eyes for the next stage of her journey back through time. To 2022.

Vire, Normandy, June 2022

EVERYDAY SPIRITS

This time Anna sought her friend, Jeanne Rajaonarison. She watched the seasons roll forward and once again she saw Vire rebuild. First the rubble was cleared leaving the Porte-Horloge and the shell of Notre Dame standing like tombstones on the hill before her. Then the walls began to rise. And spread out and out. Roads wormed their way through the valleys and over the hill. Buildings crept along those roads like a living being regenerating and growing. The pool at the bottom of the hill became surrounded by new houses and businesses. The Hôtel Dieu, where the elderly folk had been evacuated, sprouted gardens and a bridge across the pool. The Liberation bunting appeared and disappeared to mark each June and Anna slowed her search as she neared the day she left.

It was a warm summer evening. The light was fading. The memorial was in shadow and a few bright stars were starting to show beyond the rooftops. A small, dark skinned young woman with a frizz of black hair and a stylish summer jacket stood against the railing, looking out towards the donjon opposite.

Anna felt as if she were waking from a long deep dream, emerging through many layers of strange and intertwining tales. She almost doubted whether this was the friend she had made on her arrival in Vire, whenever that had been. "Jeanne?" called Anna tentatively.

"Anna!" said Jeanne turning from her reverie. "Hey, that was fast! I only said goodbye ten minutes ago."

"You did?" Anna was bewildered. "I've been gone for... so long, and so far."

"Well? Did you complete your quest? Did you get your man?"

"I... I believe he's alive. I have to go back to Nottingham, to make sure but... I have so many other things to do as well now."

"You do?"

"For a start I have to return this," Anna pulled a long leather case from her shoulder and opened the flap to reveal the finely crafted red leather grip, polished pommel, crosspiece, and the top of an iridescent blade that reflected each star in the sky.

"Woah!" Jeanne was in awe. "You have been on a quest! Who will you give it to?"

"A man in Glastonbury, who lived a long time ago."

"Mysterious. May I see it?"

Anna passed Jeanne the case and sword. Her friend drew it carefully in admiration, peering at the blade as it shimmered like a rainbow. "This is exquisite. I did a few modules in archaeology when I trained for the Médiathèque. If it didn't look so new, I would say it was early dark ages. Maybe as early as the sixth century."

"Hmm." That seemed to confirm it was no dream. It really could have come from a Roman king defending the Celts. Though she dared not suggest it was Excalibur to Jeanne. Not yet.

Jeanne looked at Anna. "You didn't go all the way back to the sixth century, did you?"

"Not for the sword. But I travelled back to Neolithic Carnac."

"No! No, you are just making all this up. Aren't you?" If it were a cartoon then Jeanne's eyes would be on stalks, goggling at Anna and the fabulous sword.

"You wouldn't believe what the standing stones were for. I met some of the people who carved them."

Jeanne's eyes did a little dance on the end of their cartoon stalks, then she threw her head back and laughed.

"And I was given the sword to fight a witch-hunter in Mont Saint-Michel," added Anna, keen to get her own thoughts straight. "And by the way, why don't you hate all English people?"

Jeanne was still laughing. Tears were rolling down her face, good ones, and she threw her arms around Anna. "I never realised how boring it was in Vire until you came and turned everything inside out. Can I come with you?"

"Would you?" Anna had been sad to say au revoir to her grandma. She had secretly been hoping for moral support, so her heart leaped at Jeanne's request.

"Look how much fun you had without me! I want to see what you see."

"Fun. That isn't the word I would have gone for," Anna remembered the duel and the mournghast.

"Come, I am taking you to La Central for a bottle of Chinon and you are going to tell me everything."

"Perhaps I could put this in your flat first?" Anna nodded at the sword in her hands.

"A sixth century antique sword? In my flat?" Jeanne shrieked with laughter again. "And which channel will you go through when you return to England? Nothing to declare? Duty to pay?"

"Ah," Anna rubbed her forehead. "I hadn't thought about that..."

"We will work something out," grinned Jeanne, "The two of us."

Showing Spirit

Vire, Normandy, June 2022

Jeanne asked for a short break from her job at the Médiathèque. "You can take me back in time so that I return a few days after we leave, can't you?" She asked Anna. Anna could hardly say no. But before they left, she took a walk, alone, to the Porte-Horloge. It was a Sunday morning. Few had yet risen, so she was able to stand in quiet beside the arrow-slit in the stone tower to think about what she wanted to say. After a few moments she gathered her courage and stepped forward, touching her fingers to the stone. It was cold.

Ice cold.

She could imagine a void beyond the wall, a chasm so dark it suffocated.

"I am sorry," she began, wondering what the hell she was doing.

The stone drew warmth from her fingertips like blood draining from an open wound. The void yawned.

"I'm not sorry I protected Rob. And what you were doing was evil."

Her hand was hurting as if it had been plunged into iced water. The ice was creeping up her wrist and forearm. The chasm threatened to swallow her world.

"But I regret taking a life. And the lives that would have been."

The flow of warmth seemed to slow. A pinprick of light appeared in the eye of the darkness.

"I don't know if I can ever undo what I have done, but I want to find a way to... make amends."

Only her fingers were cold now. A dim light dawned across the void.

"I want to undo the wrong. I am sorry."

The stone felt ordinary to her touch. Sunlight warmed her back.

Anna swayed and steadied herself against the wall, then stepped cautiously over to the bench nearby to sit. For a while she was content to bask like a cat. The Virois began to busy themselves around her in the square, buying fresh bread and flowers, meeting friends for coffee. She smiled a contented smile. Had she just imagined the ice and the chasm? Had she imagined a malign spirit within those stones? No. No more would she seek to dismiss such experiences and put them to the back of her head. She had confronted enough of the extraordinary now to find it ordinary. Everyday. Whether or not it was real to others, it was real to her. With the force of her will, she had confronted her everyday spirits, her mournghasts, and looked for forgiveness.

And found it.

University Hospital Lewisham, Larch Ward, June 2022 and 2016

Jeanne had the bright idea to seek a permit for carrying an antique sword to be studied at the University of Nottingham Department of Archaeology and at Nottingham Castle under the guidance of Dr Angela Briars.

Angela wrote an email back saying how much she looked forward to meeting Jeanne and examining the antique. The sword, not Anna. Jeanne sniggered and said she liked Angela already.

The plan had the advantage of being true and answered a lot of awkward questions, if avoiding the one about how it was found. It also gave her a good reason to be travelling there with Anna. Anna was already grateful for Jeanne's company and good sense. They laughed a lot together.

The laughter paused while Anna took a detour to Lewisham.

"Would you like me to come in with you?" asked Jeanne outside the ward.

Anna shook her head. "Please wait here for me."

Jeanne only waited a bare two minutes, but Anna looked as if she had aged two years or more when she returned. Without a word, Jeanne held her friend tight then led her by the hand to a small café around the corner from the hospital. She bought them coffee and waited patiently, passing Anna chunks from a chocolate bar until she felt like talking.

Anna stared at the coffee cup in front of her and a hole appeared in the froth which receded strangely fast. She had several goes at opening her mouth before any sound came out. Eventually, "She said my father was trying to protect me."

"Protect you? From whom?" asked Jeanne.

"From his family. From himself."

Jeanne frowned, looking worried.

"No, not like that," said Anna. "I promise I'll explain later when it's sunk in. All this time I thought he never cared about me or Mum, but Mum says he did. I need to find him... after I look for Rob's grave."

Nottingham Castle, June 2022

"And you say you were given this in the sixth century?" asked Angela Briars, cradling the beautiful sword gingerly in two white gloved hands and peering over her reading glasses.

"I was given it in the fifteenth century," clarified Anna, "and asked to return it to someone in the sixth."

"Someone?" she pushed.

"His name is... was Artorius," said Anna, looking cagey.

Angela's black eyebrows rose high above the rim of her glasses. "This Artorius wouldn't happen to be a disputed character of myth, would he?"

"Hmm."

Angela looked at the sword then Anna, then Jeanne. "Judging by the style and length of the sword, and the Celtic runes on the blade, I would have said it could be anywhere between first and eighth century, though it looks almost new. Have you any idea what this sword might be?"

"Hmm," repeated Anna.

"Wait, you can't be suggesting..." started Jeanne.

"I was told he called it Calliborc," said Anna.

"Who called it Calliborc?" asked Jeanne, leaning forward.

"Artorius."

"It is a leap of faith but if it is the person Anna is suggesting then we might know him as King Arthur," explained Angela, shaking her head in disbelief. "Though I would need far more evidence than this sword."

"NO!" gasped Jeanne. "So that's... that's..."

"Excalibur," muttered Anna. "And he said Fergus mac Róich called it Caladbolg."

Jeanne sat down before she fell down. She couldn't take her eyes off the sword.

"Who said that?" asked Angela.

"Another time traveller called Michael," Anna knew she was being economical with the truth, but even that much took a lot of faith to digest. These were her only two friends who were not time travellers who would take her seriously.

Angela eyed Anna, seeming to suspect she was holding something back. "I've heard of Fergus mac Róich. A legendary King of Ulster. You seem to be fond of meeting people that historians find challenging to prove, Anna. Another of your unique gifts?"

"A perk I suppose. Michael asked if I would lend the sword to Fergus again," said Anna, "before I returned it to Artorius."

"Sounds as if you are going to be a busy woman, Anna Partington. You're lucky you have a good friend to help," Angela looked at Jeanne and smiled. Jeanne wrenched her gaze away from Excalibur long enough to smile back.

Anna was relieved to find they liked each other. It was a comfort to know, while her head swam with the many revelations of the past months. She felt pulled in many directions at once, yet there was one revelation she was determined to confirm now.

"Yes," agreed Anna, "But there is something else I must do in Nottingham first..."

Rock Cemetery, Nottingham, June 2022

'Jane Trudy Baker. 8th May 1959 – 3rd July 2018. Rest in peace.' Anna ran her fingers over the plaque and placed fresh hyacinths in the vase before standing. Beside her friend.

The two stood side by side at the edge of the graveyard, looking at the simple headstone under the canopy of a large oak tree. Sunlight dappled the grave and the path beside it. Anna looked along the grass verged path, back towards the remains of the cave that had once been a sand mine. It was now a gated recess off the main graveyard. She had burned to see inside since leaving Carnac, but now she was here her legs felt leaden.

Anna asked Jeanne to wait for her again, apologising, and promising that she would soon take her on a proper time trip. Jeanne squeezed Anna's hand.

"I'll be here for you when you come back out," Jeanne said.

Anna approached the gate slowly and drew a key from her pocket. Angela had pulled in a favour and arranged for Anna to borrow the key. Anna remembered when Rob had picked the lock to let the pair of them in out of the rain after Goose Fair. Sitting side by side in the gloom of the cave mouth, confiding their stories to each other. Arm around his waist. His arm around hers. She steadied herself then placed the key in the lock.

Just inside she could still see the sun reaching across her feet. Further in she could see a mound of stones in the back of one of the alcoves. She remembered building that mound. She remembered placing one stone on another while her tears dripped and splashed on each one.

She closed her eyes and counted back three summers, an autumn, a winter... She had been tempted to linger in October 2019 to see the two of them sitting there, but with an effort of will she kept going until she found her focus. Herself, in December 2019.

Rock Cemetery, Nottingham, December 2019

Anna stepped back into the shadow of a sandstone alcove and watched as her younger self leaned over the pile of stones. She could just see a stilled chest and face lying beneath the stones. It was Rob. Younger Anna placed the last few stones on the burial mound and for a while she lay across it, head pressed against the cold rocks. Anna recalled the emptiness and exhaustion. Then younger Anna reached inside her oversized overcoat and drew out a golden arrow, placing it to point north towards Sherwood Forest. After a while younger Anna rose and left the cave, in search of Jane Baker, her aunt's grave.

Older Anna stepped forward and knelt beside the burial mound. The thought of pulling all the stones off again seemed like sacrilege. The thought of not knowing what really happened to Rob tore at her heart. She lifted the golden arrow carefully to one side, then started pulling stones.

Despite the cool of the cave, she grew warm and had to roll her overcoat up before lifting more stones. She was lifting stones for some minutes before it dawned on her that she never placed this many on Rob's body in the first place. She had seen a loose pile and laid him in the middle of it, moving the ones at the edge to lie over his body. Now she could almost see the sandstone cave floor.

Where was he?

Anna felt an irrational panic rise within her and scrabbled to toss the last few stones aside. There was nothing but bare stone and dust.

Nothing.

Rob's body was not there.

She had just watched herself bury him under these very stones and yet now there was no sign his body had ever lain there. She snatched up the golden arrow with her overcoat and ran to the gate. Her mind was whirling. It took a huge effort of concentration to calm herself. For a moment she stood, gulping deep breaths of air, clutching the golden arrow to her chest. Then she closed her eyes...

Rock Cemetery, Nottingham, June 2022

Jeanne saw Anna running back up the path towards her, clutching something in her hand that glinted when it caught the sun.

"He's not there! Jeanne, he's not there," called Anna as she threw herself at her friend, panting for breath and sweating from lifting all the stones.

"Slow down, Anna. Tell me what that means."

"I saw me burying Rob's body. I went back to that exact moment in 2019 when I buried him. I saw his face being covered by the stones. I waited until my younger self had gone then took all the stones up again. There was nothing."

"So, did you dream it?"

"No. I dreamed, but I didn't dream Rob. It means he took his body back home."

"Home?"

"To 1215. To Sherwood Forest. Jeanne, it means Rob's alive!"

Epilogue

University Hospital Lewisham, Larch Ward, May 2018

Here she is, my Anna. I knew she would come back for me. I knew she could. She seems older, grown up, her green eyes look as if they have seen so much since we last embraced. They seem weary and yet...

"Hello Mum," she whispers and comes to kneel beside me, putting her arms around me and holding me like a mother would hold her child.

"Hello dear," I say, "you came."

"Of course. And you knew I would because you knew what I could do."

"Yes. I'm so sorry I kept it..."

"Shh, it's okay. You already apologised."

"I did? Oh! I will have. You're going to come to me again, but it will be your first time. My second. I still find it confusing."

Anna nods, "Yes Mum. Sorry. There's me travelling backwards and forwards over centuries, but I get this trip out of sequence by ten minutes!"

"It's okay. You're here. Would you pass me that cup of water?"

She hands it to me. I take a sip and then she takes it back to hold it for me. "I went to see Grandma," she says.

"Élise," I frown, "She started you on this road, didn't she? She can be tricky to get to know."

"She was. But I think I won her over."

"She was fond of you as a small child, but spiky to others. She could be spiky to me, but I never saw her have a cross word with Dad."

"Jim," she says, swirling the water around in the cup. "I met him. He's a lovely guy, good with kids."

"Yes. He spoiled me rotten. Mum laid down the law, like when she caught me eating chocolates between meals, then Dad would sneak a few more into my hand when she wasn't looking." I smile, remembering.

"Élise didn't have much of a childhood. She had to grow up kind of quick when the Nazis arrived."

I look at Anna. She looks as if she had to grow up quick as well. I squeeze her hand. "I'm sorry you missed so much school. I'm sorry I'm going to leave you to become a woman on your own."

"How can it be your fault, Mum? And I will never regret the time I spent with you. You're my mum. I know I can be a bit spiky too, like Élise, but I love you."

I get my drip all tangled up while I'm wiping a tear from my eye then give Anna a big slobbery kiss, which is the prerogative of mums the world over, whether our children want it or not.

"Anyway," continues Anna, still nursing the cup, "I'm not on my own. I've made friends, real ones now, not just ghosts of the past. I have a good friend waiting for me outside. And..." she has a far off look in her eyes.

"Yes?"

"I've fallen in love." For a moment I see a flash of that smile she can give you, just when you're least expecting it. A smile that makes me feel the world is a good place.

"That's wonderful. What's their name?"

"Rob Ahmed. I met him in Nottingham."

"Nottingham?"

"I went to find Aunt Jane... but she passed away. Will pass away."

"Ah. I'm so sorry Anna. I know you're fond of her. I am too."

"You don't sound surprised, Mum."

"Harvey told me she was very ill."

"My father came to see you here?"

I nod. I know how little she thinks of him. "He has come to see me more often than you realise. When he can. He told me his sister Jane was dying of cancer too. I could tell he felt bad not being with me through... all of this," I gesture to the drip and the drugs and my bald head and hairless eyebrows. "I told him he should be with his sister, and not to worry. I told him I had you to come visit. Jane needed him because her ex was never going to visit her."

Anna looks at me, eyes wide. I can almost hear the cogs turning. "But... I thought he didn't care."

"He's always cared. About me. About you. It tore his heart to leave, but he did it to protect you."

"What? What do you mean, Mum? Protect me from what?"

"His family are... they're dangerous to people like you."

"They're witch-hunters," says Anna, voice low, tone flat.

"Historically they were called that. I don't know what they'd call themselves now, but they know a time traveller when they see one and they won't rest until they're all gone."

"I met one of his ancestors. One of my ancestors. He wanted to kill me and Élise and another of your ancestors too."

"But he didn't."

"No. I cut his hand off."

"Too bad you didn't cut something else off."

"Mum!"

"I know, I shouldn't say that. Especially as I wouldn't have met Harvey and had you. But you were... a problem for Harvey. He realised you would be a time traveller. He could tell, even when you were a baby, he could just tell. He can do that you know, just like the rest of his family. And he knew that the rest of his family would want to see you and if they ever did, you'd be dead. So, he did the only thing he could to protect you. He left."

She looks at the cup of water in her hand. I reach forward to brush the tears from Anna's cheeks, but I'm feeling drained already.

"He loved you, Anna. Just as much as I do."

"I have to find him."

"No, please. It's too dangerous." But I can see that stubborn look in her eyes again.

"It seems I have a saint to look after me now," she says, looking at me for explanation.

"You prayed to him?"

Anna is silent, still waiting for me to say more.

"Michael came to me too," I admit. "Yesterday. He promised to look out for you. He comforted me. But please don't go searching for more trouble with the Fitzwalters."

"I have to. There are so few people left in this world who know me. I have to go find my father."

"If Rob loves you then go to him."

"I will, if he's still alive."

"What do you mean?"

"I think he's in medieval Sherwood Forest, with Tuck and Little John and Ruth. But I have to go to Nottingham to be sure."

"You fell in love with Robin Hood?"

"He became Robin Hood. He's Rob Ahmed and he's the kindest, stupidest, most infuriating man I've ever met, and I love him."

"Oh dear. He sounds a little like your father."

Anna is studying the cup intently. I see ripples form on the surface of the water, even though her hands are not moving. Suddenly the water dips in the middle like a little whirlpool without whirling. Then there's a splash and the water sloshes over the sides of the cup.

And Anna is still as a stone.

EVERYDAY SPIRITS

THE END

279

Acknowledgements & Historical Notes

My grateful thanks to Rosie Fiorie who helped and encouraged me so much with Everyday Ghosts and whose excellent questions inspired me to tell Everyday Spirits.

I learned from many sources but those which taught me most about Normandy in 1944 were Normandy's Nightmare War by Douglas Boyd and 1939-1956 Vire se Souvient… by l'Association des Collectionneurs Virois. The latter book was picked up by Anna in chapters 5 and 15. The Hundred Years War, A People's History by David Green taught me much about Normandy in the fifteenth century. I am especially grateful to Pierrick and Catherine Cinieux, who are both excellent hosts and friends in Vire. Pierrick spent much of his own time looking up details of local history for me and they took us on a grand historical tour which no guide could have given so knowledgably.

Following a failed attempt to warn the Virois, the bombing of Vire by Allied warplanes really did take place on 6th June 1944 at three minutes past eight in the evening. Thousands of French civilians died. The rest fled to the surrounding villages including Saint-Germain, the Truttemers and La Lande Vaumont. This was no isolated incident. It was only one of many French towns that were almost obliterated by British and American bombing attacks ordered by Allied commanders. Many attempts have been made to explain or excuse these attacks and the huge loss of French lives; I shall let the reader make their own mind up. The most poignant thing I learned from my friend Pierrick was that there were no air raid sirens in Vire in 1944. 'Why would they have had them?' he asked.

After the real tank battles in Martilly and Saint-Martin de Tallevende, Major-General Leonard Gerow did lead his brave GIs into a valley full of hostile gunfire and emerged victorious the other side. There were many deaths on both sides and the fight to liberate Vire was as bitter as every other town in Normandy. But Gerow and his boys made it to Paris.

I was shocked to learn of the true meaning of chivalry in the fifteenth century and of the English occupation of Normandy. The arguments for their presence there were complicated by shared ancestry, but I wonder if anything can excuse the brutality of a chevauchée.

I have deliberately moved a few events in time or location to help tell the story. Any factual mistakes are very much my own.

My greatest thanks as always to Niamh for her encouragement and patient advice.

About Chris Gregory

I live in Hertfordshire where I'm lucky to see trees and a glimpse of water from my window. Sometimes I look away from the view and get some work done. Sometimes I receive orders to provide food and attention to my demanding cat (or creative director as she is often referred to). Sometimes I have the luxury of sitting with my laptop to write a story. All these moments are golden.

I have been writing stories for over twelve years and if you enjoyed this one, I'm delighted. Please remember to leave a review of my book at your favourite retailer. If you wish to find out about the other stories I've written, then please peruse the list of other books below and my website:

http://www.chrisgregory.uk

Other books by Chris Gregory

Science Fiction by **Chris D Gregory**
Seconders
Second Generation
Distant Son

Rescue

Urban Fantasy by **Chris Gregory**
Everyday Ghosts
Everyday Spirits
Everyday Legends

Historical Fiction by **CD Gregory**
Crystal
Resister

Pendragons
Uthyr Pendragon

www.ingramcontent.com/pod-product-compliance
Lightning Source LLC
Chambersburg PA
CBHW061426150726
47987CB00001B/116